SUCH A SMALL WORLD

JORDAN CLAYDEN-LEWIS

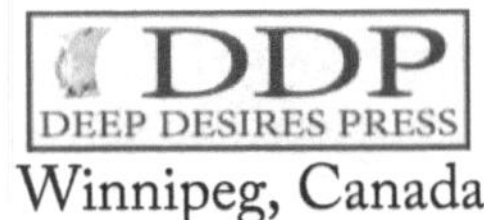

DDP
DEEP DESIRES PRESS
Winnipeg, Canada

For anyone who's ever felt different.

For anyone who's ever felt different.

Content Guidance

While this is a love story, it also
explores the darker sides of being human.

Such A Small World includes on-page
drug abuse and self-harm involving a teenager.
These scenes are depicted in Chapter 12.

If you or someone you know is struggling,
there are ways to get help.

"The only way to make sense of change is to plunge into it, move with it, and join the dance."

– Alan Watts

SUCH A
SMALL WORLD

SUCH A SMALL WORLD

Blue

LATER

Planted firmly in my allocated window seat, eyes fixed on the clouds, I wondered what would happen if the plane's engines malfunctioned, or if the aircraft just burst into flames.

What would actually happen?

If I were to survive the accident, would I then plummet ten thousand meters into the ocean like the elegant synchronized diver I was?

Fat chance: I was no synchronized diver, nor was this plane faulty, on fire, or were we in any danger whatsoever.

The first time I set my eyes on the flight attendant, with his short neat ginger hair and light green eyes, I felt as though I was about to dissolve.

Tingles, goosebumps, followed by something I like to call Mackenzie's Brain Cinema.

And this time at the movies, it was a scattered flash of camera clips yet again:

First clip: the flight attendant and I embraced in an airport, both of our eyes glassy.

Followed by a second clip: us in a bathtub with a window above that overlooked the forest at sunset.

The third: us driving along a stretch of highway, glancing over at one another.

The fourth: us on a hiking trail, vistas of valleys in view.

The fifth: him opening a black velvet box with a sparkling green ring in it.

The sixth: welcoming people into an establishment of some sort.

And finally, the seventh: his lifeless body in my arms.

What the actual fuck. No, no, this wasn't happening. Surely not.

Brain Cinema, A.K.A "My Ability in Action", was only playing tricks on itself, right?

Most of the time, Brain Cinema would only play short few-second clips, so it was undeniably rare for a whole ten-second film to screen.

I refrained from glancing at the other passengers and cabin crew as the plane's engines growled. Eye contact meant Brain Cinema activated, and sometimes, I didn't want to see a snippet of the future.

I couldn't keep my eyes off him though—the flight attendant—not after what I'd just seen.

As much as I tried to fight it, I couldn't help but notice all the little details: his creaseless black button-up shirt and slacks, the little bit of orange inlaid on his shirt. His name badge.

Jasper.

A name that rolled off the tongue over and over in my head.

I watched him from the corner of my eye as he attended to a woman and her young child, gazing at her while his fingers tapped on the seat.

After continuing down the aisle, he was so close I could've cried proper tears, as if I'd just seen the ghost of him. Though a ghost with glowing skin, probably moisturized daily.

He brushed past my row on his way to the rear, looking down at me with a bashful smile as I went red in the face, hoping to god he didn't see how much. He stifled a smirk, and in return, I stretched my lips slightly, trying not to give away the indication that, mere moments ago, I had in fact seen our distant futures.

A storm formed on our journey to Alice Springs, as did the turbulence, tossing us from side to side like clothes in a washing machine, the plane slowly edging beneath the last inch of cloud.

The aircraft soon crashed onto the runway. And for a moment, I thought it was going to tip on its wing. But like most of my other anxieties, it was one big over-exaggeration yet again.

I tried to catch sight of Jasper as I departed the aircraft, but he must've been at the opposite end of the plane. So instead of his eyes, I was met with a heat that seemed so naturally foreign. Dry heat foreign.

The air in Alice certainly was no east coast humidity, nor did I expect to see a beach anywhere in sight. The red dirt would have to do for now.

After grabbing my suitcase and standing in the airport pick-up area, I fought off flies with one hand and waved to a taxi driver with the other.

The sun poked its way through the flocculent clouds in the distance, and I checked the time. Seven past three in the afternoon. Time for a drink (question mark).

"Where to, my friend?" asked the taxi driver, rocking a silver fox beard and a bright red and yellow shirt with dot art on it.

MACKENZIE'S BRAIN CINEMA ACTIVATED

First clip: a close-up of the taxi driver's hand as he turns up the A/C.

Second clip: the driver's chesty cough as he lifts a hankie to his mouth.

I told him the name of the hotel and he replied with,

"Right on," before smiling, accelerating, and turning up the A/C, the air starting to dry the sweat patches on my face.

Every time Brain Cinema does its thing, apparently, I do this twitchy thing, like a shiver has been shot through my entire body. Fortunately, so far, I've had most people fooled into thinking it was a twitch and nothing more.

Sometimes though, I wish I didn't see these things before they actually happened. Good thing Brain Cinema only kicks into gear the first time I meet a person. So, I guess that's better than every interaction.

After checking into the hotel, I received a message from Rachel: **hey Mack, I got caught up with my mates in Kings Canyon. I won't get there till tomorrow morning.**

Turned out I'd be riding the Alice Springs rollercoaster without my best friend that night. So, I did the thing I'd been wanting to do since I got off the plane: drink some alcohol. Any alcohol. Didn't matter what it was, as long as it helped me forget what Brain Cinema had shown me earlier, albeit momentarily.

The Blue Bar, which was located just past the hotel lobby, reminded me of the Malibu Club from *Grand Theft Auto: Vice City*, except plastered with light shades of blue at each glance. Fancy, filled with groups at tables—their laughter making me break a sweat as I emerged from the lift.

As I sauntered over to the bar, I couldn't help but think everyone was staring at me, that I was the root of their laughter. They definitely weren't looking at me at all.

But sometimes, my mind has a soft spot for playing tricks on me, and not in a good way.

I pulled up a stool at the bar, a wall of crystal-clear glasses sparkling behind the three bartenders mixing drinks. On sitting, I noticed the slow ambient bass beat pulsating through the speakers.

After unburrowing my phone from my pocket, I opened a video of a drunken Rachel trying to talk to a dingo on the side of a road, the canine ultimately running away from her. Looked like *she* was having a good time. And there I was, almost too anxious to even ask for a drink.

"Yeah, can I please get another one of those Ocean Sprays?" a voice asked in earshot, in a muffled mix between a British and Australian accent. I couldn't tell which one was more prevalent.

My gaze met the side of his face. And just like that, the noise around me—the indistinct chatter, the laughter— seemed as if it all became so quiet I could hardly hear.

Can we really fight fate? It's a question I should've asked myself.

I couldn't for the life of me believe my eyes. He was *actually* here. Not a hologram or a movie playing out in my head. He wasn't in his flight attendant attire either, nor was his crisp musky cologne the cheap kind. The one that beckoned me on first scent.

After ordering his drink, our eyes met for the second time.

The second time, undistracted, utterly lost, even if short.

Found again in each other's orbs.

Lightning strikes.

The sound of thunder in a drought.

For a brief beautiful moment, I remembered we were energy, at best. Nothing more, nothing less.

We dissolved in each other's eyes.

Squiggles of sparks.

But then, I forgot again.

I forgot I was a speck, flying through space. I forgot I had a vessel. I forgot I was everything and nothing at the same time.

I forgot all of it.

And by the look of his half-moon smile, so had he.

Because now, we were just two guys, standing next to each other at a bar.

He shook his head in disbelief, and I couldn't help but do the same.

"Hey," he said, eyes squinting.

"Hey," was all I could muster, gingerly.

He held out his hand. "Jasper."

Felt like saying I already knew his name, among other things. As a safeguard, though, I shook his hand and said, "Mack," my heart hammering in my chest.

As he planted himself on the stool beside me, a rogue internal voice began to boom.

Get up and leave. You might be able to save him.

My mind prickled with discomfort. But there was something about him that made me stay for now. Might've been his exuberant energy, which implored my curiosity to take over. Perhaps, I didn't really have a choice.

He gestured his hand toward the bar. "The Ocean Sprays are really good."

I chuckled. "I'll just have to take your word for it, won't I?"

They were: the Ocean Sprays glimmered cyan from inside a freshly-polished martini glass.

Jasper asked me what I did for a living, as people do. And so, proudly, I told him I was an ecologist.

"What's that again, something to do with plants and stuff hey?" he inquired.

I nodded. "Yeah, it's like the science and biology behind plants and animals. Lots of identifying and making choices which impact the land and stuff."

He peaked a brow but it quickly softened. "Sounds…amazing," he said. "Doing a really good thing for the planet there, mate."

"I try," was my sheepish response, taking a sip of my drink. "I've always been, I dunno, connected to plants. And I love the outdoors, so it's a good gig for me. I find plants are much more reliable than people."

He extended his eyes. "You're not wrong. I've got lots of houseplants at home. Bit of an addiction really."

I wanted to scream SAME at him as loud as possible, but I had to remind myself to breathe; half hyperventilating, half all warm and fuzzy inside.

"So, what's being a flight attendant like?" I asked him. "Must be pretty cool to travel all the time."

"I mean yeah, it's great," he replied, "the travelling is wicked. But I dunno, the novelty of always being somewhere new has kind of worn off for me. I've been doing it for almost three years now, which isn't like me to stay doing the same thing for this long."

"I know exactly what you mean," I said, feeling the topic to my core. "If I stay doing the same shit for too long, I just get bored. The good thing with ecology, I guess, is there are always new things happening. But then again, working full-time does take up most of my life, so I don't have time for much else. Unfortunately."

"I get it," Jasper agreed, "but *unfortunately*, most of the world has been conditioned to the idea that we need to get a degree as quickly as possible so we can get a job and, hell, work for the rest of our lives."

I sighed, taking a generous swig from the near-empty glass in my hand. "Very true," I said, my head downcast. "I just wanna live self-sufficient, ya know. Somewhere in the forest, where there's no need for mass consumerism, and capitalism, etcetera."

He smiled. "That's the dream right there, but…it's easier said than done."

What *was* easier said than done was trying to forget the pain, the feeling of his dead body in my arms. White nothingness, and one I wanted no part of.

"You're super tanned," he observed, after his third Ocean Spray, fucking me with his eyes from the bar couch we'd migrated to.

Stop it right now, I wanted to tell him. You don't know it, but this ends badly. *We* end badly.

"It's all summer's doing," I quipped, playing it cool. "Winter's a completely different story, though. I'm as white as a ghost."

"That's one thing I wished my Mum didn't do," Jasper said, "take me over to London when I was five. I guess toddler me knew what it was like growing up on the east coast of Australia. But honestly, I don't remember now."

We both giggled.

"Maybe you'll have to spend some more time here during summer to gear yourself up for the rest of the year in London," I proposed, playfully.

Raising his glass, he said, "Maybe," with emphasis, which was followed by a lengthy silence.

"What's a secret you've never told anyone?" he soon asked, eyes glued to me, moving closer but not enough to touch.

I shook my head, scoffed. "What kind of question is that?"

"A real one," he said.

Jeez, where did I even start? A secret.

The cogs in my brain started to spin faster. Two secrets came to mind.

But could I really tell him about Brain Cinema? That I could see the relationship timeline with every new person I met. Friends, lovers, acquaintances. Everyone.

Absolutely not.

A secret. What about that night?

The one I'd been running from for years; hiding, like a spotted quoll in the darkness.

The night I'd kept buried in journals until now.

Until the flight to Central Australia. Until I met Jasper.

I couldn't deny Jasper reminded me of him. That drive. That misty night when I was only seventeen years old.

And though we'd just met, the way Jasper looked at me

seemed as if maybe I could actually speak those words without him running away from me.

"You first," I stuttered.

"Well, I first drove a car when I was eight years old," Jasper revealed.

I snickered, narrowing my eyes at him.

When he didn't join in the half-suppressed laughter, I said, "You're not joking?"

He shook his head, the corners of his mouth curling at the corners.

"Do I even want to know the story behind this?"

He shrugged, raising a finger before saying, "Maybe I'll be inclined to tell the story. But first, what's your secret?"

I gulped hard. My heart raced in a medal-worthy manner. Normally I would never tell anyone this. But somehow, I'd convinced myself that maybe it was time I finally got it off my chest. Time to stop running from the past.

But why him of all people? This man, who I assumed had no idea what I'd seen. What I'd already lived for us in snapshots.

My stomach flipped. Sweat pooled on my forehead, the chatter around us now so loud the only way was out.

"I'm sorry," I said hastily. "I have to go."

And that's what I did.

I left.

Eight Years Prior

THEN

Finn must've risen before I did. He had a habit of doing this, even on Saturdays when I wanted nothing more than a sleep-in after a week of early wake-ups and six hours of school. So, I did what I did most Saturdays: roll back into a cozy slumber for another couple of hours.

Summer was coming to an end, so Finn's farmhouse in Bower Creek was hot, but the fan in his room certainly did its job of cooling me down. Especially when it blew right in my face.

Finn's hand covered my mouth, which had me mostly alarmed, but also weirdly calm.

"Shhh," he whispered. I grabbed his hand in reflex, but he pushed into my mouth harder. "Just don't freak out when you look up, okay? And don't scream."

I nodded, turning onto my back, his hand still stretched over my face. My eyes widened and I squirmed slightly.

A brown spotted carpet python slithered across the wooden beams above us.

Finn tried to keep me from flipping out. "It's not here to hurt us, okay?"

The snake hissed softly, its two-pronged tongue poking out, feeling for the next beam to climb across.

"Let's get outta here, slowly," he said, taking his hand off my mouth.

I nodded, whispering a soft "Okay" back at him.

Finn peeled himself off me and tip-toed out of the room. I followed, a little quicker than him, holding my breath, eyeing the python as I left the room. I let out a sigh of relief as I stepped out into the humidity of the day.

Even though the air conditioner had the living room at a comfortable temperature, I was happy to be outside of the house while the snake was lurking about.

"Let's go down to the creek for a swim, it's fucking hot," Finn suggested, a tote bag draped over his shoulder.

I'd slept in my boardies so it wasn't a problem for me. Finn seemed fine, too, already shirtless, wearing a pair of thin black gym shorts.

My stomach grumbled. "What about breakfast?"

Finn jingled the tote bag. "I packed us some ham and cheese toasties, mate. Let's go."

I followed him along the dirt road that led to the back of his property. Finn lived there with his parents and older sister, Delayne.

Finn and I were best mates, so I was always there on weekends and school holidays. It was my home away from home. The place I could come to escape from my boring abode.

Growing up on the east coast of Australia was the best of both worlds. You had the beach and the farm within a short drive of one another.

I'd never been your average beach boy. I didn't surf or bodyboard as the locals did. My father, on the other hand, loved to surf. He even tried to teach me when I was younger, but I wasn't interested in the slightest.

Finn and I spent most of our days on the farm riding motorbikes, playing *Call of Duty*, and, recently, going to parties.

"What time did you get up this morning?" I asked Finn as we cut through the cow paddock to get to the creek.

"Early. I've already had a workout and argued with Mum this morning. You missed a lot while you were sleeping, ya lazy shit."

Finn had a rocky relationship with his parents, so it was uncomfortable there sometimes, mostly when he would argue with them. However, I was used to arguments with my parents at home. Just not with me in them.

"What was the argument about?"

"Ugh, you know, the normal shit," he said casually.

"They're going away for the weekend and, as usual, expect me to do fucking *everything* around the farm."

"Have you told them you wanna move to the city when school's over?" I asked.

Finn rolled his eyes. "No. I think they think I'm gonna live on this boring old farm for the rest of my life. No fucking way, I couldn't think of anything worse."

If only Finn and I could've switched lives.

"I'll happily take your place and live here on the farm," I offered.

He scoffed. "Yeah. Right…"

"So, your parents are gone for the *whole* weekend?" I asked curiously.

"Yep, Delayne is at her friend's place too."

"Ayyyyyyeeee," I piped up, waggling my eyebrows. "Maybe we should get the girls over for a bit of fun."

Finn didn't seem as enthused at the thought of Brit and Mel coming over. It wasn't a bad idea. Brit's mum could even get us alcohol.

Finn stared off into the distance for a while, then chuckled. "What's going on with you and Brit anyway?" he asked.

"I mean, I think we're a thing," I said, seeming as confident as I could, without sounding over the top. "And hey, I'm pretty sure Mel likes you, bro. I was with them at the beach last week. She thinks you're hot."

Finn stifled a snort. "Good luck, Mel."

I frowned. "Mel's cute, don't you think?"

He shrugged. "I honestly haven't even thought about it, but sure."

I talked about girls a lot, but Finn hardly ever reciprocated.

On the edge of the creek, we wandered down the rocks, jumping from one stone to the next. Half-living at Finn's during the summer served me with rock-solid feet. The first time I wandered down there would've been a few years prior and I still remember the feeling of the stones on my soles, like a hammer hitting at high speed. But now, I was a Barefoot Bushman of Bower Creek, as Finn would say.

"You and Brit better not be all weird and all over each other if they come over tonight," Finn warned. "Because that sounds like a really shit time." He stripped down to his jocks and slowly submerged himself in the creamy blue and grey water.

While I perched on a flat rock, he had his back turned to me. And for the first time ever, I glanced at his lower half in a way I had never before. His jocks, all-black with an orange stripe around the top. His bulging thighs.

"Nah, we won't be weird at all, man," I dazed, reverting my gaze to the river oak trees and their stringy green and gold leaves.

Finn turned around and looked at me with raised brows. "Good," he said, before diving into the water face-first.

After his obnoxious splash wet me all over, I stood and gripped the rope attached to the tree, hands grasped onto the metal bar tied to the end of it. And without hesitation, I swung into the middle of the creek and let go, bombing into the water next to him.

"Good to see you aren't such a pussy with the swing now," he teased me.

"Speak for yourself, Mister *I'm-gonna-crawl-into-the-creek-like-a-little-bitch*," I retaliated.

He had no comeback, so instead, he splashed me with a face full of water. Little did he realize, two could play that game, and I returned the gift with almost as much force.

After a few minutes of splashing, chasing each other around the creek, and a few rope swings, we ate our ham and cheese toasties on the creek bed.

The sun beamed directly over the water, casting a sparkle that caused me to stare.

"Thank god for this creek, hey," I said with a mouthful of food.

"Honestly, if we didn't have it, I probably would've run away by now," Finn admitted. "Or made my rents buy a pool. Probably the first one."

"This is why going for your license is your freedom," I said reassuringly. "I'm actually so keen to go for mine in a few days."

He rolled his eyes and scoffed. "As if my parents will be able to afford to buy me a car."

I shrugged. "Having a job makes things easier too. Even if it's working at some shitty takeaway joint like me."

"Tell you what else is easier? Getting a job on the coast," he said as-a-matter-of-factly. "There's fuck all out here. The quicker I move to the city the better."

Finn was set on his dream of moving to the closest big city: Brisbane. It made me feel a little strange. I'd often wondered what I would do if he really did move away and start a new life. Maybe I'd follow him and we would get an apartment together, down the road from some hip little café, conveniently in walking distance to all the nightclubs.

Real talk though, my heart didn't belong in the city. The last time I visited my cousins in Sydney, I had to breathe my way through panic attacks when walking the streets at peak hour. How on earth did I think I could survive living in it?

Daylight savings on the family farm made me want to move to the country someday—where the sun was out past seven in the summer and the paddocks turned from green to orange.

Nighttime beckoned. As soon as Finn and I had lit a fire using the teepee technique, a silver sedan pulled onto the dirt driveway.

"Yes, Mum, we'll be here waiting in the morning. Yes, seven o'clock. Love you." Brit's thunderous tone could be heard from a field away.

The car drove off, and with their phone lights and echoing giggles, the girls approached.

It didn't take them long to find us by the bonfire, which was perfectly squared off by four concrete benches. Impressed by the blaze we'd made, I stoked the fire, even though it didn't need attention.

"Hey, losers!" called out Mel, the blonder and sassier of the two.

"Hey," Finn mumbled, going all shy.

"Well, *hello there!*" I exclaimed in a muffled tone,

dropping my stoking stick and hugging Brit, her hands gripped around my waist.

"Ew," Mel muttered, taking a seat next to Finn on the bench.

"Did you end up getting it?" I asked Mel, casting my gaze on her handbag.

She winked, following it with a clicking sound from her mouth. "Of course, I got it!"

"It's so cool that your mum trusts you with the house to yourself," Brit said to Finn whilst we sipped on our glasses of vodka and orange juice, the fire raging strong before us.

Mel interrupted before Finn could respond. "Brit, bitch, that's why you're always at my place."

Could relate. I couldn't remember the last weekend I spent at home.

"I think my mum doesn't give a shit, about a lot of things," Finn admitted, his speech slightly slurred.

Brit chuckled. "She must give a lot of shits about you to leave the farm to yourself for the night."

Brit raised a fair point, one of which had me half-nodding half-shrugging at Finn.

"Who's keen for dinner?" I suggested. "I'm starving."

Since the girls bought alcohol, Finn and I were in charge of food. His mum left us twenty dollars for dinner, and I chucked in some extra money so we could buy two pizzas from the takeaway joint down the road.

Another thing I loved about the farm was the stars on a clear night. A whole blanket of them spread across the sky. No light pollution, only the bulbs of the galaxy; Milky Way and all. Nature put on a show for us and we admired it, our bellies full of pizza and vodka.

"Anyone wanna go down to the creek and see the glow worms?" Finn asked after a moment of silence.

Mel tilted her head, gaping. "Sorry, what? Did you say *glow worms?*"

Finn nodded. "Yeah."

"Oh my god, yes!" Mel squealed.

Brit didn't seem too impressed by a frolic in the forest at night, so I volunteered to hold her hand the whole way. But it wasn't her hand I wanted to hold this time.

Finn and I had trundled down to see the glow worms a few times before. We'd lay on top of a rock by the creek, on a blanket, the trees illuminated with stars brighter than the ones in the sky.

We did the same with the girls. Same blanket. Same flat rock. Just a tad less room to stretch out.

"This is actually really cool," Brit said, entranced by the twinkling dots in the trees.

I had Brit on one side of me and Finn on the other. He and I were squished between the girls, our shoulders touching, yet no complaints.

"Tell you what else is really cool," I said cheekily, planting a kiss on Brit. Her lips tasted like strawberries and cream.

Mel lay on the other side of Finn, her head nestled on his chest. He didn't seem to be enjoying himself. But once Brit and I started making out, there was no stopping Mel from mimicking those movements with him. Their kissing sounded sloppy, so much so that I pulled away from Brit to cast a glance.

"Oooooh la la," I chimed in, before kissing Brit again. Not passionately as such, more so in a way to out-kiss our opposition. A game we'd already won, but felt the need to rub in their faces.

Brit soon slipped into the creek, wearing only her bra and underwear. If it weren't for the glow worms, I wouldn't have seen her at all, wading in the water.

I looked for any excuse not to go in after her. "You know we don't have a towel, right?"

"But, but, but," Brit sputtered. "It's like thirty degrees still. We'll drip dry, cunt. Now get in."

"You go," Mel told me, waving her hand over to Brit, then to Finn. She linked her arm with his. "We'll go and get some towels from the house, yeah?"

Finn glanced from me to Mel, rolling his eyes. "If we must."

"Yay!" Mel squeaked, shepherding Finn away. "Adventure time! Enjoy your swim, love birds."

Love birds? Not sure how I felt about that, but I rolled with it, pulling off my shirt and clambering to the rope swing.

"Oh my god, Mack, you're fucking crazy!" Brit yelled.

But before she could say anything else, I swung into the creek like a drunk short-haired Tarzan.

After splashing into the water, I gasped for air on the way back up.

"Yo, you could've landed on me!" Brit shouted, hitting me on the chest playfully.

I grinned. "But, did you die?"

A smile grew on her face, one that was met with hands around my neck, lips upon mine. Brit's warm body felt good against me.

She huffed between kisses. "I've always wanted to have sex in the water. Like they do in the movies."

But before we could do anything else, a howl echoed through the trees.

"Woah, what the fuck was that?" Brit twitched, her eyes darting in the direction of the sound.

"It's probably just them coming back," I assured, pulling her closer.

She budged.

The howl again. I was even a little spooked now.

Brit shivered. A rustle from the bushes made me flinch, soon growing louder. "Who's there?" I called out, a wee whimper in my voice.

"Rawrrrrr!" a voice bellowed. A shadow emerged from behind the tree, at the bank of the creek.

Brit screamed and I followed suit, until we realized it was none other than Finn, standing on a rock. I could tell it was him by his white teeth, grinning, laughing hysterically.

"Oh my god, you dickhead!" I shouted, swimming to the bank, Brit close behind me. He held two towels out to us, swinging them as though they were pieces of cheese in front of a dog.

"Got yas good," he said, rather impressed with himself.

Brit crawled out of the water and snatched a towel from Finn. "Literally fucking hate you."

I toweled off, still on edge. "*Not* cool."

"I dunno, the look on your faces was pretty priceless," Finn teased, unable to wipe the big stupid grin off his face.

"Where's Mel?" asked Brit, making her way up to her clothes on the rock.

"She wanted to stay by the fire," Finn said. "Said she wasn't feeling well."

By the time we'd walked back, Mel was asleep in the spare room bed.

Finn wanted to sleep in his own bed, which was fair enough.

Ultimately, Brit took to the spare bed with Mel, leaving me to sleep in Finn's bed, as usual.

There was a certain calmness to sleeping next to him.

I stared up at the beams as soon as I stood in his room. "So glad the friggin snake is gone."

Finn chuckled, peeling off his shirt. "Hope it's a tarantula next time."

Eyeballing him, I said, "That's a truly sick joke."

He crawled into bed and I followed after switching off the light behind me. He then rolled onto his side, back facing me.

"Successful night," I whispered.

"Mmm. It was fun."

I paused. "So, you and Mel hey? Did you guys do anything else on your little walk back?"

Finn scoffed. "Pffft. No."

Through mindful whispers, I told him what happened in the creek.

"Nice," he replied, with tepid enthusiasm. "You like her?"

"I think so."

"Well, I think you should go for it."

I sighed. "Yeah, I dunno."

"All up to you, dude." His last words before dozing off.

Not me, though. I stared at the ceiling for a long time, searching for answers in the wooden beams of wisdom. Alas, they never revealed their secret remedies, nor did I come to a conclusion to the ever-evolving thoughts in my head. The fear people would find out what I truly desired. The fear I'd lose my friends, my family, everyone, and I'd be alone. The fight was strong, between the part of me who wanted to be free, and the part of me who wanted to continue living in secret because it was the safest option. The option we'd known for as long as we'd remembered.

Finn rolled over in his slumber, pressing up against me, his knuckle grazing my shoulder. Only then did those strange feelings I'd felt all day feel more real than ever.

The front of my shorts pushed up against the blanket.

It was confirmed. I had a crush on my best friend. And I knew, probably more than much else, that things would never be the same again.

Friend of a Friend

LATER

My phone rang at the ungodly hour of nine in the morning, waking me with a jolt.

"Hello?" I answered frantically.

"Maaaaaaate," Rachel crowed through the phone. "I'm here. You should totally come down and get me."

"Oh fuck," I cursed. "I slept in, didn't I?" I peered at the time on my phone. "Yep, I definitely slept in."

Rachel breathed hard. "Oi, you're on holiday, don't worry about that. Now come down and show me into this blue lagoon of bad decisions."

Tell you what might've been a bad decision: to take up that drink offer from Jasper. The events from the night before came pouring back, filling up my brain in true floodplain fashion. Me leaving Jasper at the bar, ever so abruptly. My past, coming back to haunt me. Real *Days of Our Lives* kind of shit.

Rachel hung up and I had no choice but to crawl out of bed, run my head under the shower, brush my hair, throw on some clothes, and amble down to the front desk, all the while craving nothing but a hashbrown. Crispy, deep-fried, golden goodness sounded like my only savior right now. And I *had* to have it, or I'd probably die.

The hangovers seemed to get worse every single time. When I was eighteen, I could go on multi-day benders without effort. Probably wake up for work at six a.m. the day after and power on through. I was now twenty-five. And honestly, if the day after a big night out didn't consist of endlessly scrolling through socials to take my mind off a spinning head, I'd consider myself the luckiest man on earth.

Rachel looked somewhat blurry to me when I finally reached the front desk. She chatted away to the tall, burly receptionist, hiding behind her sunglasses, a small orange suitcase beside her. Once she saw me, she gave the receptionist one last laugh.

"Well, here he is," Rachel called out, pointing to me. "Thanks for the recommendations, uh…"

The receptionist turned around to look at me, but I really wished he hadn't. Not only was I still half-blinded, but my eyes were probably redder than the devil's dick.

"Alvaro," he finished her sentence, smiling at her awkwardly.

Without another word, I ushered Rachel into the lift as quickly and quietly as possible.

"Yeah so, the location is super-secret apparently," Rachel rambled once we reached the hotel room.

"Some guy told me last night about the festival," she went on. "I had to pry the location out of him 'cause as soon as I'd heard, hey, *bush doof in the fucking desert,* I was like, *we gotta go*, right?"

I didn't blame her one bit. You could always count on Rachel to find something fun for us to do on our holiday. I'd always dreamed of going to Burning Man, but I'd never had the funds to jet off to the United States.

The afternoon came quicker than expected. And as much as I could've gone without returning to the bar, Rachel hadn't tried an Ocean Spray yet. I certainly couldn't let her go without. By this point, my hangover had subsided to a soft burn, one which deserved to be patched up with more exquisite blue beverages.

While Rachel and I sat at a booth and sipped on Ocean Sprays, I couldn't help but glance around at the room full of chatter, scanning faces in case any of them looked remotely familiar. Jasper-familiar.

"Yo, hello…" Rachel clicked her fingers in front of my face. "Who're you looking for?"

I was quick to say "No one," but she wasn't convinced one bit.

"Did you end up fucking someone in our hotel room last night and you're like, scared you're gonna bump into him or something?"

I rolled my eyes. "Okay, there was a guy I met last night, but he was cracking onto me so much in the bar and I wasn't into him so I…fucked off."

Half true, except for the part where I was actually *so into him* I couldn't possibly let it happen. Not after what I saw. That string of happy memories, followed by the untimely demise of all demises.

"You little fucker!" Rachel piped up, also taking a look around, her dark skin glowing against the bar's mood lights. "Well, if you can find a gay guy in the middle of Australia, surely I can find a girl out here who's into girls."

I smiled, lifting my brows up and down. "I don't doubt you at all."

Never underestimate the power of lesbian Tinder in a small town, it turned out.

Rachel swiped through the few profiles in Alice Springs, only stopping on one.

She *hmm*ed curiously, eyes squinted to get a closer look at the screen.

Now she had my attention. "Go on, give us a look."

Lily. Twenty-seven. Profile picture of her covered in glitter, wearing a rainbow cape, half-looking away and smiling, sweaty bodies taking up the rest of the photo in a lush green forest. Her bio read:

If it's gay or there's psytrance, I'm in Filipino-Australian x

"Looks like she's at a doof in the photo," I observed.

"No shit, Sherlock. She's obviously here in town for the one tomorrow!" Rachel clicked on her phone. "Oh my god. She matched!"

Rachel was officially screen-glued, messaging Lily in a huff. Meanwhile, Grindr called to me in the same desperately horny way it normally would. And not surprisingly, I was disappointed as usual. No one around who tickled my fancy, yet there was Rachel, with a reply from Lily already.

I sipped down the rest of the Ocean Spray with my bamboo straw, noticing Rachel was now consumed by her own dating app forcefield. She had this eager grin on her face and bit her lip while she typed.

I rolled my eyes and stood from the table. "I'll go grab us another drink then."

She didn't hear me, nor did I expect her to. I honestly could've got up and left the bar without a word and she probably still wouldn't have noticed.

Standing at the bar, I noticed two young guys sitting in the same seats Jasper and I were in the night before.

I was truly kidding myself if I thought I'd be able to forget about it. Even after a few pretty blue beverages.

On my return to the table, it was a surprise to see Rachel off her phone, wearing a sneaky smirk on her face, which could mean only one thing: it was *on*.

"We've got it all sorted," she winked.

"And what's that?"

"So, surprise, surprise, Lily *is* going to the festival tomorrow. She's busy tonight, so we're gonna meet at the main stage at sunset tomorrow. Front left."

"So specific," I said, arching a brow. "Promise me I won't be your third wheel. I can't deal with third wheeling."

Rachel grabbed my hand. "Don't worry. Lily has a friend with her so you and her can party if Lily and I ever feel the need to have a quickie in the tent, or somewhere in the forest."

One of the many things Rachel and I had in common: we both loved outdoor sex. There was something about being out in nature, entangled with another human. So fresh, so connected, so free. But also, as if you were breaking the rules somehow. And even though the probability of someone catching you in the act was relatively low, it still felt rebellious.

Rachel pulled her Ocean Spray closer. "Gosh, what's even in these things? The first one went straight to my head."

"As long as you don't tell the security guard that your father works for NASA, I think we'll be fine."

Rachel cackled. "Oh dear, my mouth really does run loose when I drink, doesn't it? Those people in the club must've thought I was the biggest whack job…"

This was one moment I couldn't ever let Rachel live down, even if it was two years prior.

"You were…on another planet," I reminded her.

She pouted her lips, then smiled until her eyes were slits.

"I think the planet is called Lilyville," Rachel said, slurring her words slightly.

I sighed.

"Hey, look. If I can find a chick out here in a few

swipes, I'm sure there'll be plenty of hot gay boys at the festival you can get fucking in-tents with."

I shrugged. "I dunno. I think I'd be a bit rusty, to be honest."

"You've been with a few dudes since Sam though, right?"

I placed my hand over my chin, stretching the skin down as far as it would go. "We do not speak his name."

Rachel chuckled slightly, before swiftly wiping the smile from her face. "Sorry, I shouldn't have brought it up. Fuck him."

"Yeah, fuck him for cheating on me with my ex-ex-boyfriend," I muttered, rolling my eyes.

"He was the epitome of shit," Rachel told me. "He didn't deserve you."

I sighed. "Yeah, I know. Wasn't meant to be, I guess," I admitted. "But even though it was a while ago now, the trust issues are still very much real. Although, the moving on factor…it definitely worked."

Rachel leaned in closer to me over the table. "That's why this trip will be good for us. We've both been working bloody hard, so we deserve this."

Talking about Sam made the moment come back to me yet again. Finding him and Stu, my boyfriend prior to Sam, in bed together when all I wanted to do was surprise Sam with a new house plant he'd been talking about all week. The moment of pure fury, catching them, throwing the house plant right at them in bed, soil spraying all over the white bedspread.

As it was, they got the last laugh. They got to be

together, whereas I became swamped with the possibility of never trusting a partner again. It made me angry. Angry at them for going behind my back (and not in the good way). But more so, angry at Brain Cinema for not showing me this would happen. When I met both Sam and Stu, the visions showed me all the good things. Naturally, all the lovely enticing things made me want to date them even more.

Perhaps, in the most anomalous yet simple of ways, Brain Cinema just showed me what I was meant to see.

I shook my head in disbelief, taking another sip of my Ocean Spray. "How did we end up becoming best friends?"

"We both love plants and we're both queer as fuck so I think those two things were enough to bond over."

I'd known Rachel for seven years now, since university, and I'd always appreciated how open we were with each other. She was one of those friends who you wouldn't see as often as you might want. But when you would, it was timeless. Similar to a long-lost family member, biological or not.

I shrugged in somewhat agreement. And before long, we'd finished another round of drinks, which led us back to the hotel room. We figured a good night's sleep was in order if we were going to survive a four-day music festival. Usually, it took me a while to doze off into a deep slumber. But that night, I was fading fast even after a few minutes.

The following morning, Rachel's phone alarm woke us, with a tune much calmer than mine. Instead of a screeching fire bell, we had soft bird noises over a subtle slow melody. Honestly, a far less intrusive way of waking up. I was a heavy sleeper once I sunk into REM. So perhaps the hushed wake-up worked for some people, and not for others.

Briefly, I remembered the dream I was having before I woke. The world was sinking into lava, and Jasper had to team up with me to escape from the burning hole that was now the earth. Just him and I.

I thought I'd made a notable attempt to forget about him, until this fucking dream, so thank you very much, subconscious.

Rachel was the first to inch out of bed, opening the curtains to blinding light.

Squinting on reflex, I shot her a glare of 'I haven't had a coffee yet, why the fuck would you do that?'

Unapologetically, she picked up a menu from the TV table and hummed. "Room service breakfast in a fancy hotel. It'd be rude not to, right?"

Rude it would be.

An hour later, we had Rachel's SUV hire car packed and ready for take-off to Anamnesis Festival.

"*Love* that you got a car with a rooftop tent," I mentioned, whacking on some trance music to get us in the mood.

"I just didn't wanna buy a tent and leave it there like a lot of other peeps do at festivals, you know," she explained. "Trying to be more eco-friendly and shit. It's fucking horrifying seeing post-festival campground photos. The amounts of shit people leave behind. It's really unnecessary. Event organizers say 'leave no trace' for a reason."

"True, true," I agreed, turning up the music as we left the township, the civilization of housing soon swapped out for tangerine dirt plains and sandstone canyons.

The desert had a serene calmness to it, as though the vast landscape resembled an open field of opportunity—to think without distraction, without noise.

Identifying flora came naturally to me, and there were so many plants and trees out there I knew the names of but had rarely seen for myself. Like *allocasuarina decaisneana*, or more commonly known as, desert oak trees.

Countless spinifex shrubs were scattered through the plains, in different sizes, some sharper than others. The terrain sure was different than back on the east coast, and I was loving every minute of it.

After fifteen minutes of plant spotting, Rachel turned down the music. "Remember when we went to our first festival together?" she reminisced.

I chuckled. "Oh god, when Stu stepped on a stick and we had to take him to the hospital?"

"Oh shit, I forgot about that! I was more so thinking about when you and I ended up telling everyone there were drop monkeys in the trees on our trips to and from the dancefloor. But yeah, wow, Stu really got himself into a doozy that weekend, didn't he?"

Even though it was me who broke off my two-year relationship with Stu, it was still a little painful to reflect on our memories together.

I made the same monkey sound I had years ago.

Rachel giggled, pulling into a roadhouse petrol station on the side of the road. The only building in sight.

The outback welcomed us with hefty fuel prices to make up for the untouched beauty at each glance. It seemed as if other festival-goers had the same idea to stop off. Fortunately, waiting in line for fuel meant we could spot the colorful punters who sauntered in and out of the roadhouse. Boho getups, Mad Max-style costumes; you name it. It was safe to say that Rachel and I felt rather underdressed, for now. It would only take a rummage through our bags in the back and a change of clothes, and we'd be right there with the rest.

"Imma put my party shirt on," I declared boyishly, my eyes as wide as my list of lies. "Want one too?"

She pumped the fuel while I filtered through my duffel bag of endless glad rags. "Nah nah nah, the moment I get to the party is the moment my bikini goes on, and *stays on* until someone takes it off me. And in this case, I fucking hope it's Lily."

"Rachel?!" a voice chimed in, yelling from the car park.

Rachel's eyes expanded, scanning around like she was the victim of a haunted house. Good thing for her, the owner of the voice was no evil spirit, unless slayer of the pussy counts.

Lily looked identical to her Tinder photos. Perhaps even better.

She strolled over to our car, her face already covered in glitter. She wore black fishnet stockings which crept up her legs, all the way to her short black skirt and rainbow crop top. Rachel on the other hand didn't know where to put her hand, so she ultimately stuck it into the pocket of her denim shorts, thumb sticking out.

"Uh…Lily, right?" asked Rachel, even though she knew exactly who this woman was.

The two beamed at each other, rather red on the cheeks, letting out a little laugh before uttering another word.

"This ain't no front left speaker," Lily mentioned, before popping her head into the boot of the car.

<u>MACKENZIE'S BRAIN CINEMA ACTIVATED</u>

First clip: Lily and I, eyes locked on the dancefloor, standing next to each other. She smiles at me. She has no shirt on, her breasts revealed, closing her eyes and smiling up into the sunshine.

Second clip: we're at lunch, in what seems like an alfresco café on a city side street. The smile is on her face again.

Third clip: Lily at her lowest, with dark circles under her eyes. Those of which are wet from tears.

"Hey," I said, twitching slightly, slipping on my thin rainbow overshirt.

"This is Mack, my festival buddy," Rachel sing-songed. "And best friend, of course."

Lily's contagious smile was easily mirrored. "You guys ready for a killer four days, or what?" She hoisted a brow. "Looks like we might have to be camp neighbors."

Rachel and I swapped glances.

"If you guys are keen, that is?" Lily second-guessed.

"Yeah, for sure!" Rachel piped up, trying not to sound too excited, and failing miserably.

If Rachel and Lily were two half-lit fires, Lily had metaphorically doused petrol on them both. "Groovy," she winked. "We just gotta wait on my mate and then we can follow each other out?"

She definitely spoke too soon.

"Hey," a voice called.

I was under the impression Lily's mate was a "she", but oh-so-wrong I was. Lily's mate—the one she was going to the festival with—the one who would apparently be camping with us now too—was a "he", it turned out.

And *he* now stood between Rachel and Lily.

Nope. Nope. No way. What the fuck was happening? Surely this was some sort of sick joke. I wanted to scream at a desert-echoing volume.

"Howdy howdy," Lily greeted him. She turned from Rachel to me. "Rachel, Mack, this is Jasper."

"Nice to meet you," said Rachel, bubbly and unaware, shaking his hand.

"You too!" Jasper replied cheerfully.

For a brief tick, I thought this was the moment I'd wake up and realize it was all a lava-soaked dream. But no, this didn't feel convoluted like the world we visit when we sleep. Too many intrinsic details, and a feeling I couldn't run or wake from. He was in fact here, holding his hand out to me, across the very real car in that very real petrol station. Not wanting to make a scene of any kind, I shook his hand without question.

"Nice to meet you, Mack."

I nodded, hiding from that bold stare of his. "Ditto."

An awkward silence followed. However, my brain was

far from quiet as I questioned literally everything in existence. By everything, I meant Jasper. From how the fuck something like this could happen, to why it was happening, to everything in between. Was this Brain Cinema's way of telling me I couldn't run away from what I saw, and the life I was supposed to live?

"Woo, camp buddies!" Lily announced. "How fun!"

She passed a wink to Rachel, who replied with an enthusiastic, "Woo!"

As much as I wanted to believe Jasper had planned all of this, he was noticeably as quiet as me. Processing, processing, processing. Okay, still processing. Everything was quite royally fucked and I was now exposed, vulnerable. May as well cut me open.

"Should be fun," Jasper agreed, almost for the both of us.

Would it be, though? Perhaps, if and when my state of panic decided it would regress to a less-consuming prod as it trudged through my body.

And so, we said our "See you's there," to our now camp crew of four, setting back on the wide-open road to my uncontrollable fate.

One thing I'd always hated was not having control, and I felt that more than ever. Maybe I was the problem. I couldn't, for the most part, let things be the way they were anymore. A constant burning desire to change the things I saw.

"Everything okay, mate?" Rachel asked, after releasing one of her favorite trance songs through the car speakers.

I'd been deep in thought without realizing how much so. "Yeah, girl, just taking in the scenery."

She shot me a devilish smirk and, somehow, I knew what she was going to say. "So, you reckon Jasper's cute?"

I chuckled. "Yeah, he is."

It felt as if this had now turned into some sort of fucked up game, upon which I was the protagonist and had to make my move before the first act turning point. Needless to say, I hoped the conclusion wasn't what I'd first seen it to be.

"What did you see when you first met him?" Rachel asked.

Honestly, sometimes I wish I'd never told anybody about the things I can see. There are always questions. And some, like this one, I would've rather not answered.

"Not a whole lot," I lied. "A few snapshots of us partying together." Could've told her, but I didn't want to make things more awkward than they already were. It was better to keep her in the dark for now, I thought. At least until the next four days were over. Until I could figure out what the fuck was going on.

"What about Lily?" Rachel interrogated.

I shrugged. "Same same."

She smacked her hand on the steering wheel. "I was afraid this would be nothin' but a four-day affair!"

After driving another hour or so, we followed the map to a dirt road that pulled off to the left. Kicking up dust, with cars beelining to the gate, we kept on crunching through.

"Along a doof road we go," declared Rachel, clicking up our windows.

Nothing new, though. All of our favorite raves and festivals in Australia were off the beaten track. Far enough from civilization that the ground-vibrating music was only heard by those who consented to its sheer force. This one was no different, and so, the dirt road led us over a rolling hill, down into a sandstone-surrounded valley.

After showing our tickets and slapping on wristbands, it was time to find a campsite amongst the sea of colors. In the distance, markets were being erected along a narrow line. Music chattered from campsites as we drove through.

"Hey!" bellowed a voice from the car behind us. Lily hung out of the window to gather our attention. Rachel stopped our car.

"Yeah?" Rachel called back.

"We should camp a little further away from the music!" Lily pointed further into the valley, away from the already tight-knit sites near the market stalls and stages.

Rachel laughed. "You're absolutely right." She stuck a thumb out the window and turned to the left, slowing right down so she could swoon over Lily some more.

"This chick's a fucking doof veteran," she mentioned to me, biting her lip.

Lily overtook us in her electric blue Jeep, beeping the horn furiously as if to say *I'm choosing where we camp. Follow me, fuckers.* I laughed.

"That turns me on," Rachel added, grinning, speeding up a little. She followed Lily's Jeep over to a grove of ghost gums, reversing rear-first toward the trees before hopping out of the car. "Woo, we made it!" Rachel trilled, lifting her hands in the air. First in celebration, then to stretch.

Lily high-fived her. "Fuck yeah we did." She swooped in and unashamedly pecked her on the lips.

"Well well well." Instantly, Rachel went red as Lily started unpacking from the back of her car.

Jasper and I glanced at each other. I rolled my eyes, looked away, and started helping Rachel unpack camping equipment from the car.

"So, I know Lily's usually based in Brisbane, close to our turf," Rachel said as I ripped the covering off our rooftop tent. "What about you, Jasper?"

When Jasper gave us his life lowdown, I pretended I didn't already half-know his story. He'd met Lily a few years back in Brisbane when he was living there, and the two had planned a road trip in Central Australia together.

I chimed in with a few "Oh, cool's" and an "Aw, awesome". I even snuck in, "It would be nice knowing you technically have two homes since you have family in Australia too." I thought I was playing the stranger game famously; despite the fact all games came to an end at some point.

After setting up the tents, tables, and chairs under the gums, we sat back and cracked open a beverage. I instantly felt more relaxed once an ice-cold beer from the esky washed down my throat. Sitting back and sighing in accomplishment, I let the midday desert sun spray me.

"Shit, we forgot to buy ice," Lily groaned.

"All good, you guys help yourselves to our beers for now," Rachel insisted.

"Tell you what I love about bush doofs," I mentioned to the others as we all sipped. "The fact that we can bring our own drinks and not pay close to fifteen bucks for a pre-mixed can like you do at mainstream festivals."

"Yeah, especially if you buy ten of them in one day," Jasper agreed. "Which is around the price of three bottles of spirits."

Rachel scoffed, tying her dark brown hair up. "It sure stops idiots who don't know their limits, though. It's probably why the cans are only one standard drink at those festivals."

"Oh god, I definitely learned my limits the hard way at doofs when I was younger," Lily added.

An intrusive thought arrived, of me crawling in the mud on the dancefloor of a sloshy, rainy bush doof when I was eighteen. "Yeah, me too."

"I never found any bush doofs in the UK," Jasper put forth.

"You got Boomtown though, right?" I cut in. "I met a guy from London last year and he said that festival was his yearly ritual or something."

"Yeah, I've been to Boomtown with friends a few times. It's good fun."

The beer made me stop thinking about the pure mindfuck everything had so suddenly become. Even if for a short while. Until Lily finished the dregs of her beer.

"I'm gonna go buy some ice from the market stalls." She turned to Rachel. "Wanna join me for a walk?"

Rachel raised her brows and smiled. "I'd be honored."

Lily cast a glance at Jasper and me. "Hold down the

fort, boys. The lesbians are gonna scope out the vibe in this playground."

"Okay," said Jasper.

Half-lifting my hand to say I was coming with them, I ultimately refrained when I saw the "stay right here" stare from Rachel to me. The lesbians cracked another beer and wandered into the field, leaving Jasper and me, to what, plan out our destined love and funeral(s)?

Unsure of what to even say to him, and vice versa it seemed; we sat in silence. A silence that made me want to get up and run into the hills. A silence that unabashedly dragged on.

"Fuckin' crazy, hey?" he finally said, biting his lip. "If it makes you feel any better, I'm as mind-boggled as you are."

Shaking my head dismissively, I sighed and downed the rest of my beer. "I highly doubt that."

I fished another bottle out of the esky and cracked it, guzzling down a mouthful.

Jasper shrugged. "I…I honestly don't know what to think. I'm shook. But hey, coincidences happen all the time, right?"

"Right." If only he knew what I knew.

His eyebrows squished together. "What happened the other night?"

I felt my body heat rise in true lava dream fashion. "Honestly, the last thing I wanna talk about right now."

He put his hands up to face height. "You're right. It's none of my business. I hardly know you."

"Correct."

"I just…ah, I wanna get to know you."

It was harder than it should've been.

Staring at the ground, I cleared my throat with another gulp. "Sorry, but I don't wanna get to know you. Not like that. I'll be your festival friend here and we'll take a bunch of drugs with the girls and be friendly. But, I'm, ah…not interested in you in that way."

All lies. Lies, lies, fucking lies, and Jasper's face was all disappointed. But I needed to protect him. I couldn't let someone else die because of me. History couldn't repeat itself this time. Not on my watch.

Melting Moments

THEN

"If you could have one superpower, what would it be?" asked Finn, next to me as we trudged down a row of passion fruit vines.

The scorching summer sun belted down on us while a swarm of cicadas hummed in earshot.

"Uh, probably telekinesis so these passion fruits would pick themselves." I knelt, scooping up another bit of fruit, huffing before adding it to Finn's bucket.

I wiped the sweat from my brow, knowing quite well I smelt atrocious. But Finn also had a perspired scent, so it certainly wasn't a one-way street in the body odor department.

Stretching his back before bending down, Finn collected a handful of passion fruits—some green, some dark purple, shriveled—and threw them in the bucket.

"Oh c'mon, it's good Saturday morning exercise," he said. I wasn't convinced, not even a little. "Plus," he continued, "my parents are paying you better for this than the takeaway joint."

Finn's parents grew a slew of fruits and vegetables on the farm and sold them at the local markets some weekends.

I chuckled. "Yeah, why do you think I canceled my greasy ol' shift at the shop today?"

My back ached each time I bent down. Glad we were on the second-last row, at least. We'd been at it for two hours. Two hours too long, in my opinion.

"What superpower would you choose?" I said, after a prolonged silence. Silence from us, that was. Not the god-awful cicadas.

Reaching the end of the row, it was my turn to open the potato sack as Finn poured the bucket full of fruit into it.

"Hmmm," he said, "I'd say teleportation. Or flying."

"Flying would be cool."

"Yeah. When you hate it somewhere, you could be like, 'All right, catchyas'."

At every chance possible, Finn would talk about how much he wanted to leave Bower Creek. Sometimes, without even specifically saying it. I, on the other hand, continued

to dream of Bower Creek—my nook in the forest. And so, I nodded in agreement like the best friend I was.

"Ugh, I gotta chuck a piss," he groaned, handing me the bucket. "One sec."

He turned around and shuffled close to the vine. Everything seemed slow-motion when he unzipped his pants and started urinating.

As much as I tried to refrain, I couldn't help but stare in a daze, thinking things I wished I wouldn't. Mostly what the view looked like from a front-on angle. Not his back turned.

I had to say something. Anything. "Dude, be careful. I saw your dad running around before, checking the rows."

With a scoff, Finn tucked a handful into the front hole of his shorts and zipped back up. "Hey, I read somewhere that piss can actually help plants thrive."

"Questionable. Just like picking fruit in this humidity."

He shrugged. "At least working early this morning means the weekend is pretty much paid for."

We tackled the final row of passion fruits which lay helpless on the muddy ground.

"You said your sister can get us alcohol for the party tonight, right?"

He threw a thumbs-up. "Yeah. Also, I forgot to tell ya. I nicked something from her stash last night."

"What is it?"

We stopped. After resting the bucket on the ground, Finn reached into his pocket and pulled out his slim black leather wallet. He fished out a slice of foil burrowed in one of the pockets, peeling it open to reveal two tiny squares of cardboard, perhaps only a centimeter on each side, colored rainbow.

"It's LSD," he said, wearing a rebellious grin I wasn't completely convinced of.

Finn had always erred on the side of defiance, ever since I'd known him. But it'd never involved drugs. I was seventeen. I'd never done drugs. Unless a few tokes of weed counted. So, my reaction to seeing those little cardboard pieces was one of downright skepticism.

"So, after you and I watched *Fear and Loathing in Las Vegas* last week..." I began. "Did you...get inspired or something?"

"Hehe. Maybe," he said devilishly.

"Look, I dunno how I feel about doing that at the party tonight," I confessed, my forehead creasing.

Finn chuckled. "There's no way we'd do it at the party tonight," he laughed. "I've asked Delayne about acid before. She said it's more of a thing you'd wanna do with close friends or at a doof with all the pretty lights."

"Oh yeah, I forgot she goes to *bush doofs*," I said, using inverted commas with my fingers.

"Apparently, they're lots of fun. She said she'd take me some time. Who knows, maybe you and I could both go to one?"

I stuck my nose up. "Eh, I dunno if they'd be my thing. But look, you know I'll try anything once."

Regretfully, I smirked.

The afternoon arrived, and we versed each other in *Call of*

Duty while an ambrosial baked dinner aroma wafted through the house. Notably into Finn's room, since it was right next to the kitchen.

Delayne soon popped into the room, in the midst of us pressing buttons on the controllers and blurting out commentary toward the TV screen. She wore a white tie-dyed T-shirt that hung to her thighs. We paused the game.

"What time am I dropping you losers off at your little party?" she asked.

Finn narrowed his eyes on her. "I thought Mum was dropping us off?"

A short laugh left Delayne's mouth. "No. Mum and Dad are leaving right after dinner at around six and won't be back until tomorrow."

"Typical," scoffed Finn. "Um, could you maybe drop us off at, like, seven?"

"How are you guys getting back? Cause I'm going to a party tonight too, and I'll be drinking and stuff, so…"

"Uh," I began, swapping glances with Finn. "We hadn't even thought of that."

"The party's pretty close to your place, isn't it?" he asked me.

"Yeah."

"Maybe you could take your car over, too, and then we drop it off at your house before Delayne takes us to the party," he suggested to me.

I nodded my head, lips pursed. "Could do." I'd forgotten that I now had my provisional license.

"Hmm," he continued, "or we could either walk back

to your house…or would your parents pick us up from Mel's?"

"Pffft," I rolled my eyes. "Like your parents, mine drink on a Friday night too. Actually, they drink from four p.m. on a Friday. They won't be able to pick us up."

Finn shrugged his shoulders. "The walk wouldn't be too bad."

"It's only a few kilometers," I said.

"Piece of piss after all the passion fruits we picked today."

Delayne cut in. "Can't believe you two got conned into that. Also, Finn. I needa ask you somethin'." She leaned in close and receded to a whisper. "You know the stuff I showed you last night, the stuff we were speaking about?"

Finn nodded so inconspicuously he could've been a professional liar. "Yeah."

"Have you seen it lying around anywhere? I can't seem to find it, and thought you might've picked it up possibly?"

I swallowed, hard. My skin prickled with discomfort.

"Nah, haven't seen it, hey," said Finn, shaking his head.

Delayne sighed, cursing a "shit" and a "dammit" before starting an actual sentence. "I hope Mum or Dad didn't find it. Ah well, I haven't exactly been in the best headspace this week so it's probably a sign I wasn't meant to trip tonight."

"Probably," was Finn's reply.

"Dinner's ready," Their mum, Kerry, called out.

As much as Finn talked ill of his parents, I loved Kerry. She was the cool hip mum, partying on weekends more often than not. She even let Finn and I smoke a joint once the year prior, but that was top-secret information.

"So, boys, where are we going tonight?" Charles, Finn's dad, wanted to know.

"Party at Mel's," answered Finn, mid-mouthful of roast lamb.

"I'm off to a party tonight, too, Dad. Thanks for asking," Delayne interrupted, the sarcasm radiating from her like a slow cooker.

Charles sure was swift with his response. "Delayne, you're twenty-one. You can do whatever you please. These two on the other hand…"

"Who's Mel?" Kerry questioned with curiosity.

"Finn's girl," I winked, at the same time knowing quite well it was the last thing I wanted to manifest.

Finn's mouth fell agape, his forehead following with a frown. "Okay, that's bullshit and you know it."

"Naw, Finn's going all red in the face," Delayne teased. "Is this who you were texting all last night when we were hanging out?"

Laughing, I was there for the drama, ready for whatever magnitude it was to reach.

"She somehow got my number," Finn said, casting his gaze back to me, wider-eyed this time.

I grimaced. "Mel pretty much begged me for it, so I gave it to her."

"Well," Kerry chimed in, "it sounds as if you've been enjoying the friendly texts."

Delayne rolled her eyes. "Ugh, teenage boys," she groaned. "It's times like these I wish I had a sister instead."

Kerry shot her a stern look. "I grew up with two sisters, Delayne. And trust me, it wasn't all rainbows and smiles."

Finn stifled a smirk. "I text plenty of people. Doesn't mean anything."

He washed his bold statement down with a generous gulp of H20.

At Finn's house, there was always banter of some sort at the dinner table. At mine, it was mostly silverware hitting plates and the occasional, "Can you pass me XYZ?"

"Why'd you have to bring up Mel?" Finn asked me as we got ready for the party.

"Oh, c'mon man. It was a joke."

"I know, it's just...I don't want people getting the wrong idea."

"What do you mean?"

"I dunno if I even like her in that way. I don't know what you told her. But I don't want her to get the wrong impression. I mean, she's nice and all but, yeah. I guess I've never really spoken to a girl in that way, like, ever."

Even if I couldn't be honest with Finn about some things, I had to be honest with him about this. "Yeah, look. I gave her your number, but she was pretty damn forceful in prying it out of me. She asked me if I thought you might fancy her after you guys kissed last weekend, and I said it was worth a shot."

He released a long sigh. "Fine. Look, I'll consider it."

"Atta boy," I piped up. "Plus, I'm pretty sure me and Brit are gonna have sex tonight."

"Brit and *I*." Okay, how long had Delayne been standing there? "Ready to go, losers?"

Standing to attention, I took a moment to process the fact that Delayne had heard me talking about potentially having sex with a girl, before following her and Finn out of the room.

My silver thousand-dollar Nissan sedan with the sunroof was a fresh breath of freedom. I could drive anywhere I pleased—(mostly) whenever I wanted—and didn't have to depend on anyone else.

We cruised over the hinterland, Delayne following us in her car. Finn was perched in my passenger seat, arm out the window, wind on his face. Looking over and smiling, I waited for him to smile back. He did, but he also told me to keep my fucking eyes on the road. A not-so-gentle reminder, and one that was absolutely needed.

My family home was the definition of suburbia, planted neatly in a street away from the beach, wedged within a line of houses that looked almost the same; in shape and size, but not color. Ours had a maroon roof, the one to the left black, and the one on the right, I wasn't exactly sure what color that was. A mix of red and pink, though the sticky summer sun had certainly faded those tiles over the years.

After parking my car on the street, Finn and I walked into the house while Delayne waited in her car. Looked like Mum and Dad had cleaned it earlier. The place was spotless, walls whiter than ever. The family Golden Retriever, Rufus barked from the backyard to greet us.

Mum bellowed at Rufus to stop barking, then continued to bicker with Dad on the back deck.

You could say it was a conventional Friday afternoon in the McMillan household. Lucas, my twelve-year-old brother had his eyes glued to the Xbox. Mum and Dad were having a pre-drink before heading to the beach club, listening to country music. Of course, they liked to get themselves a little tipsy so they didn't have to buy as many drinks at the bar.

Even though they were, I'd say, well-off, Mum and Dad didn't spend much of their money. They kept it locked up in investment properties and accounts they couldn't touch.

I'd ask for things. It could be anything. A new DVD. A game for my Xbox. And they'd say no. They had the money but didn't give it away, even to their own kids. They did it for a reason. So, Lucas and I would grow up with the intention of earning our own way. Still, as a teenager, I didn't understand it in the slightest.

Mum and Dad didn't notice Finn and I drop our bags off. They thought I was staying at his. Instead, I'd text them later when they were filled up on drink to tell them to leave a key out for us. That we were hanging out at Mel's place for the night. They were less inclined to ask questions when they were drunk anyway.

We were in and out within a few minutes, jumping back in Delayne's car. She tore off up the street, then down the coastal road leading to Mel's.

Mel lived in possibly the most secluded part of the local coastline, her house located on a sequestered lot away from any other homes. This ultimately made her place perfect for parties.

Before leaving us in front of the house, Delayne gave

us the whole "don't do anything I wouldn't do" spiel before driving off.

As we sauntered toward the entrance, the beats and laughter grew louder. The daylight savings sun started to set. I even heard whooshing wave breaks over the music, which wasn't surprising, since Mel lived right on the beach.

We weren't early to the party, it seemed. The yard on the side of the house was already filled with humans, some of whom we knew, some not so much. Several of Mel's friends lived down in Byron Bay, so it was as expected. Levels by Avicii blared on the speakers.

Finn and I spent the first moments of the party standing to the side of the house, against a wall. Cracking a can of Smirnoff Double Black, I let my crowd-fueled anxiety mitigate to a functional potency.

Of course, it wasn't long before we were spotted by none other than my worst nightmare: Noah Daniels, the school bully. He often made people's lives a living hell because he hadn't yet learned how to live and process his own problems. Preferably those whom he deemed weak. Easy targets. For example, Finn and I, who never looked up to Noah and his cronies as most people did at school.

It wasn't as if Noah and company were praised as such. They sadistically had everyone scared of them. Scared—that if they didn't treat those shit-stains like gods—they would be subject to daily doom.

Resisting their best efforts, Finn and I treated Noah and his pals as the absolute jokes they were.

"Looky what we found," came Noah's provoking, prolonged tone. You know, the one which made you want to completely and utterly rip out tongues. But look, violence is not the answer.

I turned my head slowly, not giving Noah or his two goons any startlement. Finn didn't even waste him a glance.

"Two fags drinking in the corner," Noah taunted. "Talking about who's gonna blow who tonight?" The two silent bullies on either side of him sniggered.

"Nope," I said, smirking, "just talking about how good it was when we tag-teamed your mum."

Finn chuckled softly, causing Noah to move in so close I almost thought he was either going to headbutt me or kiss me. He spoke through gritted teeth. "If I wasn't trying so hard to get with Brit tonight, I would bash the fuckin' shit out of you right now."

I arched my brows. "Oh yeah?"

"Yeah," Noah hissed. "Stay the fuck away from Brit. She's mine."

My eyes bulged; nostrils flared. "You don't own her."

"Neither do you. Now, I'm warning you. I know you've been hookin' up with her, and it stops now. I'm gonna make her my girlfriend soon. And what you're gonna do is back the fuck off or you'll be sorry."

He was everything wrong with teenage etiquette, and I wanted nothing more than to hurt him like he had hurt the majority of our school. I could see Finn's fists clenched from the corner of my eye. But again, violence isn't the answer.

"Good luck," was all I said, waggling my eyebrows at Noah.

He shook his head while his two mates stayed silent. Once they realized, however, that Finn and I wouldn't give them the satisfaction of retaliation, all three of them stalked off.

When we emerged from our not-so-comfy corner, Finn and I joined the party, steering clear of the germ Noah Daniels was. It wasn't hard, because the people he and his friends hung out with at parties were not, I repeat *not*, the people we hung out with.

Naturally, we were all divided into the same groups we split into at school. High school parties for us were similar to being on the playground. But throw in a bucket full of alcohol, more swear words, and a sprinkle of PDA, and we were good to go.

It didn't take long for Mel to find us inside, doing shots from mini red cups. *Heads Will Roll* played on the speakers.

"Oh my god, where have you guys been?" she blurted out shrilly, holding herself up on the kitchen counter. "Come with me."

Mel grabbed Finn's hand and led us both into her bedroom, away from the noise of the party. A majority of Mel's room was lit up with fairy lights, which created an ambient glow against the Buddha statue planted next to her bedside table. Crystals lined her windowsill, and the room smelled predominantly of incense. Finn released himself from her grip the moment we entered.

"Soooooo," Mel began. "I heard what happened with Noah. What the fuck?"

I scoffed. "Him trying to be big and strong as usual."

"Uh, he's going around telling everyone he and Brit are a thing because he hooked up with her a few weeks ago," Mel sighed. "Not that consent was involved…. He kinda forced himself on her at a party and kissed her. And Brit, well, she kissed him back. But she didn't really want to. She likes you, Mack. She doesn't want this to create a big drama, y'know?"

"Fuck him," I cursed, shaking my head, fists clenched. "He's such a fuckin' snake."

"He can fight too," Finn warned. "I've seen him beat the absolute shit out of people, so don't try and do anything stupid. It's honestly not worth it. And I don't wanna have to jump into the ring and get my ass kicked too."

"I'm a lover, not a fighter," I said, my eyes meeting Finn's.

A long pause followed. We all perched on Mel's bed, Mel in between Finn and me.

"Okay good, 'cause yeah, no fights at my party is always a plus," Mel mentioned, looking from me to Finn, back to me. "Talking about Brit, let's go find her. Without Noah seeing, of course."

The unwelcome game of avoiding Noah Daniels commenced, which proved rather easy since he'd first threatened me, so surely finding Brit without him knowing would be a walk in the…

"Brit's in the greenhouse," Mel added as we shimmied our way through the crowd. "She's been hiding from him."

The three of us scurried along the side of the shed, down the dirt driveway, leading to a large oddly placed greenhouse with fragments of sand at its base.

Mel swiped open the plastic to the greenhouse door, shepherding us to the back. Brit sat behind one of the garden beds, a half-drank Vodka Cruiser in hand, her red raspberry mouth visible in the moonlight. Full moon. No wonder Noah was crazier than usual.

"Guys, what took you so fuckin' long?" Brit blurted out, her eyes rolling around. "I thought I was gonna have to become one with the plants. I mean, would've been wholesome and all, but—"

"We had to be extra stealth," Mel reminded her.

Brit rolled her eyes. "Noah is such a cunt. Oh my god."

"Agreed," Finn said. "You really shouldn't have kissed him."

Brit scowled at him as I sat beside her. "You think I wanted to?"

"Hey, Finn, let's leave these lovebirds to catch up," suggested Mel in the most unsubtle way she possibly could. "Wanna check on the party with me?"

Finn peered from us—now holding hands—back to Mel. "Uh…yeah, sure."

And so, they left without another word. Pretty sure Mel tried to skip but Finn didn't follow. I'd never seen him skip, yet the thought in my head was one of eternal bliss.

"Sorry I got you into this mess with Noah," Brit said once they left the greenhouse. "I know you and Noah are—"

"Sworn enemies?" I finished.

Brit chuckled. "Yeah. Something like that. It's so stupid. *He's* so stupid."

She popped her head onto my shoulder, and, with my hand outstretched, I massaged her back. After an awkward beat, she lifted her head off my shoulder and turned it in my direction, gazing into my eyes. Brit was the definition of beauty. No wonder she had multiple guys after her. But was I the right guy?

We kissed, hard, our messy mouths sloshing through interspersed huffs. Placing her hand on my thigh, she rubbed closer to my groin. And convincing myself I should've been feeling something by now, I began to rub down there myself with my right hand while I massaged her breasts with my left hand.

Brit drew away and eyeballed me, biting her bottom lip eagerly. "We should do it."

"Here?" I replied on reflex.

"Well, yeah. Who's first time is even in a bed these days anyway?"

She lay down on the ground and I joined her. A solemn escape from the humidity.

Brit ran her fingers from my chest down to my belly button. I quivered, but not from horniness. More so because I'd never been touched in that way before.

Massaging the placidness in my pants, she pointed to her mouth. "Want me to, uh…?"

Feeling an onset of embarrassment, I said, "Yeah, sure," then asked, "Have you done this before?"

"What?"

"Like, sex…and oral?"

"Yeah, both. But look, my first time having sex wasn't in a bed," she explained, following through with a wink. "So, we can both be outdoor first-timers."

It did feel good. It felt great actually. Except for one thing. The whole time, as I stared up at the tent-like ceiling of the greenhouse, I couldn't help but think it was Finn down there, bobbing his head up and down. I thought about him having sex with Mel, sweat patches growing on his forehead from deep, fast thrusts, his muscles contracting, his veins popping through.

Brit stopped. "Everything okay?"

The images of Finn disappeared, and so did the hardness in my penis, which deflated as soon as I said, "Uh, yeah. I'm really drunk. Sorry."

Brit giggled. "Don't be sorry. Alcohol is known to affect sexual function. Don't worry."

Wiping my brow, I said, "Phew. I thought something was wrong with my dick."

Brit looked at me with puppy-eyed sympathy. Though, she quickly broke the stare and kissed me. "There's nothing wrong with you. Trust me."

We split in opposite directions on our stroll back to the house. The prospect of having Noah find us together was certainly not the conflict either of us wanted, or needed.

I checked the time on my phone. Ten thirty already.

Slinking past groups of people in a forcefield of drunken nonsense, I found Finn in the kitchen, sipping on what seemed to be a…glass of water.

"There you are," he hollered.

"You on the waters, pal?"

He nodded, beaming. "Yeah, boy. Just having a breather. Don't wanna wake up with my head spinning tomorrow morning."

Realizing it was a notable idea, I poured one myself. Health in a glass.

"How did things go with Brit?" he asked.

"Eh, it was okay," I lied.

I wanted to tell him about everything. But, how did one do that when it involved having a crush on your best friend?

I wanted to escape. "Hey, random question: did you bring the acid tonight?"

Finn seemed taken aback. "Uh, yeah. But I dunno if we should do it here."

My mood and tone suddenly perked up, as if I'd already taken an upper and couldn't shut up. "We don't have to do it here. We could always leave early and go on an adventure on the walk home. You said something about it being best out in nature, right?"

"Yeah, I mean, it's pretty spontaneous for our first time though, dude," he mentioned, "but I'm not opposed to it."

My gaze drifted to the sloppy humans before us. It was like we were stuck in slow motion while they were sped up. Running around, dancing, singing.

I looked over at Finn, he'd finished his glass of water. I still had a few mouthfuls to go.

Finn pointed behind us. "Let's go to the bathroom," he said, grabbing his tote bag from underneath the sink.

I turned toward the back of the house, to the line of people already waiting to use the toilet.

"No, not that one," he said. "Follow me."

He led me out of the backdoor, before continuing toward the greenhouse.

"Yo, where are we going?" I asked, trying to keep up as we power-walked past the partygoers without a word. Without anyone noticing or stopping us. "There's no bathroom back here."

"Yeah, there is, shhh." I'd been to Mel's house more times than he had, yet he seemed so sure of himself. Not one ounce of doubt.

After passing the greenhouse, I followed Finn into the scrub, along a narrow coastal track. He was lit up by the moonlight seeping through the trees.

We trekked over a clearing, stopping outside a bathroom block that connected to an empty car park. The waves crashed in the distance, the moon glowing over the dark dreamy ocean.

"Woah, what beach is this?" I asked, catching my breath.

"Mel said it was the nude beach," he said, walking me into the bathroom block. "Not many people know about it apparently."

It was clean for a public bathroom. It didn't smell like fermenting piss, which was a definite plus. The lights were brighter than the ones in the house, making me squint slightly.

"I needa take a leak," I said, stepping past Finn to get to the right side of the urinal.

"Oh my god, so do I, come to think of it," he said, taking the left side.

I really wished he hadn't. More often than not, I'd get stage fright if I pissed next to another guy, let alone one I had a big fat crush on.

Thank fuck I'd already started flowing by the time he joined me. Keep staring forward, I thought, trying not to glance in his direction, even though I could see glimpses out of the corner of my left eye.

Finishing up before he did, I washed my hands, trying to keep it cool, and hide the fact I may have grown a semi. After washing his hands, Finn approached me, getting so close I thought he might…

"Should we do it?" he asked, not taking his eyes off me.

"Sorry, what?"

Pointing at the foil in his hand, he said, "The acid. Should we do it?"

I snapped out of my daze. "Oh, yeah. Fuckin' oath."

He unraveled the foil and placed one of the squares of cardboard in my hand. The colorful slice of board that would hopefully bring some color to my night.

"How do we do it?" I asked.

"You put it under your tongue and let it dissolve," he said. "I'm guessing you swallow it once it ends up a mushy bit of paper."

"Right, okay," I said, skeptical, yet curious.

He held up his piece of board as though he was a priest about to give communion, and I followed suit.

Finn lowered his voice, started counting down. "Three. Two. One."

At the same time, we stuck the squares into our mouths. For some reason, I thought it would taste like something. Similar to alcohol, or the taste you got when you smoked something. But nope, nothing. Tasted like plain old cardboard.

"Now we wait," Finn told me, fishing into the tote bag, pulling out two cans of Double Black and handing one to me.

With the understanding Finn knew more about this

than me, I kept the questions rolling. "How long does it usually take to kick in?"

He shrugged. "Maybe half an hour-ish or a little more. Enough time to tell you the story of how I know this bathroom's here." He gave me a cheeky, toothy grin.

I cracked my can, smiling. "I'm all ears, matey."

"Okay, so…" He paused for dramatic effect. "I lost my virginity here tonight."

Uh, excuse me? Finn? Losing his *virginity*?

"What?" I spat out, trying to sound excited by hitting him on the shoulder.

He gulped down a generous swig. "Okay so, when Mel and I left you and Brit in the greenhouse, Mel said she wanted to show me something, and then ran off down this track. And yeah, we ended up here and…" He couldn't wipe the proud smile off his face. "I dunno what came over me, 'cause I wasn't sure about her at first."

"How was it?"

He nodded in a sound sort of way. "It was good. Quick. I mean, we could've picked a better spot than the grass next to a public bathroom, but hey—"

"First times are hardly ever amazing, or like the movies," I said.

"Agreed. And I mean, you and Brit got it on in a greenhouse tonight, so I guess we both roughed it?"

I took a long pause before saying, "Guess so." Not a complete lie. Just depended on what one classified as "sex".

Finn stared at himself in the mirror, leaning in closer to inspect his face.

"So, you think you and Mel will be a thing now?" I asked.

Finn was transfixed in his reflection. "Psssht. Uh…I honestly dunno. I mean, what's the point really when I'm thinking of leaving the area in like a year?"

I shrugged. "Dude, that's a year away. Things could change in a year, as they usually do. You never know, you might end up falling in love with her and wanting to stay here."

Scoffing, Finn said, "I highly doubt it."

My skin started to prickle. A warm sensation corrupted my body. Was this what I was meant to be feeling?

"Has yours kicked in yet?" I asked Finn, who still couldn't seem to take his eyes off his face in the glass.

"I'm not sure yet," he said ever so casually.

After another mouthful, I'd finished my drink. Sighing, I crouched down and started fishing through the tote bag for another can. It still felt wet inside from condensation. But the cans weren't the only thing in the bag catching my attention.

"You brought playing cards?" I questioned Finn.

He finally turned his gaze from the mirror to me, following through with a cheeky child-like grin.

"Yeah, I *obviously* knew we wanted to play red or black tonight while we came up on LSD," he exclaimed, crossing his arms into an X-shape. "Cause I'm psychic."

"You thought they might come in handy at the party, didn't you?" I said wryly, "and that we wouldn't just be drinking, or dancing, or…doing drugs instead."

"Well, they're coming in useful now, aren't they? I'll go

first since you're already onto another can. I've still got a quarter left."

I shuffled the cards, then dealt to Finn. He stretched his shoulders up and down before starting the game. I didn't blame him. Red or black could monumentally break someone, especially when you had to sip for every card you got wrong.

"Red or black?"

"Red." "Dammit."

Finn took a sip.

"Red or black?"

"Red." "Fuck yeah."

"Higher or lower?"

A queen. "Lower, of course." "Hell yeah."

The game went on for quite a while. Or maybe it wasn't long at all. Our perception of time started distorting by the minute, so it was hard to tell. Finn downed the rest of his can before we even got to my turn. And it wasn't until he put down the first card—the red ten of hearts—that it hit me. The hearts shifted a smidgeon, almost as if they were dancing on the cardboard.

Instantly holding my focus, the numbers seemed to be wiggling too.

"Um…are those numbers—"

"Moving? Yeah, they are," Finn confirmed, the glee radiating from him. He was now glowing in more ways than one, and it wasn't from the bright bathroom lights. The brown in his eyes was more defined than ever. He even seemed a tad cartoonish, though drawn up in such detail the illustration of him seemed too real to question.

"This is just…" I trailed off.

I walked around the bathroom, taking it all in, my heart hammering in my chest, a bash on its door. The bricks looked as if they were melting down the wall. The graffiti on the wall shook from side to side, its letters growing little thorns. Finn faced the mirror again, as close to the glass as he could get, his two index fingers to his cheek.

"Whatcha doin', dude?" I sang in a tune.

"Popping a pimple. I've nearly got it."

Head down, I became rather engaged with the creases and lines on my palms. The way each line broke off its branch. A tiny twig.

I stopped after a beat, getting lost in the lines, a bit like I was getting lost in most things at the minute.

Finn's pimple started to bleed, yet he still kept hacking at it with his now-bloody nails.

I grabbed him by the shoulder. "Finn, stop it, pretty sure it's popped."

He finally stepped away from the mirror, taking a deep breath. "Thanks, mate. I obviously needed to be snapped out of that. Got carried away. Fuck, this stuff is strong. I keep getting lost."

He pulled off some paper towels, wiping his face, then washing his hands with soap.

"Yeah, me too. It's really strong," I admitted. "Maybe we should go for a walk outside."

We were not prepared for that. I repeat: NOT PREPARED.

The outside was not what it used to be. Not anymore.

Last time I checked, the outlines of the trees didn't look

like a Tetris game, emitting neon red and green lights. Last time I checked, the sky wasn't purple either.

Good thing the moon provided us with enough light to vaguely see our surroundings. The dark patches, however—or rather, the parts of the outside we couldn't see—didn't look so inviting. Faces formed in those patches, with devilish features I couldn't watch, not even for a few seconds.

White strips of light slithered through the grass and sand, leading us down to the beach. At first, we were hesitant to step out of our humble bathroom abode. But once realizing we weren't going to fall into an endless pit of darkness, we followed the snake-shaped lights onto the sand. The sand on the other hand seemed kind of blue to me. And so, we started walking along the beach.

"Thiiiiiiis is craaaaaazy," I slurred, my head turned heavenward. To the stars, the Milky Way. "I swear I've never seen the stars as bright as this. Not even at the farm."

"It's fucking dope, isn't it?" said Finn, also encapsulated in a dazed wonder. "Hey, I wanna spin around in circles."

He did so, whilst running, as fast as he possibly could, stumbling away from me.

"Woah!" he yelled out. "I'm seeing some weird shit!"

I joined him in spinning. Fractal patterns formed from the dizziness. It felt as if I was slowly sinking into the sand, not fazed by the idea.

Finn dropped to the sand with a thud. I immediately stopped spinning, attempting to regain my vision. It didn't work, and I had no choice but to be horizontal. Though, the sand didn't catch me. Finn's chest did.

My arms curled over him, more or less like a wilting plant.

We both huffed and puffed. I half-lifted myself off him, instantly met with a dose of dizziness.

"Ugh, my head is spinning," I groaned, laying over him again.

He was still catching his breath, so I hoped he didn't mind me.

"Mine too. Bad idea."

His chest and stomach were warm. At first, I thought there was someone else there, with their hands on my back—rubbing it—and hugging me in.

There wasn't anyone else there. No one but Finn.

I lay there while he tickled my back with his hands, not daring to look at him, or stop him either. I was too busy picking up grains of sand and letting them sprinkle back onto the moonlit shore.

"Acid hey," Finn said, moving his hands up to my head, giggling. "Your hair feels like mashed potato."

Finn's excitement inspired me to finally meet his gaze. I let my finger wander to his bottom lip. "Your lip feels like a…burrito."

We both cackled, studying each other's eyes. He still looked frighteningly comparable to a Playstation 1 video game character.

Our laughing soon faded. Our contact, however, did not.

I then did it. The one thing I wished I hadn't. Not that night. Not there. But how could it possibly have gone any other way?

I leaned in and kissed him, hoping to god I wasn't met with a punch in the face. His lips tasted like lemonade. Felt sweet and soft, like a burrito, ironically.

We kept kissing, and I wondered if the punch would ever come, or if he would push me off him and tell me to never talk to him again. He did none of these things, and I was happier than I'd ever been, his lips concentrated euphoria, getting me high the further I pressed into them.

We finally pulled apart.

I leaned off him.

He swallowed, hard.

"That was uh…" he mumbled. "Funky."

My insides were consumed by a fluttering feeling, so much so that I hopped off him. "Acid hey."

"Yeah, this shit's weird," he blurted out, making sand angels.

After standing, I fished through our bag, pulling out the last two cans. "Should we keep going?"

He grabbed a can off me before standing up. His smile faded.

I held up the empty tote bag. "What should we do with this?"

He laughed obnoxiously. "It's not even real. Nothing's real."

I laughed, but in a much more sarcastic tone. "Well, we can't leave it here. You got any pockets?"

He ignored me, his eyes glued to the horizon, hardly even blinking. "Shit, I really am feeling this stuff," he said. "I want to go running."

So, we ran along the beach until we couldn't run

anymore. We stopped, looked around, realized everything was still alive, and kept going. Over and over, but slower each time. Tiring ourselves out. Finn didn't seem to want to stay still for too long. He became restless.

And by the time we reached my house, the outgoing, crazy, high Finn was replaced with a brooding, anxious, quiet Finn.

I checked the time on my phone once we got inside. Four a.m. But I didn't feel tired whatsoever.

Once I got back from brushing my teeth, Finn was asleep on the mattress at the bottom of my bed.

Now I wasn't so high, so objects seemed less distorted. Everything looked much more normal, sure, but I undoubtedly felt drained of all energy.

I wanted to wake him up and talk to him about what had happened on the beach. Though, as much as I wanted to, I knew the walls in the house were paper thin. And not one person would appreciate traveling voices at this early hour. I whacked on the late-night infomercials instead. On mute, the promotion of an all-in-one fitness machine appeared ever-so strange to me.

After flicking open my window blinds, I noticed the sky had become light, and I knew, that even though it was a Saturday, I really needed to try and get some sleep.

Ultimately, I switched off the television and pulled the baby blue sheets over me, closing my eyes.

The fractal patterns were still there, playing in my head. More or less a video. I didn't open my eyes, even when I heard a rustle in the sheets below.

Finn was up. Now it was my turn to pretend to be asleep.

He sighed.

And without a word, he left my room and never came back.

5

Cranberry Juice

LATER

Rachel's snoring woke me. I'd never heard her snore this loud, akin to a truck pulling up to a rest stop.

I nudged her more than gently, to which she flicked her eyes open with fright, frowning as she did so.

"What?" she groaned.

"You're snoring."

"Oh, come off it. I don't snore."

"Well, you were. *Really* fucking loud."

"Ha! Must be this dry heat."

We lay there for a few ticks, watching the last bits of condensation roll off the top of the tent.

I cocooned myself in the blankets a little longer, shielding myself from the cold morning air.

"Honestly, I don't remember what happened last night," I confessed, trying to piece it all together.

A hearty laugh escaped Rachel's mouth. "You were *so* drunk. Quite possibly the drunkest I've ever seen you."

I sighed. "Oh dear, did I embarrass myself?"

"Not…quite. You weren't exactly awake long enough to fully embarrass yourself."

Without question, I blamed it on the many cosmopolitans I downed.

A little snippet slotted itself back into my memory bank. Of me, slurring different phrases in an awful attempt at a British accent: "Gosh, I love cranberry juice." "Oh, deary me, how good is the cranberry juice?" Followed by me yelling out to campers walking by: "Hi, yes, hello, would you like any cranberry juice?"

"Look, you were actually quite funny," Rachel said, unconvincingly. "You only made it to the dance floor once, though. You couldn't exactly stand so you came back to camp and passed out."

I giggled, softly, so it wouldn't set off my headache. "Sounds about right," I admitted nonchalantly. "At least I got enough sleep. I feel well rested." I paused. "Kind of."

I needed to stop turning to alcohol when I couldn't deal with the world around me.

The afternoon prior, I remembered telling Jasper that I didn't want him in the way I wanted him most. Knowing it was a pretty daft decision, I still drank and drank, until I couldn't drink anymore. Did it work? Momentarily, like a home-brand band-aid which came off overnight, exposing my deep wound all over again. But, as they say, you need to air wounds out so they can fully dry up and heal. I just hoped the arid desert would help me out here. Alas, it would help even more if I knew what kind of wound I had, let alone how to treat it.

"What else did I do last night?" I asked Rachel. "Do I have to apologize to anyone? Should I steer clear of certain people?"

Rachel turned on her side to face me. "You might wanna apologize to Jasper actually," she whispered.

"Why?" I was quick to say, also crawling onto my side, surprised at how comfortable the mattress was.

"Do you remember putting on a British accent most of the night?"

"Vaguely. But yes. Go on."

"So, it all started because Jasper was having trouble saying the word 'rural'. He was a little drunk. But anyway, we all kinda laughed at him. But then you started with the British accent for the rest of the night and I think he got a little offended."

"Oh, for suck's fake," I hissed.

Rachel chuckled. "But yeah, you weren't overly offensive or anything, and it was quite funny. But you might wanna have a chat with him today and, I dunno, confirm you were, in fact, just being a drunk idiot and didn't mean anything by it."

With a sigh, I ultimately agreed. "Yeah. Probs should. Gosh, I can't believe I got that drunk on the first night."

"Not gonna lie, I was a little surprised at you," Rachel admitted. "But, look, it happens to the best of us, hon."

She then asked me if I was okay. "I hope our chat the other night didn't bring up anything you didn't want to be brought up. About Sam and…ugh, sorry. I did it again. I'm a shit best friend."

Little did she know, after talking about Sam and Stu the other night, I'd realized those two were the least of my worries. Time had healed that shitfuckery. It was the more recent shitfuckery which had me dwelling. The shitfuckery I had to refrain from telling Rachel—only for a few more days—so she could enjoy her weekend without worrying.

"It's okay," I said. "I'm totally fine. Guilty as charged, I went a little silly last night. Sam and Stu are honestly old news. Who even are they? I don't know."

After ripping the blanket off, I unzipped the tent with ease. The morning sun had fully risen, and upon poking my head through the hole, I was met with a blinding beam, one which took more than a moment to adjust to.

I squinted until my vision returned.

When it did, I felt somewhat alive, as if I didn't sink as much booze as I did the night before. Oh yeah, I was probably still drunk.

My outlook from the rooftop tent had a prime view of the campers and colors.

"He's alive!" called a voice from below. None other than Lily, in one of the camp chairs, sipping a coffee from a keep-cup.

"Good morning," I said, as merrily as possible.

"How're you feeling?"

I scrambled down the ladder, instantly jealous of her sunglasses. "I'll be better once I find my—" I scanned the camp table, thrilled to locate my condensation-coated sunglasses on it. I slipped them on and pulled up a chair next to Lily.

"Much better," I sighed.

"Coffee?" Lily offered, pointing to the plunger on the table.

Indeed, I was almost in a state where coffee mightn't do wonders for my stomach. But, after a strong nod, I felt as if I needed it.

"I don't have any coffee cups left though," said Lily.

Studying the table, I picked up the plastic martini cup I'd been drinking out of the night before. "This'll do."

After rinsing the cup out with water, I filled it up with coffee from the plunger, topped it up with soy milk, and cradled it in my hands.

I took a sip and smiled. "Mmm, yes." A warm hug from the caffeine gods.

"Coffee and a good feed will make us good as new," Lily assured me, looking out into the distance.

I managed to laugh. "I hope you're right there."

More campers awoke. More chatter. Even some light music from a Bluetooth speaker.

"I'm glad we camped a little bit further away from the stages," Lily noted. "I dunno about you but I slept great. We even hit the hay before the music shut off."

"What time does the stage close?"

"Three a.m. till noon each day, except for Saturday night where the music goes all the way through," she explained. "I'm not mad about it though. Need my beauty sleep, hey."

I lifted my cup, announcing, "Cheers to that."

After clanging our coffee cups together, I could've sworn the presumed hangover of mine was ninety percent non-existent. Might've been Lily's bubbly morning self that ignited enough energy to share. Might've been the coffee. Might've been the beats. The sun. But yes, I was in fact back, baby.

"Rachel up?" asked Lily.

"Yes, I'm awake!" Rachel yelled from the tent. "I…can't move yet."

"Just checking on a fellow pack leader," Lily called back.

Rachel howled. "Still here. Still kicking."

I'd obviously missed something.

Lily turned to me. "Man, you missed some funny shit last night when you passed out. Actually, it was pretty much Rachel and I being the dickheads we are."

"Oh god, what did yas do?"

Lily shook her head, which was followed by a cackle. "Fuck, it's coming back to me now."

"It's been coming back to me since I woke up," Rachel added, "and if last night set the vibe for what the rest of the party is gonna entail, we're in for some serious trouble."

Lily started decoding for me. "So, we met these guys last night on the dancefloor and went back to their campsite for a few drinks. They said they had heaps of coke to go around so me, Rachel, and Jasper were like *why not?* Anyway, Rachel and I kinda got the inkling that two of the guys were really into us, but it was past the point of refusing the free coke, so we kinda went along with it. And we got our free lines and then…couldn't help but start kissing each other and the two guys were—"

"Shocked," Rachel finished her sentence, poking her head out of the tent and into the sunshine. "I felt kinda bad, but I also didn't."

"Dude, yeah same," Lily said, her head turned to Rachel, "But they were kinda luring us in with the free drugs, don't you think? I could feel it. And they were being all touchy-feely. Ew. Anywho, they might have been nice, *however*, sometimes you gotta do what you gotta do in those situations."

I shrugged. "Coke ain't cheap in Australia."

Lily lifted her cup to me. "Cheers to that."

Rachel's eyes wandered around the camp. "Jasper not up yet?"

Lily giggled, mischievous brows raised. "*Jasper* never slept here."

Say what now?

Rachel gaped. "No way! You reckon…the guy from the campsite's neighbor last night?"

Lily nodded. "Oh, one hundred percent!"

As I took another sip of coffee, a bout of nausea bubbled in my stomach. "I really did miss a lot last night."

Rachel descended the ladder. "Yeah, you really did."

"Honestly, the level you were on last night," Lily added, "wasn't a wandering pack level."

"No comment," I said, my head downcast. "I do half-blame the cranberry juice, though."

Lily erupted with laughter.

Rachel tapped me on the back of the head. "Fuck I love you."

I loved Rachel too, but as much as I could've been spared the looming jealousy, I wanted nothing more than to know every detail about Jasper's whereabouts. "So, Jasper found a guy, did he?" I queried.

"Yeah, at the same campsite where we had the coke," Rachel replied, boiling up some more water on the gas stove and casting a glance at Lily. "I wasn't a fan of the guy, to be honest."

"Oi, me either," Lily piped up. "He was kinda rude actually. Rachel, that's why we left. And when we asked Jasper if he wanted to come back to the dance floor with us, he *insisted* he stay there. Mind you, he was pretty high at this point."

Indeed, I knew Jasper hooking up with someone the night before was some sort of karma from my actions. Or rather, my inaction to do anything.

Unfortunately, it didn't stop my gut from sinking, making me want to be the guy he slept with. Tangled within blankets together. Body warmth seeing us through the night.

"Well, let's hope he actually is with this guy and not passed out in a bush somewhere," Lily mentioned. "Jasper may seem like he's put together most of the time. Which he is. But I've seen the crazy in that boy be brought right to the fore."

As harsh as it seemed, I hoped for the latter. At least if he *had* passed out in a bush, he couldn't exact his jealousy curse upon me with a gorgeous guy by his side the rest of the festival.

"If that's the case, maybe we should go find him," Rachel suggested, "and save him if we have to."

"And we can get a hot breakfast," Lily added, standing swiftly.

"Did someone say hash browns?" I sang.

Rachel eyeballed me. "Stop it right now. The hash brown mission is on."

Surely one of the food stalls would be willing and able to make our hash brown dreams come true, one crunchy bite at a time. To our luck, we didn't even have to search. Hash Brown Brunch came to us, and it was literally a whole stall dedicated to breakfast and brunch food with hash browns in it.

After ordering double hash brown breakfast wraps, we waited inside a gazebo on some pillows while our crispy saviors fried away.

The gazebo smelled musky, with incense smoke wafting through it.

Trying to distract myself from the sound of sizzling deep fryer oil coupled with how hungry I was, I pulled out a book from the shelf by the pillows. *HOW TO LIVE IN THE NOW AND KICK A** DOING SO*, the title read. Very fitting; thanks Hash Brown Brunch. But a timely book and wholesome breakfast wraps weren't the only things we encountered in the cozy gazebo.

"There's the gang!" cried out one of the three vibrant young guys who stumbled into the gazebo, almost tripping on pillows.

What, with his sparkly painted face, purple cape, and sunflower glasses, if Jasper's voice wasn't so identifiable, I wouldn't have recognized him.

"There he is!" Lily rejoiced.

The other two guys followed Jasper to the back of the gazebo. Rachel, Lily and I scooched together so they could sit with us on the pillows around the table. Only one of the three wasn't wearing sunglasses, and he was the tanned, brown-eyed guy who took a seat next to me. He passed a soft smile in my direction.

"The Pack of Gays has officially gotten bigger!" Jasper announced. "Lily, Mack, Rachel, this is Seb, he's from Melbourne."

Jasper turned to Lily and Rachel. "You met him last night." Then, "And this is…"

The brown-eyed guy finished his sentence. "…Julian."

An exchange of handshakes and smiles danced around the table.

MACKENZIE'S BRAIN CINEMA ACTIVATED

First clip: Julian and I in a tent together, kissing as we hear moans and groans from the tent next to us.

Second clip: Julian butt-naked on the dancefloor, his hairy uncut cock flying around like a helicopter rotor blade.

Interesting.

"Order for Destiny!" a voice shouted from the little kitchen.

Rachel immediately rose to her feet.

Lily's narrowed eyes followed her. "Destiny?"

"Rachel loves to fuck with herself and give a different name for food orders," I explained.

Rachel returned to the table with a big toothy grin. "I'm fuckin' Destiny today."

Lily waggled her eyebrows. "Do you mean you are Destiny or are you fucking Destiny today? Cause I mean, if it's the second one, I want to be Destiny."

Rachel winked at her. "I can call you Destiny anytime you want."

When Rachel passed me my wrap, I couldn't have opened it any quicker.

"Ooooft, smells fresh," said Seb.

Jasper was also salivating over our crunchy, hash brown-filled feed. He turned to Seb and Julian. "Let's order some food."

Julian reached into his pockets, then sighed. "Ooh, I left my money at the campsite."

"Pffft, don't worry about it, lad," Jasper said, standing as he did so. "Want the same as these guys? That wrap does look damn fine."

Julian shot a glance from my wrap—nestled around my lips—to me, with the same innocent twinkle, nodding his head.

Mouth filled to the brim, I returned somewhat of a smile, which resulted in a morsel of food falling out of my mouth, onto my lap. Pretending it didn't happen, I kept eating, awkwardly.

I started picking stray bits of scrambled egg from my lap, laughing it off with a mouthful, excusing myself, "Means I'm enjoying it."

Julian shrugged, stifling a smirk. "I don't doubt it at all. I can't wait to do the same thing. I forgot to eat dinner last night."

I rolled my eyes from side to side, whispering, "I'll let you in on a little secret. I think we all forgot to eat dinner last night."

"Oh," Julian chuckled. "That makes me feel better."

Before I could plunge into the possibility of a connection with Julian, Jasper and Seb returned, their glittery faces glowing in the sun.

So far, Jasper had been rather masterful at pretending nothing had happened between him and me. And even though he began treating me as the friend I told him I wanted to be, somehow the way he acted around me seemed a little off. Might've seemed normal to everyone else, but certainly not to me.

"So, Mack, fancy a cosmo after breakfast?" Jasper joshed. Rachel and Lily broke into laughter.

As much as I wanted to rip Jasper's throat out and/or skull-fuck it, I knew I deserved every sprinkle of mockery toward me at the moment, especially for taking the piss out of his accent—the one I now found both unique and sexy.

"Unfortunately, we're all out of cranberry juice," I retorted. "I drank it all."

"We're gonna have to settle for caps and vodka colas

instead then," Jasper said gleefully, whipping out a baggie filled with clear capsules containing tiny brown crystallized powder. "We got a whole bunch. We can share it if you want."

"We must get on the same level, mister Jasper," Seb said.

Seb flirted with Jasper every moment he got. Grabbing his thigh, kissing his cheek, even making these noises that were like a weird mix between a baby and a fucking velociraptor.

If that was going to set the tone for the day, I needed a Bloody Mary ASAP, two of those caps, and endless music to cancel out the fucking dinosaur.

"Let's wait and get on it tonight when the music gets good," suggested Lily.

Her plan was pretty solid: wait until night so we could dance into the sunrise.

Rachel studied a brochure with the set times on it. "You're right. The lineup is amazing all night. I hate it when they do that."

I yawned. "Might need a nap today."

My yawn spread to Julian. "I feel you there."

Jasper turned to Seb. "Tell you where would be perfect for a nap?"

"Oh my god, yes!" Seb piped up. "The chillout tent!"

"The chillout tent?" I asked.

"Yeah!" Jasper said. "Seb and I were there this morning when we needed some calm music to chill us out and help us fall asleep. It's literally a tent full of beanbags and pillows, and they play this soft, soothing music."

Seb waved his arms in the air boisterously. "It's so good! You *have* to check it out!"

Jasper's face flattened, and it seemed I was the only one to notice. His eyes were set on a mother, father, and their child, who entered the tent to order. The child, who looked just a few years old, sat on the father's shoulders. The mother, after ordering from the cashier, grinned at them both, proceeding to lightly pinch the child's cheek. It was only then that Jasper looked away, his gaze meeting mine.

"Okay, this sounds fucking wonderful," Rachel said, her raised voice breaking our eye contact.

"We all wanna go align our chakras in the chillout tent?" Lily asked the group.

Our newly formed festival crew: Q-Pack, short for Pack of Queers.

"I've probably had about three hours of sleep," said Jasper, "so I probably should return to the land of comfy clouds."

It was settled. We were off to the chillout tent, which was on the other side of the now-crowded market stalls. Festival goers scrambled to chow down their most important meal of the day. For some, their only meal of the day.

The soft dirt road cutting through the stalls began to emit dust due to the number of people walking over it. Determined to not get more particles up my nose, I lifted my shirt over my face on our saunter to the chillout tent.

"We're all gonna be picking out some *whopping* boogers after this festival," I mentioned.

Q-Pack trundled in twos. I walked next to Jasper while the others yarned away in their own conversations.

Seb and Julian were good friends and had travelled to the festival together from Melbourne.

I didn't know what to say to Jasper as we walked side by side. I wanted to say so many things, but my mouth seemed to be hijacked by a rebellious part of my brain.

"Oh my god," Jasper gushed, stopping by a stall with bohemian overalls.

The handmade patchwork overalls certainly caught my eye, too, so I also stopped to look. The others kept on walking in the direction of a large ironwood tree, under it a teepee tent.

Jasper admired a green pair of overalls. "I fucking love these."

More preoccupied with the blue pair, I said, "They're so sick."

I now had Jasper alone, so this was my chance to set things straight.

"Hey, look," I began, "last night, I might've crossed a line when I was drunk. I didn't mean any offence by it, or your accent. I was being stupid, and I ah…wanted to say I'm…sorry. About that."

Feeling my face go red all over, I wondered why it had to be so goddamn awkward. Oh yeah, fighting fate. Destiny. All the fun stuff.

Jasper let out a giggle. "Don't worry, I know that now. Must admit, I was a little taken aback by it all at first, but then I realized I needed to let go and have fun, too." His face started to sweat the longer we stood in the patch of sun, his glitter sparkling even more. "And that's what I did," he continued. "I think there comes a point where you need to…let go…of things you can't control."

His eyes fucked me through his sunflower glasses. I wanted to tell him he was most certainly preaching to the choir, a choir not ready to listen.

"But, thanks for apologizing," he added, walking into the stall with the green pair of overalls. "I appreciate it."

"Great, well, I'm glad we cleared that up," I said, following him in with the blue pair. "So, we're buying overalls, are we?"

"Fuck yeah we are," Jasper announced, leading me to the cashier. "Friends buy matching overalls. Duh."

Friends. Friends. Friends. Fuck my life.

After exchanging *friendly* smiles, we paid for our picture-perfect new overalls and picked up where we left off.

It was quiet inside the tent. A soft soothing melody played over the sound of a fresh-flowing brook.

Jasper and I stepped over several bodies to find Q-Pack. A spot had been saved for us, in between Seb and Julian. Of course.

Rachel and Lily didn't open their eyes, but Seb and Julian did once we lay on our backs. It was squishy between them, and it meant Jasper's and my shoulders would have to touch.

Staring up at the ceiling with eyes of deep thought, I was transported back in time. To the farm. Finn and I, wedged between Brit and Mel. History felt like it really was repeating itself, and there was nothing in the world I could do about it.

My breathing quickened once we hit the floor, Jasper so close that I could feel him, even without touch.

After wriggling for an uncomfortably long moment, I finally settled in, and stopped moving altogether.

I thought back to the first time I ever tried meditation. It was in grade seven, Finn beside me on the ground, at a time when our friendship wasn't so complicated. When we were just friends. No ulterior motive, or anything to hide. I sometimes wondered what would've happened if I never kissed him on the beach. Would he still be alive?

The sounds in the chillout tent took me further away, in between the realms of asleep and awake.

I felt a brush against my hand.

My right hand.

Jasper.

My inner fight-or-flight revved its gears again. I thought about moving. Leaving. But I didn't.

I stayed, though I wasn't ready to reciprocate his hand's embrace. So, I kept pretending to be asleep.

The stroking soon stopped, and the hand stayed, rested on mine.

It then started from my left side. Julian rolled over and snuggled up to me.

Staying on my back, I took a deep breath, exhaled, and dozed off.

"Mack, wake up." A whisper, hands shaking my shoulders.

I opened my eyes to Rachel. The music inside the tent was still playing, but the trickling water had been replaced with rainforest sounds, of chirping birds and pleasant wind stirring through branches and leaves.

A near-empty tent, the rest of the Pack nowhere to be seen.

Grabbing my hand, Rachel helped me up and we walked out of the tent. I felt well rested, my new blue overalls tucked under my armpit.

The sun's rays blinded me for a slight moment, but I soon adjusted.

"How long was I asleep for?" I asked, clearing my eyes of discharge.

"Only a couple hours," Rachel said calmly as we wandered through the market. "You looked too peaceful to wake up, to be honest."

"Where're the others?"

"They're on the dance floor, getting a little bit loose. I said I'd go and gather the missing Pack member."

Beyond the market, bassy sounds erupted from the stage.

Rachel wrapped her hand around my shoulder. "Wanna go grab a drink and get this party started?"

Indeed, after the nap, I felt as if I could do pretty much anything.

As we moseyed on back to the campsite, I thought about what had happened in the tent earlier, with Jasper and Julian on either side of me. At what Jasper had said by the rack of overalls.

I think there comes a point where you need to…let go…of things you can't control.

"Let's start off with a tequila shot," Rachel suggested

once we reached the campsite. "Only because you needa catch up."

She shot me a devilish grin, one which screamed *You can't refuse this idea, Mack. Not this time.*

"Okay, you've convinced me," I surrendered, taking a seat in one of the camp chairs.

The campsite looked somewhat more organized than it had hours ago, in that there wasn't shit everywhere.

"Oh yeah, we did a little cleanup while you were asleep," Rachel said, fishing the tequila bottle from the esky. She threw me a singular lime. "Wanna cut this up while I get our shots ready with some..." she looked around in another box, "...salt, of course."

She cut two lime wedges, poured tequila into shot glasses, then sprinkled salt onto our licked hands.

Unsurprisingly, the tequila shot burned on the way down, even with the lime and salt.

I filled up a bottle with tequila and cold orange juice.

"Should we go to the dance floor?"

"In a sec," said Rachel, not moving from her chair. "Let's just chill for a bit."

Arching my brows playfully, I replied with a long, "Okayyyyyyy."

I felt tipsy already, taking a swig from the bottle I'd poured. "So, I apologized to Jasper before."

She grabbed the bottle off me and gulped. "Oh good. How did it go?"

I shrugged, sinking further into the chair. "It went okay, I guess. He was cool with it."

Rachel gave an awkward grimace. "He does seem that

way. He's been making out with Seb on the dance floor all afternoon."

Without warning, my heart felt as though it imploded.

"Julian seems into you, though," Rachel said, hitting me on the shoulder.

"Julian's cute," I smirked. "Maybe it'll happen tonight."

"Oh, I can see it happening!" Rachel piped up.

Was this the moment I should've told her about the whole Jasper thing, The *whole thing?* I wanted to.

"Oh yeah, I was gonna ask you," she continued. "How's Brain Cinema going here at the festival with all these new people?"

Shrugging, I said, "Eh, it's not too bad. Avoiding eye contact wherever I can."

"You know, something I don't think I've ever asked," Rachel said. "I don't think you've ever told me the whole story of when you realized you had this…future-telling thing. "Brain Cinema". You told me it all started happening all of a sudden when you were seventeen. But you never talked about the moment, you know. Of when you realized. How you felt and whatnot."

Here we go, I thought.

Summer, Where Are You?

THEN

The sun was still out by the time I woke again.

From my bed, I cast a weak glance to my right—to the mattress on the floor with tangled blankets—realizing Finn was still gone. After he'd left my room in the early hours, he hadn't returned.

I stared at the fan whirling above, my mind collapsing on itself.

Had I kissed Finn last night, and he kissed me back?

If I could remember clearly, that had totally happened. Now he was gone, and fuck, I had to text him.

Hey dude, woahhhh big night. I only just woke up.
How are you feeling?

With it being four o'clock in the afternoon, I was surprised Mum or Dad hadn't already come in to wake me up, or check I was alive at least. Perhaps interrogate me into why I'd slept way past midday.

A light knock on my bedroom door shifted my focus.

"Yeah, come in," I answered, pulling the covers over my half-naked body.

Slowly opening the door, Lucas popped his head in, but not the whole way so his face was partially hidden.

"So, uh, Mum and Dad wanted to do fish and chips for dinner and told me to wake you up to drive us down," Lucas said shyly. "I told them I could walk down by myself, but you know how they are."

Indeed, I knew how protective they were of me at twelve, so it was no surprise they wouldn't let Lucas walk into town on his own.

"Sure thing," I said, clearing my throat. "Wanna head down at five?"

"Sounds good." Lucas closed the door, leaving me with my scattered thoughts.

Five o'clock came around quickly. I felt vastly different than I had the day before, but I couldn't quite put my finger on why. It was still plain old me in the mirror. Yet my body felt somewhat alien in a way.

Finn hadn't replied to my text, which was alarming. He would usually respond pretty promptly.

I gave him the benefit of the doubt, that he could still be asleep, and hopped into the car with Lucas.

Driving seemed weird, unnatural even. Having been told the subtle after-effects of LSD could linger for hours, I didn't question it when the sudden urge to pull up at the headland hit me.

"What are we doing?" Lucas asked, his voice shaky with doubt. I didn't blame him. It was our first-ever drive together, and it must've seemed oddly spontaneous of me to take us on a detour.

"I wanna see the ocean for a sec," I said, parking the car.

"Okay. I might just stay in the car." He went back to playing his Nintendo DS.

"Nah, c'mon, little brother. We haven't been to our spot in ages."

Lucas rolled his eyes. "Ugh, fine." He turned the DS off and hopped out of the car with me.

We spotted a string of surfers out in the sea, catching some late afternoon waves. The swell raged below the headland. The ocean smelled fishy, but not an overwhelming scent. The wind tickled us softly, not blowing a gust.

"Gosh, I can't remember the last time we came here," I said, leading the way down a set of stairs, onto some rocks.

"Yeah, years," Lucas said.

Both barefoot, Lucas and I gripped the rocks as we walked to the lookout. Lucas struggled a little but got used to the feeling after a few stones.

Once reaching the lookout, we stood on a boulder overlooking the deep blue below.

"I've never been overly excited about the beach, or the ocean in general," I said, looking out to the cerulean sea. "But whenever I do come here, it does feel calming, you know?"

Wearing a slight frown, he mumbled, "Yeah, it is."

I kept staring out to sea. "I feel as if we've lived on the beach our whole lives, but only really been when Mum and Dad forced us to come. We should come more often."

Lucas arched a brow. "Yeah, we should also go get fish and chips. I'm hungry."

I chuckled, and after taking one last glance out to the water, we left.

I checked my phone as we sauntered to the fish and chip shop front. Still no reply from Finn. Almost five-thirty p.m. Surely, he was awake, right?

Worry crept closer. But that worry was suddenly halted once we stepped foot in the shop.

A new worker stood behind the counter. A plump woman I'd never seen before, with short hair and skin red from sunburn, wearing a rather dirty apron.

As soon as she asked what Lucas and I wanted, I froze, my body instantly riddled with goosebumps, from feet to face.

For the first time ever, my vision was infiltrated with camera flashes that came and went in swift, detailed slides.

MACKENZIE'S BRAIN CINEMA ACTIVATED

First clip: the woman standing behind the counter, smiling, her skin a little less red.

Second clip: the woman at a beach, holding the hand of a younger, blonde woman next to her. They both turn to look at me and smile.

Third clip: the woman behind the fish and chip shop counter again, her apron clean and her skin glowing, but also a deep sadness in her eyes, as if she's holding back tears.

"You all right, mate?" the woman asked me.

"Uh, yeah." I snapped out of it, though my eyes were still bulging at her.

What. The. Fuck? The only three words spinning around my brain.

Lucas furrowed his brow at me, interrupting, "Four pieces of beer battered barra and five dollars' worth of chips, please."

The woman gave me a weird look, as if I was a prime suspect in a criminal investigation. "Twenty-one, thanks."

With the same blank look, I handed over the thirty dollars Dad had given us. She gave us the change, told us our food wouldn't be long.

Lucas and I stood outside.

"Um, what was that?" Lucas questioned me.

"What?" I acted dumb, trying to get my own head around what had just happened.

"As soon as the chick started speaking to you, you went quiet and then did this weird twitching thing."

Twitching thing? I'd seen a movie play in my head, one which Lucas obviously hadn't seen with me.

I shrugged. "Weird. I don't remember a twitch. Maybe I'm having a stroke."

"Maybe you need to stop drinking so much with your friends," Lucas said.

I snorted with laughter, then said, "I don't drink."

Lucas narrowed his eyes. "Don't lie. I know what you and Finn get up to. I'm not dumb."

I smirked, shaking his hair. "Whatever game you wanna live in, little brother."

Weekend dinners were a little more lively in our household, in that Mum and Dad seemed noticeably high-spirited on those evenings.

"How was the party last night, Macky?" Mum asked me.

She was the only person who called me Macky. Wasn't sure how I felt about it either.

I wondered whether Finn had replied yet. "It was fine."

"Sounded like it was a bit more than fine," Dad joshed. "Heard you guys get in at bloody four a.m. And you slept all day."

Trying to keep myself from smirking but half-failing, I said, "Yeah. I was super tired."

"*And* he did this weird twitching thing down at the fish and chip shop," Lucas butted in. "It was soooo awkward."

A frown formed on Mum's face as she glanced from Dad to me. "Twitching thing? Mack?" She only called me Mack when she was serious.

"It was nothing," I tried to say.

Lucas, of course, went on to tell them the whole story. The story of what he'd seen anyway. The prospect of telling my parents the truth, though—about the hallucinations or whatever they were—had anxiety scratching at my insides.

"Are you feeling ill?" Mum asked, checking my temperature with her hand, naturally making me pull away.

Dad shrugged, taking a swig of beer. "Or maybe…he's just hungover."

"Brian," Mum chastised.

"Maybe he should get some tests done," Lucas added.

I'd had enough. "Guys! I'm fine."

I was far from fine, but the narrative of me being fine was better than the thought of people in white coats taking blood samples and prodding me with foreign objects.

Eventually, I left the table without another word, to go check my phone, or perhaps call myself a freak over and over in my head.

I did both of those things. And by seven o'clock, still no word from Finn.

Two days passed. My worry meter was at an all-time high. Had he gotten home safe? He'd been in a questionable state when leaving my house. But surely, his parents would've contacted me if he hadn't been home for a few days.

On the brink of insanity, I texted Brit while sprawled on my bed: hey, what's doing?

She didn't take long to text back: hey, chilling at my place. You?

Nothing. Super bored

Damn. You can come over if you want. I've got the house to myself for the afternoon

Desperate to get outside, I drove to Brit's in a jiffy. She lived in the next town over so it wasn't a tremendous feat. It meant I got to spot a view of the coastline on my drive over.

One thing I wasn't expecting on my little adventure, however, was my fuel light to flash orange at me. It was the first time it had ever happened, and I wondered how I even let the petrol get that low in the first place.

Since getting my own car, anything below a quarter on the gauge had me freaking the fuck out.

I pulled into the closest petrol station, where it came to my attention that I'd never been to this one before, likely because it was on the outskirts of town, next to the highway, on a route seldom used.

After filling the tank with twenty dollars' worth, I walked into the station to pay. I'd loosely forgotten about what happened the last time I met someone for the first time.

He looked around the same age as me, but with sandy blonde hair and tanned skin glowing in his green uniform. His name badge flashed: *Nate.*

"Cash or card?" he asked.

MACKENZIE'S BRAIN CINEMA ACTIVATED

First clip: blonde guy at the beach, a surfboard under his shoulder.

Second clip: I'm at a party and the blonde guy is grinning at me.

Third clip: blonde guy and I in the back of a car, naked, kissing each other.

Um, sorry what?

Again?!

"Cash or card?" he asked a second time, furrowing his brows at me as if I were some obscure creature from outer space. I sure felt obscure, and somewhat creature-like.

"Card," I said quickly, sticking it into the machine and frantically typing my passcode.

Left the store as quickly as I fucking could.

Brit lived in one of the more modern suburbs. Every house had a pool, was predominantly white, and had been built in a weird shape. I would call them mongulated because, to be quite frank, there was no other word to describe them at the time.

Brit's house was as mongulated as the rest, the home consisting of two obscenely slanted rectangles on top of each other. A crooked rectangle home for a far-from-crooked family. Two wealthy parents who gave their kids whatever they wanted, living in a house that could be mistaken for a small mansion.

I rang the bell and, soon after, the door yawned open. Brit stood in the doorway, wearing a bright red bikini.

"Hey," she said, a welcoming smile on her face.

"Hey."

"How are you?"

"Yeah, good."

She let me in. "I've been laying by the pool all day," she said, leading me through the house.

"Damn, I should've brought my towel," I small-talked.

"Don't worry. I've got plenty of spares," she offered hospitably. "No one will be home for a while either."

Once we stepped onto the back deck, Brit threw me a towel from the cupboard and stretched out on a sun lounge. I took my shirt off and crawled onto the lounge next to her, letting the summer sun consume me.

Brit sighed. "I'm *so* not keen to go back to school next week. It's been a six-week holiday, but I feel like it's gone way too quickly."

I nodded. "It always does." I scrolled through Facebook, thinking of messaging Finn on there since he hadn't responded to my text.

"What's Mel up to today?" I asked Brit.

A dainty laugh broke through Brit's lips. "Surely Finn told you he's hanging out with Mel today?"

My stomach took a sharp U-turn. I shook my head. "No. He didn't," I said sullenly. "Haven't spoken to him since the party. At least I know he's not dead."

I felt betrayed, as if he'd killed me in a real-life *Call of Duty* game. Was he serious? He could hang out with her but not reply to his best friend's texts. The best friend he'd kissed just nights ago.

I wanted to get in the car, drive to wherever the fuck they were, and yell at the top of my lungs.

"What do you think about those two?" Brit asked. "I personally think they're cute. But they're also complete opposites. I still can't believe they fucked the other night. Was not expecting it from them two."

I studied the pool cleaner whirring around in the water. My anger brewed like a bubbling kettle.

"Mack?" Brit turned to me.

My daydream of going and professing my love for Finn rapidly diminished. "I think they're cute too," I flat-out lied.

Leaning over, I smiled at Brit, attempting to distract myself.

I kissed her, hoping my feelings for Finn would magically fade into nothing, and things would go back to normal. Start of summer normal.

The school bus pulled up at seven thirty-one on Tuesday morning. My long socks were pulled up, tie freshly wrapped, and my backpack filled with notebooks and food.

Brit locked eyes with me the moment I stepped on the bus. She sat next to Mel toward the back. My heartbeat picked up, and I drew a few deep breaths before taking the seat behind them.

Brit turned around. "Hey, you," she whispered.

"Hey," I said tiredly, untangling my earphones.

Mel also turned around, smiling, as though she hadn't stolen my best friend from me. "Hey, Mack. How was the rest of your summer?"

I hated Mel. But I didn't want to. I didn't hate her as a person. I hated her because of Finn, even if it wasn't her fault. Maybe I was to blame for kissing him and creating this big fat mess in the first place.

Still, he kissed me back, and that was something he couldn't fix. However, he sure could avoid it, and run from it. Run from me. Run from himself.

"It was fine," I fibbed.

"Hey, Mel," called out a voice from the seat across from us.

Holly and Jen: two of the most gossipy girls in our grade.

"Is it true you're dating Finn?" Holly asked in her normal whiny voice.

I have to move schools.

First day of year twelve, my final year in high school. How royally fucked.

Usually, Finn would be the first person I'd see at school. But not that day. Finn made sure he sat with Mel at recess and lunch, holding her hand, kissing her so everyone would feed into the narrative of their high school sweetheart romance.

He didn't talk to me, nor would he even stay in the same room as me. Whenever I stepped into the vicinity of him, he'd whisk Mel away and move on.

I held back tears the whole first day back. It was like, after six years of friendship, I had regressed into a mere ghost.

Where are you? Brit texted me at lunch.

I was hiding in the library so no one could find me.

I didn't text her back.

So, she texted me again, **we need to talk.**

Sunk into a bean bag with a Lemony Snicket book in my hand, I rolled my eyes and replied, meet me in the hallway next to the library.

I wondered what she wanted to talk about, beginning to breathe deeper and heavier at the thought of it. Was my big secret about to be exposed? The secret I'd successfully kept without complication. Until I fell in love with my best friend and kissed him.

I couldn't get up for the rest of lunch. Couldn't get up to meet Brit. Couldn't read about the *Series of Unfortunate Events* because I was in the middle of my own—the series I hoped had some sort of happy ending.

I'm in the hallway, where are you? Brit messaged me.

Having an anxiety attack in the library, can't make it, sorry. I felt as though it would've been a truthful reply at least. Yet instead, I ignored her.

After lunch, I arrived late to fifth period.

"And why would you be late, Mackenzie?" Mr. Thompson asked once I finally rocked up to Maths. With arched brows, he looked at me sternly once I'd completely interrupted his whiteboard diagramming.

The whole class eyeballed me. And just when I thought my anxiety was gone…

"Uh, I was in the t—"

"Tripping," finished a voice from the middle of the room.

To add to my growing misfortune, Noah Daniels sat

there all smug. If there was a day that dickhead wasn't making snide comments, it was an unusual day indeed. A few students sniggered.

Mr. Thompson shot a glare at Noah. "Noah, you can see me after class. And Mackenzie, next time, go to the toilet five minutes before the bell."

He pointed his whiteboard marker to the empty desk at the back of the room.

I had a choice of two seats: one next to Finn, or at the empty desk behind him. Before the summer holidays, we sat next to each other in every class. But times had changed it seemed, and dropping out and doing a trade sounded more inviting than ever. Anything so I didn't have to be at that fucking prison of a school.

Finn didn't even roll his eyes in my direction when I sat at the desk behind him. Mr. Thompson continued with his algebra diagram on the whiteboard, until Mrs. Smith came to the classroom, making Mr. Thompson sigh loudly at his second interruption.

The two teachers spoke outside. Noah sat at the desk in front of Finn, close enough for him to turn around and taunt me.

"Hey, faggot," Noah whispered in my direction. "Why aren't you sitting next to your boyfriend? You two fighting now 'cause he's dating Mel?"

I narrowed my eyes at Noah, wanting nothing more than to take this black pen and gauge his eyes out.

"Shut the fuck up, cunt," Finn hissed at Noah. "Turn around and mind your own business."

Mr. Thompson returned to the room and the class fell silent again.

After a smirk, Noah turned back around.

Even though Finn wasn't talking to me at the moment, at least he hadn't turned on me. At least he hadn't fed into the bullying like some backstabbing teenagers would.

I didn't know the solution to the algebra equation on the board, and I sure as hell didn't know the solution to fixing my problem with Finn.

I watched him kiss Mel at the bus stop that afternoon before I hopped on the bus, sitting as far away from her as I could. The seats were packed by the time Brit got on, and she chose to sit next to me instead of Mel, instantly folding her arms in my direction.

"What the fuck, Mack?" Brit seethed. "Why didn't you meet me today? I waited for you near the library."

"Sorry," I apologized with tepid enthusiasm. "I had to go to the toilet. Wasn't feeling well."

Her anger reduced to a deep sigh. "What's going on?" she whispered, tucking her head below the seat. "I asked Finn why you guys aren't talking and he just kinda shrugged and palmed it off. Is that why you disappeared today?"

I made my own shrug, speaking as softly as Brit so nobody could hear. "He just stopped talking to me, and it sucks."

"I don't understand why he'd do that. You guys have been best friends for years."

Revealing the real reason why would blow everything to pieces, I thought. I'd lose Brit, the only person I spoke to at school now. I'd become even more of a target for Noah.

And I'd still have to see Finn and Mel together every day whilst everyone knew the truth about me.

After arriving home from school, I walked to the headland solo, knowing I had to come up with some sort of game plan. Any plan, to make the mess a little lighter. Part of that meant messaging Finn again. I promised myself it would be the last time.

Hey, can we talk? I think we need to clear some stuff up.

I thought he would respond. But it ended up being another blue text box added to the conversation with myself.

As the sun set, I started to cry. Feeling abandoned, I sobbed for quite some time. I felt slightly better after letting it all out.

Back at home, I made it most of the way through the house before being summoned by Mum, to which I sighed.

"Yeah?" I kept my head down when I presented myself to her in the living room. Didn't want her to see my red eyes.

She watched *Home and Away* and I really hoped she wasn't going to ask me to watch it with her, because it would be an enormous "no" from me.

"Come sit," Mum smiled, patting the lounge next to her.

"I really don't wanna watch TV," I admitted.

She turned the TV off. "I wanna have a chat. C'mon."

"Okay." I ambled in and sat next to her; my head kept down.

"How was your first day of year twelve?" she asked, taking a sip from the wine glass next to her. "Last year, hey? Must feel good."

I sighed. "I'm thinking I wanna drop out. I hate that school."

Mum frowned. "Hey, what makes you say that? You've got friends at that school."

"Pffft. What friends?"

"Uh, you *do* go to school with your best friend," Mum said as-a-matter-of-factly. Little did she know.

"Me and Finn aren't talking," I confessed.

Mum put her hand on my shoulder. "What happened?"

I shrugged.

"Maybe it's time to make some new friends then," Mum suggested.

"Like who?"

"C'mon, even though our community isn't near any big cities or anything, there's still a lot of people who live here. And I bet there's plenty of young people who would wanna be your friend." Mum always had a calming nature about her. She always knew what to say at the right time.

"Sometimes, things can change quite drastically," Mum put forth, "and it's gonna happen many times in your life. The best thing we can do is know things aren't going to stay the same."

Things already weren't the same, and they were going to stay that way for a long while. I took Mum's advice, though. I would try and make some new friends.

And so, the next day, I sat with the new guy, Nate, who'd just started at our school.

Nate, the worker I'd seen at the petrol station. The one who'd moved to the coast recently. The one I'd already seen naked in a vision.

"It feels like a silver lining when you see a familiar face on the first day of school," Nate told me at lunchtime when we hung out under a tree, eating our sandwiches.

I thought about how weird I must've seemed to him when we first met in the petrol station, with my twitch and all that. I never brought it up, so it seemed as if he didn't judge.

The more I hung out with him, the less I thought about Finn. In fact, over the next few days, I had nearly forgotten about him, until the two of us ended up in the locker room together after recess.

Sadly, his locker still sat next to mine. But since we'd been back at school, he had successfully avoided me in the locker room. Not today, though. Today, we were forced to be within arm's reach.

After collecting my books first, I looked over at him. "Finn," I uttered.

No response. A mirror to my text messages.

"Finn," I said again.

Finn swiftly ripped his books out, his facial features deflated. He closed his locker and went to walk away.

I grabbed his shoulder, but he shoved me off. My voice rose. "At least fucking talk to me before you drop our friendship."

He kept on walking.

"Finn!" I called out, hiding back tears. "Is it because we kissed, and we both liked it?"

All of a sudden, Finn turned around and slammed me against a set of lockers with a thud, his fist wrapped around my shirt, face about as close to mine as it was on the beach. "Nothing happened, understood?!" he growled through gritted teeth. His eyes were knives. He glared at me for a few moments, but even that seemed too much for him.

He scowled, let me go, and stalked away.

Even though his first words spoken to me in over a week were ones of a threatening nature, I somehow felt better than I had after he gave me the attention. Even if it left me with a bruised back, a crinkled-up shirt, and a right old shock.

The following afternoon, I had to stop the Playstation. I needed to do something which didn't remind me of Finn.

I texted Brit, wyd?

Sighing, I threw my Playstation controller in the bin next to my desk.

Was literally about to message you but you beat me to it lol we needa talk. Can you meet me at the beach near Mel's?

Okay, I messaged back. And to self-sabotage myself even more, I drove down to the same beach Finn and I were on the night of Mel's party, trying to find the exact spot we kissed.

Waves crashed onto the shoreline, the high tide rolling in. I sat in the dunes while I waited for Brit, the afternoon sun glowing against the water's surface. I scooped up handfuls of sand and let it sprinkle out, slowly, back to its majority.

"Hey," a voice called from behind me, hastier than I'd ever heard it.

Brit sat down next to me in the sand.

We didn't speak for a few moments.

She sighed. "I have to ask you something. Are you…gay?"

My forehead furrowed. "No! No…I'm into girls," I was quick to say.

Lifting my knees up, I switched my gaze out to the water, a frown still on my face.

How much longer could I possibly keep this a secret?

Brit placed a hand on my shoulder. "Look, it's okay if you are. It's honestly fine. Even though I do like you more than a friend, I'm not going to judge you if you're into guys."

I shook my head, trying to pull at straws again, but now, they were non-existent. "I do like you," I said.

"Yeah, but not in the same way you like Finn, right?" she asked.

My stomach tightened into a knot. Exposed. May as well have been stripped of my clothes and left naked in a crowd full of people all jeering at me.

"What do you mean?" I tried to play dumb, far past the point of being able to lie to Brit anymore.

"Mack, I'm the girl who fell for a guy who doesn't want her the way she wants," Brit said. "I see more than you might think."

Obviously, I couldn't deny it. We sat there in silence,

watching the tide creep closer. She didn't slap me or tell me I was a terrible person for lying to her for as long as I did.

"Is that the reason you and him aren't talking?" she asked, looking over at me.

"Not quite," I sighed.

I told her everything, and she listened with empathic ears. It made sense to her. All of it.

"Do you hate me?" I had to ask her. I low-key hated myself, but I did feel better after telling someone. Even though Brit was the last person I thought I'd confide in.

She smiled. "No. I don't hate you. It just means I can take up some date offers I've been passing down for the past month or so."

I chuckled at the conversation I thought would be incredibly hard but wasn't so bad after all.

Bread and Butter Pickles

LATER

Jasper, Seb, Julian, and I were having a cheeky drink whilst the girls were off canoodling, when a wall of dust billowed through, one which had us retreating to the two small tents that, of course, could only fit two at any given time.

If it wasn't for an abrupt afternoon dust storm, I wouldn't have crawled into the tent so quickly with Julian.

My tongue wandered inside his mouth. Yet I couldn't help but think of Jasper. He and Seb were in the tent next to us, some faint but pleasure-heavy noises chiming in from them.

Julian's lips felt soft. Recently-applied lip balm soft. His cock pulsed through his shorts as his body rubbed against mine. I had a tonne of energy to release, and I sure as hell would use some of it now, to distract myself from the pangs of Jasper-and-Seb jealousy.

Julian and I rubbed our cocks together. His dick had much more foreskin than mine by the feel of it. We couldn't see much in the tent, though, so I couldn't know for sure.

We sixty-nined each other, my indiscreet huffs blocking out the noise of any other sexual activity going on around me.

But before either of us could come, there came the call of a lesbian.

"Where are the gays?" Rachel sang from outside the tent.

"They're probs fucking in the tents," Lily said. "Bet it's fucking intense too."

Jasper and Seb giggled. Julian joined in.

"I'm guessing it's dust-free out there?" I called out, pulling a stray pube from my tongue. Bass music grumbled from afar, something I very much fancied being a part of. The music and I, having the time of our lives together.

"Yeah, it is, thank god," Rachel chuckled. "We got a little bit coated, but nothing baby wipes couldn't fix."

Baby wipes were, in fact, a godsend at any music festival. And I was glad Rachel remembered to bring them. She always did, and it had saved my life on countless occasions.

Scrambling for my clothes and pulling them on, I crawled out of the tent through a small opening in the zip.

I could've opened up the door like a normal person, but I felt a far grander entrance was in order.

I poked my whole body through, looking up at Rachel and Lily with a cheeky, "Hiiiii".

"Hello, little caterpillar," Rachel said, patting my head.

Last light sprayed onto the rugged crags surrounding the valley.

Once I'd crawled the rest of the way out of the tent, Julian followed. I lay on the earth, rolling around in the dirt. One could say I was grounding myself. Another could say I was cooked and needed serious help. Believe both.

Jasper emerged from the next tent, shirtless, glitter still sparkly on his chest, smirking at me. "It looks…comfortable down there."

"I'm just being at one with the ground for now," I said, which turned out didn't need any more explaining. It was what it was.

I couldn't help but focus my gaze on Jasper's bare body. He had a tattoo of an orchid stretched across his left rib cage.

I started making dirt angels.

"Are you sure you didn't take any molly?" Rachel asked, arching her brows.

I wasn't high, but I'd drank a little before hopping in the tent, when the sun still packed a punch upon my skin.

Seb came out of the tent and started sculling from a water bottle.

Jasper walked over to me. "Is there any room in your earth circle?"

I laughed. "Not for you." A little harsh. "I mean, there's room near me. *Near* my earth circle. But not inside it."

"Perfect!" Jasper said gleefully, becoming horizontal in the dirt next to me.

Lily giggled at the sight of us both making dust angels on the ground. "It's great to see you two have lost your fucking marbles," she said. I wasn't sure if she was being sarcastic or serious. Indeed, both would've been okay.

As quick as he could, Jasper pointed to the sky. "I just saw a—"

"Shooting star!" I shouted.

"Oh, fuck yes," Seb cussed, tilting his head toward the sky. "I wanna see a shooting star."

"Well, you gotta get down to this level and you might," Jasper teased.

"Yeah, the level of the dirt monsters," I added.

Truthfully, I could've stayed there all night and stared up at the stars. But Seb wouldn't allow it. Jasper had put a spell on him, albeit an unintentional one.

I guessed it would've been a lot more convenient if Jasper hadn't made Seb keen in the first place. Yet I probably would've done the same thing if I was rejected by a boy I fancied. That boy was me, and now I regretted ever rejecting Jasper in the first place.

Seb sighed, taking a swig from a bottle of Fireball. "All right, who's keen on the dance floor?"

"Yes, bitch," Julian instantly agreed, equally unimpressed with Jasper's and my ground antics.

"Maybe after you give me some of that Fireball," Lily winked.

"Be my guest," he quipped, handing her the bottle. "There's plenty to go around."

Both Lily and Rachel took sips of the cinnamon whiskey. In fact, we all did.

Stepping from the ground, I wiped a layer of dust from my unbuttoned shirt.

Jasper rubbed his bare shoulders. "Is it me, or did the temperature drop a wee bit?"

I pressed my pointer finger against my lip. "I think you're right there."

Jasper snuck into Seb's tent and threw a T-shirt on.

"Some more whiskey and you won't notice a thing," Seb butted in.

Rachel cocked an unconvinced eyebrow at him.

"Oh my god, I know what I need," Jasper said, as if a revelation was coming. "My *overalls*. I left them at camp 'cause it was too hot to wear them today."

"I completely forgot we bought those overalls!" I laughed.

Naturally, the material was quite thick so wearing them today would've been comparable to wearing a black long-sleeve on a summer's day.

"I might go get mine," announced Jasper.

"Well, I've gotta wear mine, too, obviously," I told him.

"I'm going to the dance floor," Seb said, rather rudely.

"Same," Julian joined in.

Awkward. So fucking awkward that I could've dug myself a hole in the dirt and crawled into it so I didn't have to face anyone.

"All right, let's leave these losers to go get their

overalls," Rachel suggested, "and we'll wait for them on the dance floor until they make their grand, dusted-off entrance."

I finally locked eyes with Rachel. Her brows were still raised, and she now had a devilish smirk on her face.

Even though nighttime had welcomed us, I could still see Seb narrow his eyes at me before he said, "Fine by me."

The four of them walked toward the dance floor whilst Jasper and I walked in the opposite direction.

"We've gotten ourselves into a little pickle, haven't we?" were the first words Jasper said on our quest for the overalls.

I couldn't help but chuckle. "I mean, if I'm thinking what you're thinking, then yes. It's a big pickle. Like a big big large gherkin, still swimming in its own juices?"

"Yeah, bread and butter pickles with all the mustard seeds and peppercorns."

I chuckled, picturing it, and so much more. Undeniably, Jasper's juices were what I was imagining.

We frolicked through a cluster of campsites. Jasper sighed. "So, when I was in the tent with Seb, I uh…could hear you and Julian, and all I could think about was—"

A girl squealed from a campsite up ahead. Jasper's attention fixed on whatever was at the end of the path. I couldn't make out what it was myself.

"Uh, since when did they set up *that!*" he gushed.

At the end of the path was a structure held together by massive wooden poles, a blue light illuminating a circular dome created with the poles. Inside were a slew of hammocks. A patterned shade sail covered the dome.

"Woah, how have we not come the long way back to the campsite," I said in awe.

"I dunno, but it's epic, let's go."

Jasper started speed-walking, making me keep up with him.

Although the dome wasn't enclosed at all, it felt as if Hammock City was our own little spaceship. A few hammocks were already occupied, so we each took one at the back. It was oddly quiet in there. We lay back and watched the lights beaming from above, which created projections of sacred geometry in the dirt.

"Weird, I can hardly hear the music in here," Jasper mentioned.

Indeed, the thumps of bass echoing from the stage had lessened to background noise.

"Yeah, what a fun little pit-stop," I said, casting him a glance.

My gaze drifted upward. The more I mused, the more my face softened. I tried to communicate my thoughts and feelings to him, without words. But alas, telepathy was in no way my forte. It would be a cool power to have, but who knew if people could actually do that, or if it was merely a preconceived idea from someone who wrote a book, or a movie, and thought the concept would wow an audience. Then again, if I could see the things I saw, I wouldn't be completely surprised if I found out telepathy was real.

I cleared my throat. "What were you saying back there?"

"Hmm?"

"Back there. You were telling me about how you were in the tent and—"

Jasper chuckled. "Dammit. I nearly got off the hook from confrontation."

I simpered, cocking my head in his direction. "Nope, not that easy."

Jasper shrugged. "I'm really into you," he said, straight up. "And I know you're into me, too."

"How do you know that?" I asked, still unsure why I was still playing *this* game with him.

He scoffed. "I'm surprised you haven't picked up on it yet, honestly."

Had I missed something?

"I mean, I guess my twitches aren't *as* noticeable as yours," he went on, "but they're still a thing, I guess. I've learned to control them."

What? Um, wait, what?

I went to speak but kept holding back.

My smile waned. "What do you mean?" I decided to play the dumb card one more time.

Jasper rolled his eyes. "Oh, c'mon, you don't need to hide it," he said playfully. "We can both see the future, right? In everyone we meet."

As confronting as the moment was, it felt like a weight had been lifted off my shoulders.

What had *he* seen when he first met me? Did he see what I saw? Did he see his own death, at an age no older than forty, yet still want me?

"Well, fuck, hi," were the only words I could speak.

Jasper leaned forward and stood out of the hammock, towering over me with a twinkle in his eye.

"Hi," he said back, holding out his hand. "I have so many questions."

I went first. "D-did you see…us?"

"Yeah," he breathed hard.

How had I not recognized Jasper's twitch this whole time? I guessed I was too consumed by my own feelings to even notice him. That aside, it all made sense. The question he asked me when we first met in The Blue Bar—about the secrets.

He'd seen his own snapshot of what our future held. Yet he still pursued me, waiting until he was sure I was like him, until I'd twitched for the right number of new acquaintances to zero in on me.

Besides Jasper's untimely demise, I wanted all those things with him. But for now, I had to let go of the future, of the thought of him dying.

"We've got a lot to talk about," he admitted.

I nodded, hoping it would help the words take shape.

"We don't have to rush to do that," he said.

Ten years was a decent amount of time, so I said, "We don't."

Unable to deny his penetrating stare, I reached out and grabbed his hand. It was as cold as mine. He pulled me up and we both stood in this dome of sacred geometry, looking into each other's eyes bewitchingly.

My whole body tingled the closer we inched to touch. Jasper let go of my hands and rubbed my shoulders.

Not letting go of his gaze, his face moved closer to

mine, slowly. I mirrored his movements, a few centimeters from a kiss. I was ready to feel those lips for the first time. To have the one freckle on his bottom lip press against my skin.

So close.

Closer.

A deep and echoing *bang* blew, sending sparks into the sky.

The fireworks made us flinch away from our moment, but we laughed it off.

"Let's go get those overalls," I winked.

They fit perfectly, as I'd undoubtedly hoped. And after pouring a bottle of vodka and strawberry soda to take, we walked back to the stage, to the sea of colors, hand in hand.

After finding out what was going on, inhibitionless to begin with, it started to make sense. It was as though the real estate on my shoulders became less loud and heavy, from the voice telling me to desperately change things, to the weight of that character resting on my bone.

By the minute, Jasper felt more familiar, a continuation of my first love familiar.

Maneuvering through the lasers, we couldn't put two feet forward without bouncing to the beat.

As the night grew, so did the BPM of the music.

Jasper looked immaculate in his overalls. I kept checking him out every chance I got. Most of the moments I passed a glance at him, he met it with a smile.

Now and again, someone in the crowd howled into the night, which would follow with another howl, and so forth.

Jasper and I stood in front of each other, swaying from side to side as we gravitated toward one another.

When he finally kissed me, the music, the howls, and everything else—canceled out.

Dissolving.

Our first kiss was equal measures of softness and passion. So much so that my eyes were closed, our lips moving in sync, his breath purring through the bass.

When we pulled away, he beamed at me, his face rosy pink, and my heart fuller than the volume of the speakers.

We finally reached Rachel and Lily, who were dancing on the front left side of the crowd. I should've known they'd be there.

"Aren't you two cute!" I shouted over the music, popping my head in between them. "Wasn't this where you two were meant to meet for the first time?"

Both their eyes lit up. Rachel pulled me in for a tight hug. We stayed glued in the embrace for at least fifteen seconds. Actually, I think it was the longest hug we'd ever had with each other, to be honest.

"I fucking love you," Rachel said quickly, her pupils dilated. "Thank you for joining me on this trip, honestly. It's been fucking *amazing!*" She handed me a hefty grin before letting go. "And I'm not just saying this because I'm high."

"You left your boyfriends, Seb and Julian, waiting a

little too long," Lily called out to Jasper and I. "They're now hooking up, but based on how long you both took to get your overalls, I don't think they're your boyfriends anymore."

Jasper and I looked at each other. Lily had her arm around Rachel.

"We called it on the first day of the festival," Rachel mentioned.

"Yeah, we knew it was only a matter of time," Lily added with a wink.

Lily gave us the two-finger *I've got my eye on you* and turned around to face the stage. Rachel put out her hand, placing a clear capsule in my palm and one in Jasper's.

"They're fun," she said cheekily, arching her brows.

Rachel didn't need to convince me twice. Jasper and I downed our caps with sweet vodka strawberry, a drink refill most definitely on the cards.

After the caps kicked in, the rest of the night flew by. Our drinks needed filling up, so we filled them. We danced some more.

By midnight, the music turned to dark progressive trance. We danced harder. Refilled twice in an hour.

Two in the morning swung by to say hello. We popped another cap.

The sun peeked through the hills. We basked in the first shine, silently, a welcome break from the dance floor, before going on to talk about our own Brain Cinemas.

"I discovered mine a lot younger than you," Jasper

explained, in response to me asking when he first discovered it. "Pretty much when I learned to read and write is when it started happening. My parents thought I just had a wild imagination, then I started predicting things that could not have been made up. I can remember the first time they were shocked by something I'd already said would happen. It was a car accident involving one of the students at school."

I swallowed a lump in my throat, and Jasper went on, "I remember when I first met Henry, one of the vision clips was him, like, all bruised and beaten up in his school uniform. And in the vision, I'd asked him if he remembered anything from the car accident. Naturally, I went home and told my parents about it, but they said I shouldn't make up such horrible things about someone else. Then, it would've been maybe three months later, and Henry was in a car accident with his family, and when he recovered, the vision played out exactly as it had in my head."

Jasper stopped talking when we passed a group of festival-goers. We, then, continued along a narrow dirt trail and climbed to the top of a surrounding range, which overlooked the whole festival, watching on as the morning glow sprayed across the valley.

The music echoed, even from far away, the dance floor still packed with people, like little ants dancing in the distance.

Jasper put his arm around me. My hand massaged his thigh. We still wore our overalls. However, they were a lot dustier than when we first bought them.

"Do you have any siblings?" I asked him.

"No biological siblings, but I have a half-sister who's older than me" he said. "What about you?"

"I have a little brother," I said. "We hardly ever see each other 'cause he's out living the university life now."

Jasper sighed. "I hardly ever see my sister either. We've been reconnected recently, but under not-so-good circumstances. To settle my adoptive mother's estate back in London."

I looked into his hazy eyes. "I'm sorry to hear about your mum."

"It's fine," he shrugged it off. "I actually had two mums. I was adopted when I was eleven, by my two mums who got me through to eighteen. They were such an amazing couple, and it really made coming out easy to them when I was young."

I gaped at him. "Wow. I've never met someone with same-sex parents before."

"Yeah, and they did a much better job than my actual parents did," Jasper said, rolling his eyes.

I paused a moment before asking, "What's the story with your biological parents, if you don't mind me asking?"

Jasper sighed, then smiled and caressed my hand, as if he'd told enough people the story to be comfortable with it. "My biological mother was pretty troubled, and she really couldn't look after me properly. When I was five, my dad died, so she took me to London. She had family over there. I was super young when we relocated from Australia to the UK, but I remember spending nights at random houses of guys she would be fucking for a hit. It wasn't pleasant. Eventually, she didn't have enough money to feed me, so she gave me up. Hell, I'm glad she did. She wasn't a terrible woman. I do actually remember a lot of good qualities about her. Before she spiraled into that dark hole, I remember how great she was at cooking. Sometimes she'd spend hours cooking, just to make something nice for her and me. But when she became dependent on the drugs, she stopped cooking. She stopped looking after herself. She stopped looking after me. It did teach me a lesson at a young age though: that it's one thing to use drugs recreationally, but another for them to consume you, to the point you can't go a day without them or you'll feel like you're already dead."

Tears welled in my eyes, feeling the last part to my core. "I'm so sorry."

"It's okay," he was quick to say, swinging a courageous smile my way. "I don't remember my dad, and my mum failed, but I ended up with two new amazing mums who wanted nothing more than to look after me." His voice became vibrant again. "And they did. They made me feel so loved it felt as if I'd been with them my whole life. I did lots of things with them. We went traveling and they took me on *so many* adventures. And even though I hardly knew my actual parents, I'm grateful for how things turned out…most of the time anyway."

"I'm proud of you," I said, moving my finger up and down, and in circles on his thumb.

"Thanks," he said. Then, "So, my adoptive mums separated a few years ago, but this was before one of them got rich off an app she created."

"What was the app?"

"Oh, some business communication platform that went bonkers when more people started working from home."

"Right."

"Yeah, and I kept in touch, but it was weird not having both my mums together, you know?"

I sighed. "Same. My parents are separated. I guess after the kids leave home, sometimes the parents realize they don't love each other anymore. That they only stuck together because of the kids."

"Yeah." He paused. "Anyway, Helen, my mum with the estate from her app, got coronary heart disease and it was a big shock, especially to her company, and to us. She ended up selling the company before she passed. She gave a little bit of her estate to my other adoptive mum and her family, but most of it went to me and my sister. I was surprised when I saw how much money I was about to get. I just didn't know what to do with such a big amount."

"She probably wanted you to do something useful with it," I said. "She must've disrupted the business world with what she created and what she earned from it."

"Yeah, I guess I haven't worked out what to do with it yet, and my visions haven't given me any clues so far. I want it to go toward something good for the world or something. But two years ago, when I acquired the inheritance, I got scared to tell anybody about it. I was living in fear that if I told anyone, they would treat me differently and hate me in a way. So, I've kept living a normal life ever since, even though I do have enough to quit working if I wanted to."

I nodded. "Sounds like it hasn't gone to your head, which is good."

His lips flattened even more. "And I never want it to. Money can be dangerous."

"And it makes the world go round, so it's a catch-twenty-two, isn't it?"

Jasper sighed. "Yeah. You're right."

I kissed him on the cheek and said confidently, "You'll figure it out."

We basked in the sun through another silence, and soon, I said, "I wanna tell you about Finn."

No Going Back

THEN

When I stepped onto the school grounds, I got the gist something wasn't right. People whispered to each other as I walked past. But it wasn't until the bell rang and I went to the locker room that I was swamped with the sheer brunt of the chatter.

I was gathering books from my locker when Holly approached me with her shrill voice. "Mack, is it true you and Finn are more than friends?"

Brit glanced over at me from a few lockers away, the guilt wafting from her. Even she wasn't aware of how quickly her words would get around.

I sighed. "Honestly, Holly, piss off and mind your own business."

But Holly wasn't the only one. When it came to recess, I was cornered on the playground by none other than Noah Daniels. And of course, he was accompanied by his two favorite henchmen on either side of him.

"Always knew I was right about you and Finn," Noah teased. "Yet you're still trying to come between me and Brit."

Standing against the side of a tree, I put my head down. Nate sat next to me on one of the tree roots, as speechless as he'd been in the locker room. I knew he wanted to back me up, but being the new kid in school, I didn't blame him for not.

"Brit doesn't even like you," I mumbled, though I wished I would've ignored Noah instead.

Noah gritted his teeth. "What did you say, fuckwit?"

"You heard me," I said, clenching my jaw.

Noah Daniels then did the one thing that embarrassed me even more than being outed to the whole school: he ripped my pants down, underwear and all. And to my dismay, there were far too many groups sitting under the trees for my liking.

Gaping, it took me a fraction of a second to realize what had happened before pulling my pants back up. But it was too late. Most of the students under the trees had already seen me, and those who didn't were already told by their friends who had.

They all giggled. Noah and his henchmen laughed the

loudest. Tears filled my eyes. I ran off before I let any of them fall down my face.

Brit must've seen me crossing the school grounds and followed me to the east wing bathrooms.

"Mack," she called out from behind me.

Already sobbing, I ignored her at all costs. I'd finally cracked and I wished it was locked away in my bedroom, alone, not at school, where I had to face all these people.

I stopped at a corner before the toilets.

"Mack," Brit said again.

"What the fuck do *you* want?" I cried, wiping my eyes and nose.

"Mack, I-I'm sorry," she stammered, placing a hand on my shoulder. I shook it off immediately.

"I didn't mean for it to get out," she said. "Mel kept asking questions about you, and me, and it kind of just slipped out."

"Yeah, and now I'm the laughing stock. Thank you very much."

Brit sighed. "Mack…do you really think you would've been able to hide it forever? Especially something like this, where hiding it just hurts people more."

I cried harder, unable to stop. "I should be able to come out on my own fucking terms!"

"I'm sorry. I really am. I just…felt as if Mel needed to know," Brit went on. She sighed again. "But you know Mel, and I didn't realize she would react so much. She flipped out. Told a bunch of people. Broke up with Finn. Now I feel like I've fucked everything up."

"You have," I sniffed, walking off.

The bell rang for third period. Yet I couldn't for the life of me prepare myself for Maths. Maths meant I had to sit in the same room as Finn and Noah, which was a big no from me.

Instead, I walked to sick bay. I wanted to go home. I didn't look any of the office ladies in the eye so they couldn't tell I'd been crying. At least I had a blocked nose, so it was easy enough to tell them I felt a flu coming on.

They called my parents and got their permission for me to go home. Thank god I'd driven to school, so I didn't have to wait for any buses, or be around anyone.

Everything felt much calmer once I'd left the school grounds. I walked to the car park, almost forgetting to pick my feet up.

After reaching my car, I noticed one person at a picnic table in the nearby park.

Him.

Turns out he'd had enough of school for the day too. He wasn't trying to escape me this time, though. He started by shooting a glare in my direction, then stood from the picnic table and stalked over to me while I unlocked my car.

"Finn?" I said gingerly.

Stepping onto the driver's side, Finn grabbed me by the shirt and shoved me up against the car before I could open the door.

"What the fuck is your problem?" he shouted begrudgingly, his jaw clenched. "Are you trying to ruin my life?"

Adrenaline leaked into my blood. I shoved him off me. "What's *my* problem?" I yelled. "What's *your* problem?!"

He seemed taken aback after my retaliation.

"You'd rather cut me out of your life rather than be true to yourself?" I hissed, pointing at him. "Is that it?"

"Shut the fuck up," he growled. "You don't know anything."

"I know you kissed me," I said, feeling my eyes glaze over again. "And then, you just stopped talking to me. Do you know how it made me feel?"

Finn narrowed his eyes on me even more. "Oh, don't act like you're not hiding too. You led Brit on for fucking ages and now you can't hide it anymore so you used me as what, your fucking experiment?"

"It's not like that!"

"What's it fucking like then, Mack? Do you even know your own truth anymore?"

My voice softened. "You wanna know the truth?"

He folded his arms. "Go on. Humor me."

I looked right into his eyes. He looked tired, but still as beautiful as I had remembered before summer ended.

"I like you," I said, more sure of myself than I'd ever been. "More than a friend."

I was waiting for a punch in the face, but it never came. He breathed in and out deeply, taming the anger I'd triggered in him.

He held my gaze for a few moments, then looked away and sighed, shaking his head. "I'm not like that," he denied, starting to walk away.

"Aren't you?" I called after him.

He stopped walking. I wanted him to turn around, let me know I wasn't alone. Even if he didn't feel the same way about me, I still wanted a friendship with him. We couldn't throw it all away, I thought. All those years spent together surely meant more than nothing.

"What are we going to tell everyone at school?" I asked. "If we don't say something, the gossip won't stop. You know how they are. If we don't settle on a truth—"

He sighed. "According to me, it's all a rumor."

"But it's not, and you know it."

Without another word, Finn left me in the car park. I cried again and drove home.

I didn't return to school for the rest of the week. Didn't leave my room much, either, especially when Mum and Dad were home. I had to play the gravely ill card to the best of my ability.

During the day, I snuck across to the beach while Mum and Dad were at work. At night, I played *GTA* and watched DVDs of movies I hadn't watched in a while. Mostly old-school slasher films to distract me from the real horror I'd left behind at school.

I received a text message on Wednesday and one on Thursday.

The one on Wednesday was from Nate. **Are we still going to Holly's party on Friday night? Totally understand if you don't wanna go man**

Honestly, parties were the last thing I could think about. Worse yet, the thought of a party with people from my school.

I don't think so, I messaged back.

No worries Mack hope you're feeling better soon

The text on Thursday was from Brit. **Are you okay Mack? Both you and Finn haven't been at school all week**

Honestly, I wasn't surprised Finn hadn't been at school either. But I wondered if it would spark even more talk amongst the students. I imagined they would come up with as many scenarios as their imaginations could let loose.

I didn't reply to Brit right away, mostly because I didn't know how to answer her question.

Was I okay? Short answer: no.

Though, when I didn't reply by four-thirty, she called me.

I sighed before answering, "Hello?" pretending I didn't know who called.

"You didn't reply to my text," she said, a hint of worry in her tone.

"Yeah, sorry. Didn't really feel like talking."

"Fair enough. But I still thought maybe you were dead."

"Nope, plot twist: still kicking," I said sarcastically.

"So, I was ringing to let you know…the gossip has totally died down at school," she informed me. "The talk of the town is Holly's party this weekend and…"

The over-phone silence sparked a quiver in my stomach. "And what?"

Brit guffawed before gathering herself again. "So, Noah Daniels may have had to go to the hospital yesterday because he took so much Viagra his dick wouldn't go down. Which I thought was *hilarious*."

I laughed for what felt like the first time in a while.

"Didn't think that douchebag needed Viagra, the way he talks himself up…"

"Oh, everyone has their secrets," said Brit. "He got his karma, though. Had it coming to him."

I exhaled heavily. "Yeah."

"How are you with everything? I know I'm not your favorite person at the moment and I broke your trust, which I'm really sorry for. But I do care about you, Mack. As a friend."

After sighing again, I told her about the heated encounter in the car park.

"It sounds as if he's just really embarrassed and doesn't know how to take it," Brit admitted. "Cause, you know, it never would've happened in the first place if he didn't want it. Tripping on acid or not."

"Yeah, I dunno what to do," I said. "I wanna rock up at his house and tell him I'm into him and scream it out and kiss him again."

"Probably don't do that," Brit advised. "But I think you need to talk to him again about it. Face to face. Otherwise, you guys won't be able to get closure from any of this."

"Hmmm, yeah you're right."

"And look, I wouldn't be telling you this if I didn't think Finn was secretly into you," she went on. "Mel fancies him but their short relationship was messy and I could tell Finn wasn't really into her—there was something else at play there. But god, ever since I've known you two, you and Finn have been *really close*. I mean, even before me and you started hooking up, I kinda thought you guys were a thing."

This gave me hope. Maybe I wasn't crazy for thinking

Finn and I could possibly be more than friends without us even knowing it.

"Well, how do I get the chance to talk to him face-to-face without scaring him off?" I asked. "He ignores my messages if it's about anything even remotely related to what happened that night."

"Hmmm," Brit pondered. "Did you leave any of your stuff at his house?"

"Uh, a few Playstation games I think."

"So, there's your excuse to go over and talk to him," Brit blurted out. "I'll take fifty dollars for this scheme consultation, thanks."

We both laughed. I needed a good laugh. I needed several, but this was a good start.

"Let me know how it goes, okay?"

"Sure thing. Thanks for the call."

"You better come to Holly's party on Friday and get drunk with me, dickhead."

"Ha ha, maybe."

Finn appeared online when I clicked on his Facebook profile.

Hey Finn, I know you're at home, so am I, but I was wondering if I could come round and grab those games I lent you?

It took him a while to open the message, and I almost expected him to ignore it.

But he actually replied: uh yeah sure. But come

tomorrow while my parents are gone. I'm meant to be sick

I was sick too. Sick of a slew of things. Sick of the person I'd pretended to be all these years. Sick of hiding the person I really was. Sick of the toxic societal pressures that made me this way in the first place. I was sick of feeling like a fucking alien.

I wondered if Finn got the twitching thing after that night on the beach. Was he, too, seeing things he couldn't for the life of him explain? The flashes. The camera roll playing out inside the mind. But not flashes you would create with your imagination.

I finally texted him back: sure thing. I'll message you tomorrow when I'm leaving. Won't be too early.

For dinner, Mum cooked her famous spaghetti bolognese (as she always called it). I had no idea how she did it, but it sure tasted delicious, every single time she served it up. Between the four of us, there wasn't much conversation over the table. Mostly, it was the slurping of spaghetti and a gulp from a drink every few mouthfuls, Mum and Dad with their red wine, and Lucas and I with our lemon lime bitters.

Thursday was the day Dad and Lucas were assigned wash-up duty, which left Mum and I still at the outside table, staring into the abyss of our own food comas.

"You feeling a bit better, hon?" asked Mum.

I shrugged. "Kind of."

If only she knew what was really going on in my

exploding brain of doom and sorrow and endless questions that may or may not have answers.

Mum sighed, folding her hands together and placing them on the table. She tucked her chair in, sat up straight, and gave me an awkward smile, to which I looked away in response.

"So, I got a call from the school today," she said.

My stomach sank, and I kind of hoped it would be all my problems sitting in there, so I could ultimately shit them out once I'd digested my spaghetti.

I rolled my eyes. "What about?"

"They wanted to know how you were doing," Mum continued. She bit her lip. "They also told me about this rumor going around the school. About you…and Finn."

I locked eyes with Mum, about to deny it all. But I didn't want this anymore. I wanted to stop hiding, at least from who I was. The rest could come later.

"Do you wanna talk about it?" she asked softly.

I half-sarcastically chuckled. "It's a long story."

She took a sip of red wine. "I've got all night, Macky. However long it takes. Just know that whatever you identify yourself as, I will love you unconditionally. Forever."

"But what about Dad?" I said sullenly. "He's such a macho guy, and he's into footy and stuff and I'm…not."

"Who said you need to be like your father?" Mum put forth. "Surely you got some genes from both of us."

I shrugged.

Before Mum gave birth to me, she completed an arts degree at university, where she met Dad while studying. Dad always said Mum was an incredible writer, that she had a way with words. But when she finally completed her degree, children became her priority, and her incomplete book of poems got dustier and dustier as the years went on.

Dad became the breadwinner of the family when Mum had to give up her job at the pub to have me. He worked his nine-to-five in marketing while Mum stayed at home looking after me.

Mum forgot about her writing. When I was old enough to go to school, she went on to work with troubled youth. I asked her why she chose youth work over writing, and she told me she wanted to help people. Writing was too hard of a road for her to take.

"I'm pretty sure I'm gay," I told her, after our longest conversation in years.

She took it a lot better than I thought she would. And while Dad and Lucas watched television inside, Mum and I kept on chatting.

"I kind of had an inkling you were," she said, her mouth slightly stained from the red wine.

"How?"

"Well, when you were about thirteen or fourteen, you didn't quite erase the search history on the computer," she joshed. "And I know I didn't look up *nude male celebrities* and your dad had his own computer and Lucas was seven or something, so…"

I went red in the face and subsequently laughed it off whilst I drowned in embarrassment. Mum laughed too.

We stopped and sat in silence, before I broke it again. "Hey, Mum?"

"Yeah?"

"Do you ever regret not pursuing your writing?"

Mum looked to the left. "Yeah, it comes up from time to time. But I also love doing what I do. You know, I went from being a youth worker to now managing the residential houses I used to work in. The progression and growth have been great."

"So, you don't ever imagine what life would've been like if you took that path?"

"I do, but if I was meant to, I believe it would've happened already," Mum said, finishing off her glass. "Plus, who knows, it's been so long. I might not even love writing anymore."

Our conversation ended with Mum telling me she wanted me back at school on Monday. She said I could have one more day off, but next week, it was time I faced the world, the world being my school, which I only had to put up with for less than a year.

She said I should start thinking about what I wanted to do after high school. I had no idea, though I promised her I would think about it.

"Hey Macky, is there anything else you want to talk about? Any other changes you've noticed about yourself?"

Oh yeah, pretty sure I can see the future now.

"No," I lied.

I slept in on Friday morning. By the time I rose, Lucas had gone to school, Mum and Dad to work. While the house was as quiet as it had been all week, something about that Friday seemed unexplainably different. Might've been the chat with Mum the night before, making me wake up far less anxious. Or was it because I was going to see Finn at the Bower Creek farm in T-minus two hours? Also, highly likely.

I cooked a sausage roll in the oven for lunch and ate it outside, role-playing the looming dialogue between Finn and I. What would he even say to me when I arrived? Better yet, what would I say to *him*?

"Finn, I think we should explore the part of us we discovered on the beach."

"Finn, I want you to be happy and to be yourself."

"Finn. I love you."

After finishing my sausage roll, I showered and slipped on the best summer clothes I owned: navy chino shorts, white sneakers, and a blue Ralph Lauren polo shirt.

I doubted myself in the mirror.

Is this too much?

Will he even care what I wear anyway?

Should I just not go?

I shook my head and left the mirror before the racing thoughts could consume me.

The drive into the hinterland was lush. The sun coated everything in sight, and the oaky smell of the trees wafted through the car window. The wind blew against my hand as it glided through the air in a wave-like motion. I had a habit of doing this almost every time I drove across the range to Bower Creek, cruising around the bends I knew all too well. It felt good to do it again after some time.

I drove down the dirt road to Finn's farmhouse, taking deep breaths. Good thing his family wasn't there in case I was awkward around them too.

I parked my car and hopped out. The chickens ran around freely. I kept my distance, even though they weren't a threat as such.

Finn was exercising in the gym at the front of the house, underneath the verandah. His shirt was off, his skin glossed with sweat.

"I forgot how quick it was to get over here from the coast," he said, wiping himself with a towel.

I tried my best to only look at his face and not his abs. "All good, man. How've you been?"

"Been all right," he mumbled. "Anything's better than being at school."

I chuckled. "True."

"I'll go get your games. They're on my bed."

"Can I come in?"

He hesitated. "Uh, yeah."

I followed him inside the house and through to his room. It was a mess, to say the least. Bed unmade, clutter over his bedside table, clothes scattered on the floor. I didn't remember Finn being a clean freak, but this was the messiest I'd seen his room. I stood on the very inside of it, pretty much in the doorway.

"Sorry, I should've said no to you coming in," he said hastily, picking up some of the clothes and throwing them into a basket on the other side of the room.

"It's fine," I said, entering once I could actually step on some carpet and not one of his old T-shirts or wank socks.

He sighed, reaching over and grabbing a pile of video games sitting on his television cabinet. He handed them to me. "Here."

We finally locked eyes as he placed them in my hand. Though, he didn't just place them in my hand. He touched my hand, too, and didn't pull away.

Our fingers touched, the video games between them.

He pulled away after a few seconds.

"Thanks...for the games," I said.

"No worries."

I had so much to say to him but didn't know where to start. I hoped it wouldn't be word vomit. None of the sort.

"I'm sorry," was what came out of my mouth, "for how everything went down. I didn't mean for it to happen the way it did."

He shrugged off my words with, "Whatever."

"*Whatever?*" I retorted. "Is that what our six years of friendship were to you? *Whatever?*"

He shook his head. "I never said that."

"What is it then?" I raised my voice, far earlier than I thought I would, my eyes already narrowed and ready for answers.

Finn kept calm. "What's what?" he riddled me.

"All of this!" I cried out. "I need closure. I can't do this anymore."

"Can't do what?"

"Fucking stop it, man. You know exactly what I mean," I told him. "Tell me the truth."

His eyes appeared glassy, which was unlike him. Finn had always been as tough as cheap steak on the outside.

"What do you wanna know?" he asked me.

I sighed. "What do you think of me? What did you think about the night on the beach?"

He swallowed hard. "You wanna know the truth?"

"Yes. I do."

"I'm scared," he revealed, folding his arms and rubbing his elbows. "I'm scared of you. I'm scared of me."

He started crying, resisting with all his might from fully breaking down.

I moved closer to him, slowly. He must've known deep down he could trust me. To not only cry in front of me, but for me to wrap my arms around him.

It felt whole to hug him and for him to hug me back.

Finn. My best friend.

"It's okay to be scared," I whispered. "We're in this together."

We were, even if he wouldn't care to admit it right away.

Finn cried in my arms for what I thought might've been five minutes, his tears soaking into the nape of my neck.

He pulled away slowly, bowing his head for a moment longer before looking up into my eyes. He smelled of lustful sweat. Placing both my hands on his cheeks, I wiped away his tears before they fell further.

Then, I kissed him. I kissed him, and he didn't pull away. In fact, he kissed me back with force, as if the doubt we'd been plagued with intrinsically dissolved to dust. But we weren't innocent like we were in the sand those weeks ago. Our intentions weren't masked by fragments of psychedelic hallucination. And although I could tell it hurt him to be this close to me, perhaps it was hurt that would soon turn into something else. Something more elegant, more time-stopping.

Lips kept locked, we huffed and puffed between kisses. We looked at each other for a moment, both nodding as though a mutual consent to keep going. He peeled off my shirt. I ran my finger down his sternum, stroking his abs. He turned his gaze to his bed, not needing to breathe a word. I smiled and nodded.

Even though I'd dreamed of this exact moment, I didn't think it would actually come to fruition.

Finn lay down first on his back.

"I've never done this before," he admitted.

"Neither," I said, crawling on top of him and kissing him again.

The bath was big enough for both of us to lay comfortably, tucked within one another. It didn't feel weird at all, to soak in the suds with him.

Submerged in silence, I stroked the hairs on his leg. "So…what do you think you identify as? Gay or bi, or?"

He shrugged, rubbing my fingers with his. "I think bi," he said. "I'm still attracted to girls. I've always known this. I guess my attraction to guys is still new to me. What about you?"

"Honestly, I think I'm gay," I blurted out, becoming surer of myself each time I said it. "I think I've been trying too hard to try and be sexually attracted to girls, but it's definitely not me." I paused. "None of the girls or other guys are you though, which is a dilemma."

Finn went red in the face, his temporary skin tone followed by a smile. He leaned over and kissed me softly.

We hopped out of the bath before pruning up too much. Late afternoon settled in. We played some *Call of Duty*, like we had before things got complicated.

"Are you thinking of going to Holly's party?" Finn asked me in between our second game.

"Hmm, I dunno hey. I was a little hesitant," I admitted, placing my controller on the bed and looking at him. "But hey, it could be fun."

Finn came out with a nod of consideration. "This is true."

We sat in silence for a few moments, scrolling through our phones.

"Well, if we are gonna go, I don't wanna be sober," he announced, standing up and rolling his neck around. "Delayne won't be home, and my parents are up in Brisbane visiting my aunt and cousins."

I glanced at the time. "It's four-thirty, but hey, a drink wouldn't go astray."

We migrated to the kitchen. Finn rummaged through some cabinets, pushing bottles aside.

"Bleh, there's only red wine," he grimaced. "Dunno how my parents drink this shit."

I chuckled. "I think it's the kind of alcohol people drink as they get older."

"Kind of like how I hated onions as a kid but now I actually don't mind them?"

"I think so."

There were several bottles of red wine in the cupboard, but neither he nor I wanted to drink it at all.

"Why don't we make sangria?" I suggested, a metaphorical light bulb buzzing above my head.

"What's that?" he asked.

"You got orange juice?"

He opened the fridge. "Yeah. Lots."

We made red wine sangria with a handy online recipe. Finn didn't even care about his parents noticing. I always worried my parents would pick up on the scent of their alcohol being taken away from them.

I texted Mum after our second glass: hey I'm at Finn's. It's going well. We are going to Holly's party tonight so I'll be home tomorrow, or maybe tonight

I was too wrapped up in Finn's presence to even realize Mum texted back almost immediately. No worries, Mack. Glad you and him are speaking again. Be safe xo

As the sunset crested the hills, we both thought we had a future together. For how long, we did not know. No one could have known.

The thought of being there, at the party, with Finn, with everyone we knew, and finally being open with who we were, clouded me in fantasy. Clouded both of us.

The sunroof was wide open while we cruised over the range. The wind cleared out the smoke from the cigarette we puffed down. We were halfway to the Utopia we'd imagined, Finn out the sunroof at eighty kilometers per hour, screaming into the night.

"You can feel the G-Force!" he yelled out, popping his head back down and kissing me on the cheek. "Pull over somewhere and you can try it. It's so much fun."

"I dunno if that's a good idea," I said.

"Oh, c'mon."

He reeled a smile out of me.

I pulled up.

Finn drove us down a dirt road and back onto the range.

He was right. It felt invigorating with my upper body out of the sunroof. At the same time, it felt as if my face was about to fall right off, the skin exposing nothing but blood and bone.

When Finn and I first met in seventh grade, we'd gone for a drive with Delayne and her boyfriend. It was when I didn't know Finn would become my best friend. It was a taste of what our weekends would become. Delayne's boyfriend had a sunroof we all took turns in climbing out of.

Delayne's boyfriend had passed his driver's test, though.

And, so had I.

I never should've let Finn drive.

We unraveled our layers, became complacent.

If only I could rewrite the past instead of seeing the future.

I popped my head down, my mouth falling open at the figure jumping toward the headlights.

A near miss, followed by a hard break.

A skid.

An ear-deafening screech.

Bitter burnt rubber, the smell of impending doom.

I only saw the wallaby for a split second as it hopped across the road.

The car skidded onto its side with a jolt.

It flipped upside down.

The windows smashed.

I caught his eyes one last time before the car rolled.

He didn't look scared.

It was like he somehow knew at that moment, that it was his time.

Road Trip

LATER

After another day of dancing, Anamnesis Festival ended in a whirlwind of longing. Longing for more. But not more of the festival as such.

"Instead of flying back to the coast, why don't you join me and Jasper on a road trip back?" Lily suggested to Rachel and me, her invitation almost a serotonin boost for the amount lost over the last few days.

Just like that, Q-Pack was down to four and the white-sanded east called. We had to enjoy the red dirt for a little while longer. Which, unsurprisingly, wasn't hard at all.

Two thousand two hundred and fifty-three kilometers. Alice Springs to the Queensland coastline. The longest road trip I'd ever been on.

Lily's four-wheel drive was packed high with camping gear as we drove through the middle of endless red and tangerine plains, ones as far as the eye could see. There wasn't much out there. A few roadhouses to stock up on fuel and food was about as far as it went. And it stayed the same for quite some time. Hours, in fact.

Lily's car wasn't automatic, so I was the only one who couldn't drive it. It made me think maybe I should've learned manual driving, with all the gears and whatnot. But Mum and Dad both drove automatics when I first got my license, and they chose my first car. The one which ended up totaled mere weeks after owning it.

The more we switched drivers that weren't me, the more it made me wonder. Perhaps if I had my manual license from the start, Finn wouldn't have been able to drive my car. Maybe we would've made it over the range and confessed our love for one another at the party.

You can't change it.

Rachel and Lily drove the first stretch from Central Australia.

Sometime later, Jasper handled the wheel while I sat in the passenger seat. As he kept his eyes on the road, I couldn't help but think about the two of us, on top of the festival lookout at sunrise the morning before, when we unpacked our secrets.

No one's life was perfect, even if they made it out to be. And meeting Jasper was a perfect reminder of that.

"So, you said you have family who live in Australia, right?" I asked Jasper whilst the girls slept in the backseat.

Jasper yawned. "Yeah, so, my biological mum's sister has lived over here pretty much her whole life."

"Oh yeah? Nice."

"Yeah," said Jasper. "So, you know how I said I relocated from Australia to the UK when I was five? Well, I came back over here when I was eighteen since I had dual citizenship, and I was only meant to stay with my aunt for a while. My aunt on my foster mum's side, that is. But yeah, then I ended up living in Brisbane for three years before moving back to London. Started being a flight attendant. And the rest is history."

"And a damn fine flight attendant you turned out to be," I added smoothly.

Jasper waggled his eyebrows twice, followed by a subtle wink, not taking his eyes off the road.

"When do you have to be back at work?" he asked me.

"I've still got another week off," I said.

"Same."

"Great. Then have you gotta be back in London?"

"Yep. I've got a flight booked for Sunday."

I lowered my head, lifting it again as I said, "Well, we'd better make the most of it then. I'm gonna have to teach you about *all* the plants once we get into more…forest-y kind of terrain."

Jasper let an amorous laugh escape. "I was hoping you'd offer me some of your flora knowledge."

Outside, the sun started to set and the plains glowed a vibrant orange.

We kept driving across the sunburnt country. And even though I'd fallen in love with the desert, I was ready for some more familiar territory. Ready for plants I could identify at first glance. Ready to be consumed by the forest. To spot Brigalow trees scattered through valleys like silver snow. For bustard birds to fly alongside the car. For families of emus to run together through fields of cream and green. For kangaroos to watch from underneath trees, cooling themselves from the coarse day's heat.

It was dark before we hit Mt. Isa to bed down for the night. It felt strange to have driven through the desert all day and then hit a country city with a population of twenty-two thousand.

Jasper and I had shared a tent on the last night of the festival but eventually passed out next to each other. Nothing happened between us. So now, once we hopped into that same tent in the caravan park, we discovered we had much more energy, even after driving for nine hours.

We were too tired to speak, but we lay facing each other. Full moon beckoned outside. Jasper's eyes gleamed through the darkness, his breath smelling of fresh mint. He leaned in and kissed me, and I immediately closed my eyes. Jasper, shirtless. Me, running my fingers down his sternum while I kissed him, my other hand wrapped around his waist. He stroked my cheek as he pressed his lips upon mine, harder now.

As soon as he grabbed my thigh, my semi-hard cock twitched.

We settled for jerking each other off. I'd been wondering what his cock looked like for days now. And I wouldn't even get to see it yet, being in a darkened tent and all. Feeling it was good for now, though, and his load was more than I expected, spraying me in the face and all over my chest.

"I've been saving that for a few days now," he huffed, regaining his breath.

I thought my load was heavy. But Jasper, wow. Jasper was a completely different story when it came to shooting his bullets.

"Finally," I whispered, kissing him on the nose, on the forehead, then on the neck.

"Amazing," he breathed.

The next morning, we rose to the sun. Rachel and Lily were already up, packing their tent, throwing gear back into the car.

"Mornin', frands," Rachel called out in a deep merry voice, a touch more gleeful than she'd been the day before.

"That girl is doing things to me," she confirmed to me while Jasper and Lily were in the showers.

I hoisted my eyebrows at her, following it with a friendly nudge on her shoulder. "Get it, girrrrrl," I said zealously.

"You know it!" She placed her hand underneath her chin and looked up to the sky.

"How are you and Jasper going?" Rachel asked me, a slight twinkle in her eyes.

You and Jasper.

I placed my arm around Rachel and nodded. "It's going so well. I mean, how are we even here, right?"

As we admired the tangerine dirt, Rachel said, "I'm surprised your little *ability* didn't see this trip coming."

I didn't say anything. I'd completely forgotten I'd kept my vision on the plane from her this whole time.

She pulled away from my embrace, eyes narrowed. "Mack? What is it?"

Gosh, I really needed to stop hiding shit like this from people who were dear to me. It was hard to keep up with my own bullshit narratives.

So, I blurted it all out as fast as I could. Seeing Jasper on the plane. Our destined long-ish relationship. His death.

Rachel folded her arms and looked at me blankly while I explained everything to her. After I'd finished, she sighed and unfolded. "Lily and I have spoken *a lot* the past few days," she said, her eyes widening. "I already put the dots together that you'd most likely seen Jasper before the day of the festival, especially since I found out you were both on the same flight. Your vision with him, on the other hand, I didn't see coming. But look..." She poked me in the chest firmly with her pointer finger. "You need to stop lying to me, fuck ya."

I gulped as she eyeballed me some more.

"I'm sorry," I apologized, honestly.

She sighed and hugged me, holding onto me tightly. We stayed in an embrace for almost a minute.

"I love ya, mate," she said, her voice softening. "Don't ever forget it. You can trust me with anything."

Back on the road again. Cruising through vast farmlands, we played a game called Windmill, where we split into teams and the first to spot a windmill on the side of the road won a point. Lily seemed to be a natural at the game, her hawk-eyed observance winning them most of the points.

Afterward, we played Eye Spy which kept us occupied a while longer.

"I wonder what radio stations we have out here," Rachel said, pressing the seek button for stations.

Wild West music chimed in, a slow guitar strum mentally transporting us to another era. It was the only searchable radio station that didn't consist of static.

We passed several silos that stood tall on farmlands, giant stacks of hay bales, even a giant solar farm that occupied a whole field.

I didn't mind sitting in silence. We let the Wild West tunes take us further away, to a place far from the one we were driving in.

"Imagine a world without cars, in the Wild Wild West," Jasper said dreamily while we sat in the backseat.

"What, like on horseback?" I said, stroking the fair hairs on his leg. "Or how about horse and carriage? Would've been kinda cool."

Lily scoffed from the driver's seat before adding, "Also really fucking slow."

Rachel placed a hand on Lily's leg. "It was probably really fast to them back in the day."

Lily pouted her lips, nodding in agreement.

"You ever ridden a horse?" Jasper asked me.

My tongue made an unsubtle clucking sound as I winked at him. "Sure have."

Rachel and Lily giggled from the front seat.

"Nah, yeah, I have ridden an actual horse, once," I said truthfully. "I could hardly walk the next day. The biggest pain in my groin."

Jasper nodded, suppressing his laughter. "They tend to do that the first time you ride one."

"How about you?" I asked in return, to which he smiled devilishly. "Yeah, a few times. I didn't really fancy it, though."

I gripped his thigh, gazing at him with sheer hunger, one which made me hope we were close to our final destination for the day.

"Bit of a shame really," I flirted.

"Oh my god, emus!" Rachel squealed, whipping out her camera.

She wasn't wrong with—plural—*emus*. A whole family of them, running through the plains for us to see.

We couldn't stop talking about it for the next half hour.

"I can't believe it!"

"I've never seen so many."

"Wow. So special."

"Fuckin' emus."

After another eleven hours of driving, we stopped at Lake Maraboon near Emerald, booking a two-bedroom cabin overlooking the lake for two nights. We were going to camp again, but we thought it was time we treated ourselves to a bit of luxury. Exhibit A: a bed and not a thin camping mattress on the ground.

I didn't have a long shower at the campground in Mt. Isa. At the cabin, however, I stood under the hot water for a good ten minutes, washing off all the leftover dust and mud from the festival, which still hid in grooves I didn't know dust or mud could get to.

I opened the door to our bedroom, instantly gaping, so awe-stricken I nearly melted to the ground.

Jasper had already showered, but he hadn't clothed yet. He was horizontal, with his skull against the bedhead, legs spread, and a smirk on his face. His uncut cock and testicles held my gaze more than anything else.

I smiled, closing the door behind me.

"Where're the girls?" I asked, unable to take my eyes off him.

"They've gone to watch the sunset and drink wine at the lake together," he said. "Won't be back for a while."

I dropped my towel, revealing my naked body to him.

He shook his head, lips upturned into an eager smile, showing his teeth.

"Come here, sexy," Jasper beckoned me, shuffling to one side of the bed.

He didn't have to ask me twice, and so, I crawled onto the mattress and inched closer to him until we faced each other.

We went through bouts of looking at each other, followed by an in-depth examination from the eyes to our unshaven holiday stubble. He wasn't a clean-shaven flight attendant anymore. He was messy, hairy, and ready to let himself go to my touch.

Once I reached his stomach, I drew circles around his belly button. He opened his mouth and moaned. I looked down further, his thick hard cock pointed at me. He smiled cheekily as he stared at mine, which had also woken without touch.

We kissed, his body creeping closer, already-wet cock rubbing against me. I grabbed it, tugging his foreskin up and down, slowly, as he writhed to my touch. He cradled my balls and tickled my knob. I huffed, jerking him faster, feeling his precum trickle out. We moaned in unison. I felt close to oozing already.

Jasper bit my lip as he massaged my arse, prodding his finger against the wall to my hole.

"Is this okay?" he gasped.

"Yes," I breathed.

"Would you like me to fuck you?"

"Yes," I groaned.

I wanted him inside me, and I sighed with relief when he told me he kept a sachet of lube in his wallet.

He reached for a towel and stuck it under me, tearing open the sachet of lube with his mouth, smiling at me as he massaged his cock with it.

After covering my dick in lube, he moved his hand up and down slowly.

I moaned as he entered me; first with one finger, two, then three. My cock made a squelching sound as he rubbed it. I was ready for him.

He hovered over me, kissing me softly on the lips and neck. My hole quivering, he pushed against it with his sticky condomed cock. I let out a moan, taking a deep breath as he pushed inside, carefully. Perfect amount of lube, perfect sized dick, Jasper knew what the fuck he was doing. In and out. Slowly, before moving faster.

"Does that feel good?" Jasper asked, looking into my eyes deeply.

"Feels fucking great," I replied through a toothy grin.

"Great," he said, inching his face close to mine. "Because it feels fantastic being inside of you."

He kissed me in between thrusts and I grabbed him by the cheeks, pulling his face in forcefully. I bit his tongue hard as he stuck his shaft in deep. It only made him thrust harder, sweat multiplying on his face. Meanwhile, my dick was rock hard, bouncing around.

All I could say was, "fuck" for the next few minutes, and all he managed was, "Yeah" and, "Oh my god."

I could feel it; I was close. He started to jolt and shudder.

"I'm gonna come," I growled.

I exploded all over my belly and chest, jet after jet of warm cum. Huffing, Jasper scooped some up with his fingers and licked it while he fucked me some more.

It wasn't long before he pulled out, ripped the condom off, and shot all over my jizz-soaked stomach.

After we caught our breath, sticky upper bodies becoming one, he kissed me for a long time, making the moment last, before hopping off me.

"No mess, how good," I said, dragging the towel from underneath me. "Can't say the same for the amount of cum on my stomach, though."

Jasper let out a childish chuckle. "Oopsy," he said, before wiping his stomach clean, a grimace growing from his grin as he did so.

"We probably should've had a shower *after* having sex," I joshed, standing up and slipping my underwear back on.

"Mmm. Yeah."

I cleaned up some more in the bathroom and then walked outside onto the balcony. The sun started to set over the lake below, spilling a milky glow onto the water. Kookaburras squawked in the trees. Jasper placed his hands around my waist.

"It's beautiful," he admired, kissing my neck. "You're beautiful."

I held his arms around me, pulling him in tighter. "It really is. And so are you."

Standing in silence for a few minutes, in only our

underwear, we watched the sun disappear behind the hills at the rear of the lake.

By mid-morning the next day, it hit thirty-five degrees, and you can bet we made good use of the air-conditioned café at brunch. We stayed as long as possible, even after we'd finished our food and coffee. I wasn't expecting the servings to be so big, and when they came out, my mouth dropped. I wondered how on earth I'd be able to devour bacon in such a large quantity. Jasper, Rachel, and Lily all thought the same when their plates came out. I even looked at Jasper when we started eating, and suggested maybe we should've shared.

"Yeah, look, this is enough bacon to feed a bloody football team," Jasper mentioned, breaking his poached eggs, "but hey, I'm hungry as fuck, so I'm gonna try my very best."

After calling it quits on my meal, I looked down at the rashers of bacon still left, quite ready for the food coma to follow.

"I dunno if I can ever eat bacon again," I groaned.

"Yeeeeep," agreed Rachel, burping loudly. "Way too much."

Jasper burped as well, almost as loud. "Yeah, honestly, I might even need a nap before we go swimming at the lake," he admitted, slouching back into his seat.

Lily twisted her wrist sassily. "Oh, after a good after-bacon-bog, we'll be right."

I cocked my head at Lily. Rachel looked at her and laughed. Jasper joined in with a sneaky giggle.

"Sorry, did I hear correctly?" I asked, lifting a brow. "An *after-bacon-bog?*"

Lily bit her lip and smiled. "Yeah. It was the first thing that came to mind."

I downed the rest of the cold table water and gayly raised my glass to Lily. "Genius," I commended her.

Lily's after-bacon-bog concept had naturally come to fruition. And after feeling ten kilos lighter, I was more than ready for a splash.

We backed Lily's car onto the designated swimming spot at the lake. She'd brought two blow-up row boats in her car.

"I completely forgot I had these," Lily said after blowing them up with an air pump. "I do remember packing them, but I haven't used them the whole time. Even with all the driving I did before meeting Jasper up in Alice."

We set up a gazebo on the lake and lay on our towels under it, listening to music from my UE BOOM. Even though I had sunscreen on, I slapped on some more.

"What do you think your favorite spot was on your solo road trip from Brisbane?" I asked Lily.

"Well, I drove down the east coast from Brisbane to Victoria, across to South Australia, and then up to Northern Territory, so there were *a lot* of cool places to visit," she explained. "I've always been a beach girl, and I thought the New South Wales South Coast beaches were incredible. Jervis Bay. Mollymook. They were both amazing."

Lily's adventurous personality stimulated me, and

seeing her romance with Rachel blossom made me root for them more every day. "Did you do much hiking?"

"Yeah, I did," Lily said excitedly. "Um, the Flinders Ranges in South Australia had some *amazing* hiking trails. I'm kinda spewing we didn't have more time around here in Central Queensland 'cause I would've loved to go to Carnarvon Gorge. But we have to be back in Brisbane by Saturday for *this one* to catch his flight back to London." She kicked Jasper, who was in his own little world, swaying his hands to the music.

"You need to move back to Australia already," Lily told him.

Jasper twisted his head to her. "I'm most definitely thinking about it."

Please do, I wanted to say.

"It wouldn't be too much different than living in London, right?" Lily went on. "You could transfer to Brisbane and keep doing international flights."

Jasper sat up and looked at me with a knowing smile. "Maybe I should."

I shrugged, trying to keep it cool without screaming *YES* at the loudest volume I could muster.

"It would be nice having you close," I said in a voice soft with affection. Couldn't help it.

"Q-Pack has to stay united!" Rachel chorused.

We all howled in unison, followed by a moment of silence as we gazed out at Lake Maraboon. Queensland's second-largest lake. All hundred and fifty kilometers squared of it.

"Wouldn't be for a while, though, if I did come back to

Australia to live," Jasper sighed. "I've got my good friends' wedding in November, and I own an apartment in London now, which…I could always rent out."

"Oh yeah, your two friends…the wedding," Lily piped up. "I remember you telling me about that."

"Yeah, it'll be cute," Jasper said. "My first gay wedding."

"Naww," Rachel swooned.

I caught Jasper's grin, mentally returning to the vision on the plane. Seeing him propose to me with the jade ring. The color I knew all too well.

The scenario of marrying a person I'd known for less than a week had me both baffled and thinking about Finn, so much so that when I began journaling by the lake, I found myself writing him a letter.

<u>September 29</u>
Dear Finn,

I haven't written to you in a long time. Years, in fact. I'm sorry I haven't come to visit your site in a while. Life has been extremely busy and it doesn't show signs of slowing down anytime soon. I feel like the older I get, the busier life gets. I guess it's somewhat better than being bored with nothing to do, though.

Sometimes, I just wish there was more time to enjoy the stillness, something this holiday was meant to be. It's been so unexpected, to the point where it feels like I'm just a little character hopping around the Monopoly board.

Remember that time we played Monopoly when

camping with your parents, Delayne and her boyfriend? You were winning, and Delayne was pissed off that she went bankrupt first.

Man, those were some simpler times, when Monopoly was just a game without any real-life consequences. We were fourteen. Little shits back then, weren't we? And so naive, but we had lots of fun.

I'm thinking back to another memory, just now, of the first time Delayne's boyfriend took us motorbike riding. I nearly ran into a tree as soon as I started. You'd been on a motorbike plenty of times by that point, and you helped me get the hang of it.

I miss you, Finn. You'd love it here in Outback Queensland.

With love,

Mack

How Do I Live Without You?

THEN

The waves came and left, over and over.

Looking out to the blue, I hoped one of the barreling masses of water would be him. As a sign, a glimmer of hope, to let me know he was still somehow with us.

Where do we go when we die, Finn?

Hell, maybe I don't want to know. I already know too much.

Laughter echoed from behind me, and I turned to see several people dressed in black and white, walking in pairs down the wooden steps. A bride and groom led the pack, all of them barefoot. As their feet hit the sand, their happiness radiated like the soon-to-set sun. A moment they'd remember forever.

As the wedding party submerged ankle-deep, laughing, snapping photos, I wished I had told myself to stop trying to grow up so quickly.

After snapping a photo of the ocean, glowing against the sun, I pulled up his contact profile on my phone.

It had been a month since he died.

A month since I walked away, alive, from my totaled car.

A week since it didn't hurt when I got up and down.

Two days off the crutches.

The grief was a vortex, and I hadn't even jumped in yet.

I clicked off my phone, the reflection on the screen showing the scars on my neck and face, reminding me of that night. The one I'd had nightmares about at least once a week since.

I pressed my finger on his number and put the phone to my ear. It didn't ring. Straight to voicemail, akin to all the other times. I rang so I could hear his voice, even if the words weren't new.

"Hello?" his voicemail said.

When he first made it, I was fooled to believe he'd picked up the phone.

"Hey, can you hear me?" he continued. Then, "If you've made it this far, you've actually reached voicemail. Please don't leave a voice message. How about you text me instead?"

I'd already done that, in the form of letters in my

journal—letting him know what I got up to that day, or what was on my mind. Sometimes, how much I missed him.

"Hey," I said into the phone. "It's me. I kind of just wanted to call again to hear your voice."

My eyes burned.

"I've been thinking about you, but you probably already know this, I think. I miss you. I really fucking miss you."

My voice trembled. "I hope you're doing okay, wherever you are."

The tears fell.

"I want us to go back to the old days. Things were so much simpler. They don't feel the same without you. But hey, maybe you were too good for this world. Too smart."

I wiped my eyes and exhaled the hurt I'd been harboring.

"Anyway, I was thinking of you, so I decided to call you, to tell you."

I didn't hang up. I couldn't.

"If you can hear me, give me a sign someday, Finn. I don't want this to end."

Days passed. There was no sign. No way out of this.

One thing I noticed about the sadness, though, was the way it spread to each corner of my body, its hold thick and tough, showing no signs of letting go.

Would I have to make the first move?

"Hey, can you hear me?" he asked through my phone. It was my tenth time calling that morning, "If you've made it this far, you've actually reached voicemail. Please don't leave a voice message. How about you text me instead?"

It was always the last sentence: *how about you text me instead,* that would eventually have my breath hitching into a sob. Sometimes, it only took one phone call, other times ten.

Forty days without him, yet not a day passed that I didn't hear his voice, even if it was automated. It was still enough to hold on.

To cry.

To press my palm into a sharp object so the pain would disperse.

That Saturday, it was one of Mum's crystals from the bathroom.

I dug its jagged edge into my skin until blood trickled down my wrist.

Until I felt better.

What's doing? I messaged Nate soon after, bored, needing a distraction. In the days that followed the funeral, I felt more connected to him than anyone.

My own family, Finn's family, Brit, Mel—they all felt like strangers.

Nate answered almost instantly, **Nothin, heading to a party down in Byron later, you?**

Desperately, I replied, **Can I come with you? I need to get out of the house**

It wasn't a lie. Spending another weekend night at home sounded like a shit time. I wanted to let off some steam, drown myself, anything that didn't involve staring at my bedroom walls or dialing Finn's number.

I just needed something.

Perhaps a party could be that something.

For sure! Nate texted back. **The more the merrier. My friend who's up from Sydney is coming too. The party's on a property in the hinterland. Apparently a bush doof. Wanna ride with us?**

Better yet, a bush doof down in Byron. So, the likelihood of people from my school being there, namely Noah Daniels and company: slim to impossible.

Finn and I were meant to go to our first bush doof together, taken by Delayne. The same Delayne who couldn't even look at me at the funeral.

I didn't blame her.

It was my car.

We were drunk.

It was my fault he was gone.

I just had to accept it.

And if I could go back in time, change things, I'd make sure we spent much longer in that bath, pruned skin be damned.

After lunch, I was starting to feel a little hopeful again, and it might've been the fact I was about to do something adventurous, something I wasn't supposed to.

I told Mum I was just going to a house party, not a bush doof in the middle of nowhere, probably near to no phone reception as Nate had added in one of his messages.

"It's good to see you getting out again, Macky," Mum said on my way out of the house, backpack draped over my shoulder. "Be safe, okay?"

"Always, Mum," I lied, surprised at the smile I wore. Little did she know. "I'll be back tomorrow."

"Have fun," she called out as I rushed out the door, to the outside world I hoped would free me.

Nate's station wagon was parked in the driveway. Dad said goodbye to me as he trimmed the trees in the garden with shears. Little did he know, too.

Little did anyone know.

Since Nate's friend, Jordy was in the passenger seat, I made room in the back, greeting them both with an overenthusiastic, "Howdyyyy."

Unsurprisingly, Nate's forehead was slightly furrowed in response to my chirpiness. "Hey, dude. How you doing?"

"Never been better," I said, untruthfully.

Jordy turned around and held his hand out, to which I felt myself twitching slightly as video clips appeared in my head.

MACKENZIE'S BRAIN CINEMA ACTIVATED

First clip: Jordy and I hanging out the windows of Nate's car as we drive along a dirt road, Jordy pissing into the wind.

Second clip: Jordy, Nate and I sitting against a massive log in a field.

Third clip: Jordy passed out in the back seat of the car.

Interesting.

Feeling like I already knew him now, I reached out and gripped Jordy's hand.

He had blonde hair like Nate's, though his was notably longer, down to his shoulders. He and Nate could've been mistaken as brothers, twins even. They talked the same, too. It was as though one of them desperately mimicked the other. Naturally, it made me wonder which one was the original.

"Did you manage to get some alcohol?" Nate asked me as we cruised down the M1.

"Yeah, I did," I said, unzipping my bag and pulling out the half bottle of vodka I'd kept stashed in my room. The one I had stolen from a cupboard at Finn's wake.

The wake had changed everything.

Kerry was also using alcohol as patchwork for Finn. And at the wake, she really let loose how she was feeling. She was cold with me the whole time, and, when I tried to help her move some furniture around, said she didn't want to be in the same room as me.

I didn't feel wanted at the wake after that. So, I stole Kerry's vodka, left without anyone noticing, and called Mum, asking her to pick me up.

Nate pointed to the cask of wine on the back seat. "We bought a goon sack, but here you are bringing the goods."

"We could make a deadly punch," Jordy suggested.

"Sounds like a plan," I said, pulling a packet of cigarettes from my bag. The packet I had stolen at the wake, from Delayne. "Mind if I smoke in here?"

"Yeah, that's cool, dude," Nate pipes up. "Mind if I have one?"

"Me too," Jordy chimed in.

"Go for it," I said, pulling two out and handing them one each.

We pressed down the windows and lit up.

Nate took the Lismore exit.

Turned out he'd misread the directions, which had only been sent to him that morning. He thought it was near Byron, when the party was actually two hours inland of Byron.

So, after chipping in for petrol with the money I had saved from the takeaway shop job I was no longer employed at, we began our cruise inland, not taking long to drive past sequestered farmlands, rolling hills and valleys.

I'd never ventured this far from the coastline. The wilderness, alongside loud alien-like trance music that Jordy started playing through the AUX chord, was the recipe for otherworldly.

Perhaps I needed to experience something unknown to what I knew to shake how I'd been feeling the past month. Thankfully, the fresh mountain air was helping so far.

Soon, the dot-pointed directions took us down a long bumpy stretch of dirt road; our car engulfed in dust.

When it settled, Jordy thought it would be a good idea to piss out of the car window, to which I joined him—in the hanging out of the window part.

We drove along the dirt road for about an hour, before reaching a gate with two young people, a guy and a girl, not much older than us, standing at it, attending to the car in front of us.

"Do we need to get out or anything?" I asked while we waited.

"Nah, they'll just get us to pay with cash and direct us to the campsites," Nate said.

"They better not ask for I.D.s," Jordy hissed. "Heard they've been doing that at the Sydney doofs now. Most of them are eighteen-plus unless you're with a *responsible* adult."

"Pretty sure the ones around here are more chill, from what I've heard," Nate told him.

My face faltered. "Let's hope so," I said, carefully watching the gate staff as they finished up with the front car.

"If not, then we can just go camp somewhere else. I've got a bunch of weed," Nate laughed, inching the car forward.

Thankfully, we didn't get asked for I.D,, and the gate couple didn't see me in the back seat, so they only charged us for two. Probably a good thing, given that being unemployed now, money wasn't something I had readily available. And naturally, I was hesitant to ask my parents for any, even though they would most likely provide me with some, but only if it was for something worthwhile, like going to an arcade or a carnival. Anything but a rave in the forest with a smorgasbord of drugs at most of the campsites, or bass so powerful that you felt it more than you heard it at times.

Time was of insignificance out there, and that was what I loved about it.

Being preoccupied, I had no reason to look at my phone

either. It stayed in the glove box of Nate's car the entire time since we'd arrived. Instead, my time was spent roaming with Nate and Jordy, dancing under the psychedelic shade sails, chatting with people far different from the ones I'd met. They all dressed differently, too. I'd only ever seen hippy attire like this when visiting Byron Bay and Nimbin when I was younger. Still, it was rare for us to visit those places. Mum and Dad preferred to stay in our beachside bubble up north, away from the tourists.

When the sun disappeared behind the hills, the campsites and dance floor lit up with colorful backlights.

We met our camp neighbors, who generously gave us some caps in return for a bottle filled with the punch we'd concocted. Turned out they had underestimated how much they would drink so quickly.

A few hours after that, we bought LSD and were already coming up on this concept we'd been told was called "candy flipping", the mixing of psychedelic and stimulant. Several whooshes of euphoria folded over me as I danced, my inhibitions disappearing at a cracking pace.

Within a tight-knit bunch toward the front of the stage, I felt two arms curl around my waist. And when I turned around, there was Nate, whispering in my ear, "How good does this feel?"

My vision shuttering like a camera, I stifled a smirk and replied, "Amazing."

Jordy met a girl on the dance floor and stayed there kissing her while Nate and I returned to our campsite. We didn't have a tarp or gazebo, only an exposed table next to a four-man tent.

Nate glanced down at the powdered knife on the table and back up to me, his smile turning devilish, his eyes seeming all black and demon-like.

It only stayed that way for a brief moment before he asked, "Are you okay?"

To which I nodded my head with tepid certainty, "Yeah."

"You're really handsome, you know that?" he said with a grin.

He didn't seem evil anymore, so I presumed it was the acid playing tricks on me, unleashing thoughts from the depths of my mind's hell and forcing them into a somewhat believable reality.

"Thanks, man," I answered, blush burning my ears.

"Wanna hang out in my car?" he then asked me, and although he followed it through with a knowing nod, I still wasn't sure whether I was hallucinating or not.

I followed him to the car and he opened up the back, clearing the seats for us. Once we closed the door, the lights turned off and we were left with the whites of each other's eyes.

Nate passed me the bottle of punch, of which I took a generous swig. Couldn't even pinpoint what it tasted like anymore. It was as though my taste buds were now defective. When they'd return, I did not know.

What I did know, though, was that Nate was moving his hand up my thigh.

"I don't know why the sudden feeling, but I've been really attracted to you today," he told me. "I've always thought you were a hottie," he told, "Ever since you first came into the petrol station while I was working."

"Oh yeah?" I asked, the animalistic being inside of me wanting to get his fix.

And so, we threw ourselves at each other, lips locking, hair pulling.

I remembered, then, the first time I met Nate in the petrol station, seeing that exact moment play out in the car. Us together.

But was I seeing the future that was planned out for me, or creating the one I consciously knew already?

After we finished, Nate asked if I wanted to smoke a bong. I agreed, in such a daze that I felt like I'd do anything at this point.

I still felt weird from the acid, but it was like our time in the car together had made all of this feel somewhat controllable.

Like progress was being made.

And it felt that way, even when I breathed out the smoke from the glass bong.

But then, when the fog settled, hours passed on dance floor, and daylight beckoned, I was hit with a strong sense that something wasn't right.

There were voices in my head.

They were out for revenge.

They were all against me, plotting my death.

Hums that intended torture.

I had to get away.

From the music.

From Nate and Jordy.

They sat cackling about something in the camp chairs, and I was trapped there, staring off into the distance, trying to keep my cool.

But in my head, hell was let loose, one I couldn't escape from.

Soon, I puckered up the courage to say I was going to go find the toilet. Yet instead of walking in the direction of the portaloos, I walked to the other side of the valley, sweat forming in patches on my forehead as I traversed uphill.

Through thistle bushes, in the shade of scrub where I could hide.

The music became faint the further I walked.

Until it was nothing but the sound of my own breath.

In and out, rapidly, in a panic.

Fight or flight.

High in a gum tree, a kookaburra cackled.

Why was I so worried?

Better yet, how long would I be worried for?

My second time on psychedelics felt far more sinister than the first. The first time, it was a glitzy tetris world, and now things were dark, yet daylight shone. Not a cloud in the sky.

The branches of the gumtrees exhaled.

I closed my eyes, hoping the thoughts would disperse, those that taunted me, telling me I was going to die out there.

That it had all led to this.

A community bent on putting me to rest for what I did to Finn.

I opened my eyes just to distract the thoughts with sight.

Several ants marched along a log, carrying what looked like the remnants of a dead lizard.

We all do what we need to do to survive.

In the long grass, I survived by gazing up at the clouds, at each figure that formed in the white masses of condensed vapor.

Once it took shape, I realized it was a man in a yoga pose.

The sleeping pigeon.

<u>March 23</u>

Dear Finn,

Happy 18th Birthday. I can't believe you aren't here to celebrate this milestone. Though, you'd have to wait until May for me to turn eighteen so we could hit the clubs together. I wonder what we would've done today. Probably a party at the farm with your family, around the fire like old times.

We'd get to sleep next to each other again.

I hope this gets easier, but does that mean forgetting you?

Talking about parties, I went to my first bush doof on the weekend. Remember when we were going to go to our first one together? Anyway, I had a good time, and a not-so-good time. At one point, the psychedelics had me so paranoid I thought I was going to die out there, that these people were part of some cult out to get me.

But it never happened. They never did what I thought they were so set out to do.

At one point, I was about to give in to them if they were. Maybe because I could've been with you again, but then I thought to myself: is there even an afterlife?

If you know the answer to that last question, let me know.

Forever,

Mack

The Sleeping Pigeon

LATER

Several birds chirped as the morning sun gleamed on the lake.

While I lay on a picnic blanket, close to the shore, Jasper stayed in the sleeping pigeon yoga pose next to me.

I hadn't spoken for the past half an hour, my gaze fixed on the clouds, all cotton candy-like.

Once Jasper emerged from his pose, he shuffled closer to me, placing a hand on my sternum.

"How are you feeling?" he asked, his voice a little hoarse. "You seem a bit…down."

I snapped out of my stare, turning to him. "I've just been getting deja vu a lot since I met you, I've realized. And it's been bringing up a lot of memories of the year of the accident."

His face went crestfallen. "I'm sorry. Is there anything I can do to help?"

"No. It's something I just have to let in. Let it run its course."

"You don't have to be alone while you do that, you know?"

"I know." I kissed his hand as my eyes drifted back to the sky, sunshine entering my eyes.

"Do you have any significant exes?" I then asked him, with a slight croak.

He chuckled softly. "Yeah. I do."

"What happened?"

"Just didn't work out the way we thought it would," he said. "We went our separate ways, as heartbreaking as it was for both of us. We were both flight attendants and spent a lot of time doing long distance. We made it work for a while. A few years. And it was an amazing time together. I think we can love people, and they can love us back. But sometimes, the world takes it away from us. Either that, or we change, and the parallel journeys stop intertwining. Doesn't make it any less special, though. Or not worth it."

I wanted to say aloud, that I wasn't sure if I'd ever love anyone the way I loved Finn.

"You're right," I said.

"There's nothing like the first ones," Jasper added. "But

as time goes on, we learn from them. We grow, I guess. For the next one to come along."

I rolled my eyes. "Yeah, and then we think that person's gonna be the one. And the one after that…"

"And then you and I finally found each other," he said, my heart swelling at the mere mention of it. "And suddenly, the wonder's gone. The worry. The what ifs. We just *know* now, right? I don't know if it's better or worse than not knowing sometimes. We don't get the mystery of it all."

Contemplatively, my brain mulled it over for a moment, until I opened my mouth again. "What did the visions show you when you first saw me? Of us."

"I've wanted to ask you the same thing," he said, brushing his fingers over my leg. "It's just…"

"Just what?" I asked.

"I don't know," he shrugged. "What if we saw different things, and if we tell each other, there won't be any surprises from now on?"

I wanted to tell him what I saw in the vision. His early demise. But again, something stopped me, as if it wasn't the right time.

"I suppose you're right," I agreed, laying my head in his lap.

Firmly, he placed his hand on my heart, breathing a soft, "Trust."

Now that we'd freshened up by staying in a cabin for two nights, we drove two hours to our next camp spot for the night. It was nice to feel the wind against my hand again.

Blackdown Tableland reeled us in. The range rose abruptly, and it was a steep drive uphill to reach the National Park. A deep cruise into a dry eucalypt forest. Beautifully, the bush was scattered with granite boulders of varying sizes, those which suddenly appeared through the trees.

Once we hit the top of the range, a rugged view of parched plains and surrounding mountains welcomed us. The road back to the highway looked ever-so faint from the top, dwindling far below. The rocky escarpment sprawled across the plateau.

On the short walk back from the lookout, I stayed at the back of our group, admiring plants along the way.

Forests feel homely to me. Probably because I know most plants when I see them. Even their long Latin scientific names.

The spring wildflower season was in full swing. I picked a few flowers of each color—yellow, white, and purple—holding a bunch gently in my hand. Once we stopped walking, I tapped Jasper on the shoulder.

"Got you some flowers," I said softly.

His eyes lit up.

"Oh my god, I can't handle you," he gushed, taking hold of the flowers before smelling them.

As the afternoon settled, an overcast blanket folded over the sky. We set up our campsite in record time. Rachel and Lily started painting with watercolors in the middle of the camp while Jasper and I went for a walk. A walk on a trail that no one seemed to be on at the time.

The track had been covered in these perfectly spherical rock marbles which caused us to slip and slide, especially when we walked on the very slightest downhill segment. I regretted wearing running shoes with lousy tread on them. Jasper wore his hiking boots, and even he nearly went arse up at the wrath of the marbles.

"It's so nice to be in the forest again," he admired, musing around at the eucalypt trees and granite boulders. "I can't believe you get to be in forests at your job every day. So wicked."

"Yeah, I get to be outdoors a lot of the time, which is nice," I linked my hand in his. "No two forests are completely the same. There's always something different to look at."

"Like those flowers?"

He pointed to a tall bush of golden yellow flowers to his left, a tad off the track.

My eyes bulged. "Oh my god, it's *banksia spinulosa*."

"Whatever that means," Jasper commented, unaware of the true level of my excitement.

I led Jasper off the track and over to the bush, my widened eyes leading the way.

I couldn't help myself when it came to plants. I simply had to study them, even outside of work. Naturally, identifying plants was so ingrained in me that there was no way in the world anyone could stop me. I loved them and they loved me.

I pulled one of the hand-sized flowers from the bush

and lifted it up to Jasper's face. "All right, so this is your first bit of plant knowledge," I told him. "So essentially, the vagina part of the banksia is on the end of the stalk. It's called a stigma. And the pollen, which is the cum, is on the flower part below the stigma. See."

Jasper's mouth curved into a smile. "Yeah. I do."

"So, the birds fly in and eat the nectar and get cum all over their faces and then they go to the next flower and brush their heads over the vagina, spreading the semen between the flowers."

The corners of Jasper's eyes crinkled for a moment as he kept gazing at the banksia flower.

"Yeah, right," he replied, without sounding unduly curious. "I didn't know birds and plants were so much like humans."

I whacked him on the chest. "I'll be charging for my wisdom next time."

A smirk stretched across his cheeks. "Is that right?"
"Yeah."

He leaned in closer. "What do I have to pay to get a little bit of your wisdom every day?"

He wasn't even touching me but my cock already stood to attention. I looked down. He chuckled.

He kissed me. I held the banksia flower in my left hand, right hand wrapped around his neck.

Jasper pushed me up against a tree, out of sight from the track in case someone wandered down.

He squatted, unzipped my pants, and took a well-deserved mouthful whilst jerking his dick. I ran my fingers through his hair and moaned.

"Fuck that feels good," I huffed as he slurped my shaft. I held onto the trunk of the tree for dear life.

"Mhm," he groaned, looking up at me with lustful eyes as he swallowed an inch deeper.

Patches of sweat formed on my forehead. Jasper took my cock out of his mouth, stood, and jerked me rigorously. A thick layer of saliva covered my dick and each squelch made me squirm.

Precum oozed out of my penis. Jasper caught it with his hand and rubbed it on his erection, the sensation causing him to gape and huff.

"Fuck, you turn me on," he breathed.

"Right back at ya, stud. Fuck, you're getting me close."

"Yeah?"

"Yeah."

He slowed down his hand movements, my legs shaking with each slide down my shaft. I built up a ball of spit and let it leave my mouth. It dripped onto both of our cocks, which were now firmly grasped in his hand. He wrapped his foreskin over my knob and circled it around with saliva and precum. My whole groin tingled.

"I'm gonna come," I whimpered.

"Yeah?"

"Yeah!"

He looked down at the banksia flower still cupped in my hand.

"Come on the flower," he said, his body trembling.

"Yeah?" I yelped.

"Yeah," he moaned.

With another shudder, I lifted the flower to the head

of my cock and painted it with three thick ropes. Jasper's mouth was fully agape as he watched my cum drip from one banksia hair to the next. He immediately grabbed the flower from my hand and put it to his lips, licking it clean while he jerked his cock faster.

I shook my head, still tugging my semi-hard milked dick as I watched him swallow my cum. "Fuck that's hot," I managed, biting my tongue, thrilled for his release.

He pulled my foreskin over his tip, and with one big final gasp, he shot a load inside it, the pool trickling out, all over our shafts.

Both of our breathing slowed as we rested our foreheads together. And at the same time, we started shaking with laughter, before inching in for a long sweaty kiss.

I could really get used to this.

But first, back to our dodging marbles on the trail bullshit.

Before reaching the lookout, I pointed to some trees around us.

"I'm gonna teach you the different types of eucalypt trees next," I told him.

Jasper grabbed my butt. "Two lessons in one day? Damn, I'm a lucky boy."

Teaching Jasper about eucalypt trees made me think maybe I could be a teacher one day, teaching environmental science to university students who were similar to me once upon a time, ready to be introduced to a pond full of knowledge (frogs included). Perhaps one day I'd reach my peak of knowledge. Perhaps in the years to come, I'd reach the end of my days as a field worker, the next step to work in an office or pass my knowledge down.

For now, though, it was just us, here, with the smooth barks and half barks and stringy barks and spotted gums. All the eucalypts stood tall amongst us. Their leaves waved in the wind as we neared the lookout.

We made it just in time to watch the light show, of alpenglow upon hilltops and cotton candy clouds across the sky. And by the time we returned to camp, the girls had lit a fire. In our absence, Rachel had painted Lake Maraboon, a scene from the same spot we'd been the day before. Lily had chorizo and vegetable skewers marinating while she tossed a salad in a metal bowl.

"Jeez, it's all happening over here," I said, the mere sight of food sparking a bonfire of hunger inside me.

"Oh, the lesbians know what's good over here," Lily winked. "Just you wait."

"Need any help?" Jasper offered.

"You can crack open a bottle of red and pour me a cup?" Lily put forth, tasting the salad dressing. She moved her head from side to side, pouring in some more oyster sauce.

Jasper reached for a bottle of red wine from a cardboard box under the gazebo. "That, I can definitely do."

The red wine went down a treat. On top of the grill, the skewers sizzled over the heat of flames. It was almost therapeutic to watch, our dinner slowly cooking. The stars started blanketing the sky.

In the wilderness again, where we felt most at peace. A gourmet camp meal, drinking red wine by the fire, soon to tell ghost stories.

When we moseyed on to bed, I stared up at the stars through a gap in the tent covering, the soothing crackles of the firepit sounding off outside. Jasper snuggled up to me, breathing a soft, "Goodnight," before we both dozed off.

During the night, my dreams were whack. Jasper and I were traveling somewhere overseas in the jungle. We came across some sort of abandoned town in the middle of the forest. Because all the wooden buildings were overgrown with plants, we had no speculation we would see anyone there. We stopped our car at a tall rusty metal gate that had been dotted around a derelict town. In the dream, Jasper and I didn't speak as we walked through the gate and into what looked like the main street. The main street, however, was taken over by the forest, to restore it to the way it was before civilization came and paved its path. Vines wrapped around the buildings and grew through their interiors. We were both quite confused at what we'd stumbled upon. Though, before we could even ask each other the many questions bubbling in our brains, the front gate snapped shut behind us. The gate was far too high to climb. We were trapped in there. But neither of us seemed alarmed.

This was when I woke up, and it was morning again. We weren't trapped in the forest. If anything, we were free, in a tent with an easy zipper to get out.

After a swim in the crystal-clear Blackdown rock pools, we climbed back in the car, en route to the coast. From the passenger seat, I pensively thought about Jasper. That he wouldn't ever become elderly. Knowing this for a fact prickled my heart with discomfort, yet I wanted to help him have the best life he possibly could.

I knew I had to tell him someday, though—tell him he was going to die sooner than he might have imagined. But perhaps he hadn't even thought about it, or maybe he already saw something in his vision. A foreshadowed breadcrumb of sorts.

Would *I* want to know my estimated death date, or would I rather not know at all? It could make one crazy—obsessive even— knowing they were going to pass away at a certain age. Or, it might inspire them to live their life to the fullest with the time they have left.

And with that, I penned another letter.

<u>October 1</u>

Dear Finn,

I don't know why I'm writing again. The others think I'm just journaling our travels. That first letter was just refreshing, and it made me think of when I wrote those letters to you when you first passed.

To be honest, I've been thinking about you a lot lately.

And I think it's because I'm falling in love again, Finn. I can feel it. But it seems different than when I fell in love with Stu or Sam. Stu was completely different from you, and I think that's why he was meant to come into my life, to help me heal from you, to remind me that I could love without you. Because as you may know, I was searching for you in men for years after you died.

But now, with Jasper, I can see parts of you in him, and I think that's why I feel so comfortable around him. Is it because I'm going to have to say goodbye to him one day like I had to say goodbye to you?

At least with him, I see it coming. Not sure if it's better or worse, though.

We're headed back to the coastline today. I'll go for a swim at the beach for you.

Your dearest,

Mack

Vortex

THEN

One month turned to two since Finn died. I started losing hope. Hope that it was all a dream.

"Murderer," Noah Daniels murmured at me in the corridor.

The wounds on my face had healed, but the ones inside were still angry. And the sneers at school weren't making things any easier.

Everyone was whispering, it seemed.

Aside from the few who came with not-so-subtle

taunts, most of my peers avoided me, not making eye contact. Not that I was one for eye contact anyway.

"Murderer," they breathed in my ear. Nobody was there.

I turned almost mute. I believed them, the voices as they slurred, *murderer*.

I hopped off the bus with my earphones in and Nate tapped me on the shoulder from behind. He gestured with his hands to take my earphones out, to which I rolled my eyes and sighed.

"Hey," he said.

"Hi," I replied, my gaze as hollow as a tree.

"How are you?"

"Fucking great," I said sarcastically.

"Wanna go to the beach?"

"Why?"

He shrugged, his hands going palm-up. "Because the beach is nice. Plus, I've got some stuff you might be interested in."

I looked him in the eye. "What is it?"

He stifled a smirk. "You'll see."

I rolled my eyes again. "Whatever."

We turned around and walked in the opposite direction. I still had one earphone in, listening to *Goodbye My Lover*, which had been on repeat since I'd left school.

Down the next street and across the road, we wandered down a sand path in silence. I had nothing to say, nor did I have the energy to make small talk.

"How have you been?" Nate soon asked, five minutes along the path. "We haven't spoken much since the doof."

Murderer.

I shrugged, my eyes burning.

"It must be tough, man," Nate said, ducking his head so it didn't hit a bunch of tree branches. "I lost my cousin a couple of years ago. We were real close."

Nearly said we were much more than friends. That there was something far deeper between Finn and me that didn't even get a chance to blossom. A connection that, when perished, turned to guilt and what-ifs.

"Just saying, and I know people have probably told you this, but if you need someone to talk to, I'm here."

It was the last fucking thing I wanted to do. And so, I stopped in our tracks, turned, and faced Nate, a beguiling mix of anger and lust mixing its fighting forces inside me.

"I don't want to talk," I said, forcing a half-smile before pulling him in for a kiss.

I hoped Nate would start tasting like Finn, feel like Finn, or do or say something, anything, to at least remind me of Finn.

It never happened.

"You want some ket?" Nate asked when we arrived at the dunes.

He whipped out a bag full of white powder.

"What does it do?"

"Makes you feel as if you're walking on marshmallows."

"Okay," I said.

I snorted a bump off the tiny spoon. He did the same.

After five minutes, my body started to numb. The

water looked less dull. So did the clouds. An incandescent glow on everything around me, including Nate. I felt happy in the moment, but a moment was all it was.

By the time I returned from the beach, Mum and Dad were arguing out on the back deck, louder than usual.

The comedown came. I couldn't take it again. The voices. Shouting. The way my room looked with its stupid fucking family photo hung up on the wall. I looked at the ten-year-old boy standing in the picture, in between my parents, smiling, innocent.

Murderer.

I gritted my teeth and clenched my jaw as tight as possible, hoping it would alleviate some of the pain. It didn't work. Only made me angrier.

I opened my phone.

Nate?

Brit?

Mel?

They wouldn't understand.

They couldn't possibly understand.

Finn would. But he never came back home, so I wasn't sure where he was. I knew where his ashes had been scattered, at the same beach I found myself on most days, having one-sided conversations over the phone. I knew where his plaque was, but I hadn't been game enough to visit him.

I breathed deeper and heavier with interspersed huffs.

The argument outside grew louder.

All I could hear was: *murderer.*

I scratched at my arms, digging into the skin, but my nails weren't sharp enough, not sharp enough to relieve.

After scanning my bedroom, I zeroed in on a pencil sharpener sitting on my desk, which was surrounded by a bunch of messy open books and unorganized pieces of paper. I hadn't been able to keep up with assignments or homework since the crash. The school had exempted me, but I didn't care. I didn't care about any of it anymore. Everything was nothing and nothing was everything.

I reached for the pencil sharpener and tried to press it down into the floor with a shoe. It didn't break open. My breathing deepened. So did my desperation to stop the pain, with more pain.

Using the force of a stapler, I crushed open the sharpener, ripped the blade out of it, and held it to my bare thigh.

I'd seen them do it in movies, and it never ended well.

The blade slid across my skin like butter, blood spilling out of each fine cut. After the third, I calmed, rivulets of red trickling across my leg and its hairs.

Mum called for dinner fifteen minutes later. My breathing had subdued. The bleeding stopped after applying pressure with toilet paper. I threw on shorts a little longer than the ones I wore, only so no one could see what I'd done to myself.

Mum cooked spaghetti bolognese for dinner, but I could barely taste it. Officially, my favorite meal had joined the list of things I used to love yet couldn't find joy in anymore.

"So, tomorrow's the annual region carnival," Mum said,

breaking a silence I felt comfort in, the others not so much. "Thought we could all go as a family."

My leg stung underneath my shorts.

I wished it had been me.

Dad looked from me to Lucas. "I tried to tell her you both aren't kids anymore."

"The event is *not* just for kids," Mum protested, gripping the stem of her wine glass. "There're markets, a parade, all sorts of fun stuff. Plus, we haven't gone in years so I think it'd be good for us."

Mum smiled at me, and instantly I felt like a sympathy case. Mum, Dad, and Lucas continued to discuss the carnival, but all their words began to fade and I sat there, staring at my half-eaten bowl of spaghetti bolognese as if it had maggots growing out of it or something.

"What do you think, Macky?" Mum's voice sprung into earshot.

Her eyes, along with Dad's and Lucas', fixated on me when I didn't reply.

"Mack?" Dad reiterated.

"Huh?" I asked, one half of me scared at being locked away but the other half not giving a shit.

"What do you think about the carnival tomorrow?" Mum's smile didn't reflect someone who wanted me locked away.

I wanted to cry, but my leg kept on stinging, so it distracted the tears. I couldn't tell them about the cuts. I thought Dad would get angry and ask why I would do that to myself, and Mum would smother me to the point I couldn't breathe.

"The four of us going to the carnival tomorrow," Mum continued. She turned to Dad, hoisting a brow. "Your father and I are shouting."

My nose twitched. "Nah, I'm good."

"Oh, c'mon," Mum tried, cocking her head. "I think it'd be good for you to get out of the house."

Lucas' head was downcast.

"Yeah," Dad agreed. "You might even see some of your friends there."

I eyeballed Dad before bursting out in laughter, hysterically. And I didn't stop. Lucas' eyes started to glaze over.

"Mack, stop," Dad attempted to say, but my cackles reigned supreme.

"Mack!" Mum cried, her eyes welling with tears.

I stopped laughing. "What? I find it really hilarious that you think I still have friends."

"You do have friends," Mum said.

I huffed and left the table.

Wanna hang out tomorrow? The text from Nate read.

I wanted more ketamine. It made me happy hours ago and I wanted to feel that again. I wanted it so badly, to feel numb to it all completely. To make the voices stop.

And so, **Sure thing,** was what I replied, before smoking three bongs, secretively, and passing out.

The next day, I woke with fright, covered in sweat. Another nightmare to add to the list, and one I'd soon forget. My cuts had crusted over so they weren't stinging as much. It made me want to cut again.

By midday, I bled in the bathroom, using the same sharpener blade. Sitting on the edge of the bath, I studied the dusty exhaust fan after each fine slice, the light grumbles sending me into a state of daze. If I could hold out until I got the ket off Nate, I'd be fine. Relief swept onto me as blood seeped from my leg, but I'd also forgotten to lock the bathroom door.

It opened suddenly, but only a fraction. All I saw were Lucas' eyes on the other side as he looked from my dilated pupils to my leg.

I felt my eyes enlarge; no words.

"Sorry," Lucas said shyly, closing the door with a thud.

"Fuck," I gasped. "Fuck, fuck, fuck, fuck." My fucks grew louder with each repetition.

I turned on the shower and hopped in, blood running down my leg, washing down the drain, hoping my problems would follow.

When I got out of the shower, my tiptoes to my room felt like walking on eggshells without the crunch. I'd cleaned myself up with the same bloody towel from the night before, it slowly losing its blue with dark uneven patches.

I waited for the bleeding to stop before pulling on some shorts. The house wasn't as lively as it had been before I went to shower.

No country music was playing. No bangs from rearranging furniture. Dead silence, and no complaints from me.

What time do you want to meet? I messaged Nate.

While I waited for a reply, a coffee called to me, shooting an ample amount of life into my stomach. I only made it a few sips in before Mum called out my name from the living room.

I rolled my eyes at the request and sauntered in with my mug in hand to see Mum sitting on the couch with a worried look on her face.

"Mack, can you sit down with me, please?"

I narrowed my eyes at her, shaking my head. "Why, what's going on?"

"Please, come sit."

I sighed loudly and planted myself on the lounge next to her.

Mum started to cry. "I'm so sorry this is happening to you, darling."

I let out an exhausted chuckle. "Mum, it's fine."

"No, Mack, it's not fine," Mum sobbed.

"Please stop crying," I told her bluntly, my chest tightening.

"We need to do something about this," she said. "You're breaking my heart."

"I need to go," I said, standing up.

"Mack, please, we need to talk about this."

I ignored her and went to leave the room.

"At least let me put antiseptic cream on your leg," Mum begged.

I stopped on my way out of the living room for a moment, the anger back with a vengeance, my jaw pushed together tightly.

I rushed out of the living room and bashed into Lucas' bedroom door. He tapped away at his controller; his eyes glued to the TV screen playing Xbox. He jumped in startlement when I opened the door.

"You really need to learn how to keep your fucking mouth shut!" I yelled, approaching him with my fists clenched.

"Mack," was all that left his mouth.

"Mack!" Mum called out, following me from the living room.

"It's really gonna get you into trouble one day, you little cunt," I growled at Lucas, moving closer to him cowering on the bed. "Aw man, I could fucking kill you."

"I'm sorry," Lucas said with his hands up, tears filling his eyes. "I'm worried about you. We all are. Please, don't hurt me."

I punched the wall instead, my fist gliding through the plaster as if it were paper. I punched another hole, and another, and another.

"Oh my god," Mum pleaded after the fourth punch. "Mack, please! We love you."

"Love isn't real," I spat with force. "It's all fucking BULLSHIT."

After exiting Lucas' room, I threw my mug at the kitchen wall, and it smashed onto the ground.

My body was tense as I grabbed my shoes and phone. I left the house, even though Mum begged me to stay.

Wished I still had a car, so I could go far away. Further than on foot, anyway.

By the time I made it to the end of the street, I stopped and slipped my sneakers on.

Nate replied, **keen to meet up whenever.**

My fist throbbed from the plaster, spots of red on my knuckles.

I told Nate, **meet me now on the sand track from yesterday?**

But as I walked toward the beach, he replied saying, **I'll pick you up and we can hang at mine? No one's home.**

I waited for Nate to pick me up on the corner, two streets away, right where our school bus would drop us off. He didn't take long. His car smelled of sweat, but not to an overpowering amount. I didn't mind, it distracted me from what had happened at home and the person I had become. Except, who was that person?

I didn't want to know.

As soon as I hopped into Nate's car, I started caressing his crotch.

I let him fuck me while I was high on ket later that afternoon.

My first time.

Yet I wished it wasn't.

He didn't have any ket because he said he wouldn't be able to perform, but I insisted I be fucked after a bump so I could enjoy it. So, I could close my eyes and think it was Finn fucking me.

It worked for the most part. And it made the afternoon fly by in a flash of suppression.

"My mum's gonna be home soon," Nate told me at sundown. "Want me to drive you home?"

"All good. I'll walk," I said shortly, and started walking to the front door with a stumble. "Thanks for the ket and drinks…and dick."

"Take care of yourself, okay?" he said, almost parent-like. "Are you sure you don't want me to walk you home at least?"

"No, I'm really fine."

"Okay."

"Okay."

"Bye."

"Bye."

And I left, on my two-kilometer walk back home.

Along the way, I started to get the feeling I was being followed.

Footsteps tapped behind me. But whenever I turned around, nothing was there.

When it happened the third time, my stomach sank, making me gulp.

Darkness consumed the road, engulfed by trees, my phone light doing jack shit.

Whispers from the trees. I couldn't make out what they said, or if they were even real. Even if they weren't, I could still feel my heartbeat racing, faster, faster.

I kept walking, telling myself not to look behind. If I could make it out of the dark stretch, I'd be back in the street lights. So, I walked as quickly as my feet allowed.

The footsteps grew louder. They appeared closer, sending a shiver across my upper torso.

I let out a yelp and ran for it, branches of trees whooshing past the corners of my eyes as I picked up the pace. I became so scared that whatever followed me would catch up and do bad things to me.

But as I reached the first street light, gasping for air, I calmed a little, the posts of bright beams my safeguard.

I needed my family.

I needed to make amends.

The fight from the darkness told me that.

From the treetops, it whispered. Had I listened?

The next morning, I woke to the sound of waves and sand through my hair, the sun starting to poke its way over the water. I'd slept on the beach, tucked into sand dunes, given that nobody was at home to let me in the house, and my phone had gone dead so contacting Mum, Dad or Lucas proved rather problematic.

The memory of the night before lingered in my brain, though not overwhelmingly. More like a reminder.

As the sun rose higher, painting the water's surface and sand orange, I felt the most alive I had since the accident.

Accident.

After sunrise, I walked back down the sand track and took the two streets back home. I probably smelled disgusting in my sleep-deprived state, and I expected a mouthful from Mum and Dad, deservedly so.

I took a deep breath before ambling through the front door, expecting shouts. But instead, I was met with

OneRepublic. Not the usual country music. My favorite band. What was going on?

As the screen door shut with a thud, Mum appeared in the hallway.

Somewhere between the look she gave me, the smile, the glassy eyes, and *If I Lose Myself,* I felt the release coming. And it came with such force, a month of pent-up tears.

As I let go and cried, Mum held me in her arms, like she had when I was a child. Turned out I never stopped being her child. I'd, instead, forgotten who that little guy was.

"You go take a shower, then we're gonna take a drive, okay?"

I stepped under the warm water, which stung my cuts on impact. Yet I didn't feel the need to do more damage. Regret, however, spilled into me faster than the blood that seeped.

I wanted to heal, and I hoped I actually could.

Mum and I hadn't taken a drive together in years. Only her and I.

Pensively, I looked out the window as Mum drove, watching the trees, signs, and highway lines flash past the glass. My energy levels were at an all-time low, my urge to speak even lower. What could I say at this point? Mum knew I'd been cutting, and I presumed that was what the drive was all about. An intervention, of sorts, on the wide-open road. I thought about saying sorry. Thought about saying I wouldn't do it again.

"I'm not gonna ask why you didn't come home last night," Mum finally said. "You're nearly eighteen, so I'm going to treat you like an adult who can make their own decisions. You're mature enough now."

With this, I sighed. I wanted to say she wouldn't have to look after me much longer. I'd probably move to Brisbane soon for university. And while Mum didn't intend her conversation starter to convey a message of child-parent separation, it sure felt like it.

"But, there's still one more thing I need to guide you through," she continued, catching my undoubted attention.

"I'm not following," I admitted.

"I know you've got Brain Cinema," she said.

Now on top of the range, we pulled up at a lookout, overlooking the valley below.

"What are you talking about?" I asked.

"I've noticed a change in you, and not just your mood, Mack. I know you've got the twitch…and the visions."

I swallowed the lump in my throat. "But how?"

She chuckled. "Who do you think passed this genetic *thing* onto you?"

Mum went on to tell me all about her experience with having the same future-telling snippets as myself.

"The trick is to not look people in the eye," she said. "Especially in crowds. If you look into too many eyes in a crowd, it can end badly. Sensory overload badly."

"Does Dad know?" I asked.

"Yeah," Mum admitted. "Yeah, he does."

<u>April 14</u>

Dear Finn,

I have a confession: I'm now 100% certain that I can see visions of the future, because, so can my mum, it turns out. So, it's like a hereditary kind of thing. It's so weird. I wonder if there are others out there like us. For now, I wouldn't want to tell anyone because they'll think I'm crazy. Hopefully one day I'll be able to tell people about this secret, just like I'm telling you.

I'm tired. It feels like I haven't had a full sleep in forever. Fuck. At this rate, I'll never catch up. But I want to catch up.

And I haven't been dreaming.

I told Nate and he said it's because I've been smoking too much weed.

Yeah, I've been smoking a lot since the funeral. I know that. But it's the only thing that allows me to sleep at night, to block out the pain. Most of the time, it works and I feel numb, other times it makes me so anxious I can hardly breathe, as though I'm a burden in this world, to everyone around me.

I'm also thinking about doing an Environmental Science degree at university next year. Mum thinks that I should move away from the area, which I'm starting to think might be a good idea for me. Maybe Brisbane?

I also start seeing a psychologist in a couple of weeks. Her name is Jill, and I'm really scared.

Wish me luck.

With love, Mack

Small World

LATER

Mum moved to Agnes Water on the Queensland coast when she and Dad split. It must've been a decision they made years prior because as soon as Lucas turned eighteen and moved away to study in Brisbane, they announced the news of their separation. I was twenty-three at the time, living with Stu not far from the family home.

I wasn't too surprised when they told me. I hadn't seen them kiss or hug each other in years. Not that I was home much at the time. They talked me through it separately. It was a smooth transition for them both, so I was told.

The region was experiencing a property boom at the time, so once they sold the family home, they both had enough money to buy their own separate houses. Dad stayed in the region and downsized to a unit because he had family around there, and Mum moved up north, where the weather was warmer, and the properties cheaper.

"This will always be a home for you and your brother, holiday or not," Mum had mentioned to me a few times.

She was always trying to get me to visit. But I couldn't make it as much as I endeavored, especially working as much as I had been since she left. Once or twice a year at best.

And there I was, about to bring three people to her house, one of them my supposed future husband. Mum had already met Rachel once before. The year prior, when Rachel and I drove up for a long weekend.

ETA around 2pm, I texted Mum after we passed a town named "Dingo", the name about as Australian as it could get.

She replied almost right away, no worries, Macky. See you soon!

The tangerine terrain soon turned cerulean, the sea sparkling in the sun.

Mum's house blended in with the white sand sprawled along the shoreline.

"Finally here," I chorused with a sigh of relief as we parked in the driveway.

I was the first to hop out of the car. The front door swung open.

"Hello!" Mum called out.

She stood in the doorway, wearing her favorite white dress.

"Hey, Mum!" I beamed, hugging her before bothering with my belongings.

A radiant smile stretched over Mum's cheeks. "Ah, it's so good to see you."

"You too."

She looked over at the others.

Rachel walked forward. "Hey, Mumsy," she said enthusiastically, giving Mum a hug. "Good to see you again."

"You too, Rachel."

I turned around to Jasper and Lily. "As you can see, we found some pretty special people on our trip."

"You were telling me," Mum said politely, stepping forward with open arms. "I would say I've heard a lot about you both, but I'm sure that time will come."

"Nice to meet you, Lauren," Lily rejoiced, hugging Mum.

"It's a pleasure, Lily." Mum then turned to Jasper, her smile growing through the greetings. "Hi, Jasper. Nice to meet you."

They joined in a long embrace, which surprisingly lacked the awkwardness I thought it would.

After bringing our bags in, Mum gave Jasper and Lily the grand tour.

Mum's house in a nutshell: spacious, open floor plan, lots of plants. The only thing different was an array of new artworks she'd hung up on the walls, most of them water paintings of botanical plants. My favorite was of the most intricate Nodding Greenhood orchid I'd ever seen. I even stopped in front of it while Mum showed off her abode.

She popped up next to me. "I thought you'd like them. I got them off this lady in town. She's such a talented artist, it *baffles* me."

My lips curved upward. "They're beautiful."

"Yeah, whenever I walk through the house now, I convince myself I'm wandering through the forest."

I nodded, losing myself in the detail of the orchid print.

"The paintings make me think of you, too," she added, placing a hand on my shoulder. "You out there, conserving our world. Saving our planet with your good work."

I chuckled. "I dunno about saving the world, but…thanks, Mum."

She clapped her hands. "All right, gang, so beds…"

Jasper snuck up next to me and pecked me on the cheek.

"Two can sleep in the spare room and then there's a pull-out sofa bed in the lounge room."

"As much as I want to claim you as my mum," Rachel said, putting her arm around her, "I think Mack and Jasper get privilege on the spare room."

"That was easy," Mum concluded with a shrug.

Mum already had dinner planned out for us. She

wanted to fire up the barbecue, so Rachel, Lily, and Jasper volunteered to drive into town and do the grocery shopping for dinner, leaving me with Mum for some quality time, which involved a glass of Pinot Grigio on the back deck. I'd missed this. Having wine and chats with Mum.

Ever since I was younger, I'd always told Mum everything. Dad, too, but Mum and I had this special connection—not any more superior than mine and Dad's, but just different. We saw life similarly. We shared the same love of simplicity, and some of the same frustrations.

"So, Jasper seems nice," Mum mentioned, in a cute *spill the tea right now* kind of tone.

I took a sip of wine and lifted my glass, as though I was celebrating a win of sorts. In retrospect, I was.

"Yeah," I said, feeling my cheeks go red. "It almost doesn't feel real."

I had to tell her. All about Jasper, the vision, everything in between.

Mum went all gooey when I told her that I saw Jasper propose to me. She kept gaping and smiling and gaping again when I relayed the details.

In response, her eyes popped when I told her Jasper had a Brain Cinema of his own.

"Hmm," she mumbled, furrowing her brows. "Interesting. I…didn't know there were others out there like us. Not outside of our family anyway."

"Neither did I," I said.

"Must be nice knowing you're not alone, though," Mum mentioned, twisting the stem on her glass, "and that someone who's not your own family has lived a similar life to you." She paused. "Well, as similar as possible anyway. No one can live the exact same life we do as individuals."

I met her affirming gaze with a smile of the same caliber.

Brain Cinema, she always called it.

Her mother had it, and her mother before her.

A hereditary gift. A curious curse.

Though, as I learned to live with it over the years, it became not a gift or curse. It became a part of me. A not-so-new normal anymore.

Jasper, Rachel, and Lily weren't back with the barbecue groceries yet. So naturally, Mum and I were half a bottle of Pinot Grigio deep.

"How's your writing going?" I asked Mum, to which her eyes lit up.

"Well, I've been sitting on the news for a while now, and don't tell anyone yet because it's still under wraps," she said zealously, "but my agent has *finally* sold my book to a publisher."

My eyes widened. "No way?!"

"Yeah!" Her cheeks went rosy red. "I signed my contract this week."

I gaped. "Oh my god, Mum! Congratulations! You did it." Standing up from the outside table, a little tipsy, I stepped over and hugged her.

"Thanks, Macky. It's been a calling of mine for quite some time now, as you know."

I sat back down. "Is it the one you were telling me about? The poetry one?"

She nodded. "Sure is. And I've got another book in development, this time fiction instead of poetry."

Unable to control my excitement, I said, "Mum, I'm so proud of you. You did it. You did what you've been passionate about since you were young. All those poems sitting in the drawers for years. Now, you've written a goddamn book!"

A tear fell down her cheek. "Aw, thank you. You know what, when I first discovered I had this ability, it tore me apart. And I was alone for most of it, which is where a lot of my poetry came from, especially the poems exploring loneliness. My mother—your nan—was very closed off, so she and I didn't even have a conversation about it until just before she died. We lived for so long…so closed off. Hiding this part of ourselves. And when I found out it ran in the family, I made myself a promise that I would teach you how to use Brain Cinema. That I would run alongside you. Because I know how alone I felt."

"And you did run alongside me," I reiterated, not taking my eyes off her. "You taught me how to control it. All those times over those first few years after Finn died, I wanted to give up and I couldn't grasp what this life of mine was going to be. You were there."

Mum wiped the tears from her face. "And I always will." She paused. "And I hope this book—who knows—some people might read it, and find solace in it as I did in writing it."

She clasped my hand, letting out a little laugh.

"Hey, Mum, there's something I want to tell you."

"Anything, darling. Anything."

Stomach fluttering, I paused before saying, "It's so weird. Finn was my first love, and in the years since, I've never felt anything close to the way he made me feel when I was with him. But I don't know, Jasper reminds me so much of him. It's weird."

Mum maintained eye contact as she said, "Things happen in strange and beautiful ways. You should know this by now."

"I know. But, sometimes, it's as if they've got the same energy. It's like he's alive again. But in Jasper."

Mum didn't reply for a moment. Her gaze drifted to the pink sunset sky before she said, "Maybe he is. And who are we to say otherwise? You know, you don't have to be religious to have faith."

"Yoo-hoo!" the recognizable voice of Rachel called out.

Rachel, Jasper, and Lily stepped into the kitchen holding bags of groceries.

"Who's hungry?!" Lily said, loud enough for her voice to echo.

"My non-tipsy self would've said yes," Mum quipped, picking up her glass of wine. "But my tipsy self says I will be hungry…soon."

Mum turned on the lights.

"We got loads," Jasper added, turning to me. "Sorry we took so long. We stopped by the beach on our way home. It's so lovely down there."

He sat next to me and cracked open a beer, kissing me on the cheek.

I smiled. "All good, mister," glancing over to Mum, catching her eye. "We had some catching up to do."

Jasper looked over at the half-empty wine bottle sitting on the table and laughed. "I can see that."

So far on our road trip across Queensland, I didn't know what day it was half the time. It didn't matter. But on Saturday, it mattered to me. Because it meant I only had one more sleep with Jasper. Then he'd be gone. For how long, I did not know.

We arrived at Workman's Beach by eight in the morning, setting up underneath a wooden hut on the sand. One with raft-like beams in the middle, branches, and leaves hanging over the sides to form a circular dome.

Waves crashed onto the shoreline. The wind kept to a minimum, which meant no sand swept on our faces.

Running straight into the water, I floated on top of the ocean, eyes to the sky, reflecting on how surreal the past week had been. How far we'd traversed. How much had changed. For the better, I hoped. Surely.

Once back under the hut, Lily started playing guitar. I lay close to Jasper, more content as the minutes passed. If perfection could be described, this would've been it.

Stringy dried palm fronds cascaded down the hut, swaying in the breeze like cellophane. In a daze of euphoria, I caressed the smooth palms.

Appreciation for Country.

While Rachel and Lily were swimming, Jasper and I

kissed on our towels. Staying still, eyes locked. How could I tell him I missed him already, without sounding needy?

"Come over to London for the wedding next month," he requested of me, running his finger through my hair.

I scoffed, rolling my eyes without sounding overly rude. "I think you forget that I won't be able to afford much after this trip."

He smiled humbly. "My shout."

I shook my head. "I can't take your money."

He stopped touching me. "Why not? It's not taking. It's a gift. A gift I want you to receive." He stopped when he discovered I wasn't convinced. "Hey, if it makes you feel any better, this can be your birthday present. And in between then and the wedding, we can try and see each other when I have overnights in Brisbane between flights to London."

I sighed. "I dunno, Jasper."

"Please," he begged gently, stroking my fingers. "I'd really love for you to be my date. For you to meet Tom and Bruce and receive this plane ticket, kind of like how…you receive my dick."

My forehead creased, stomach taking a plummet. "Tom and Bruce?"

Jasper exhaled a chuckle. "Yeah. My friends. The couple who are getting married."

I picked up my phone hastily.

It couldn't be.

No fucking way.

It couldn't, could it? If it was, it would naturally be a

validation that the world we lived in was smaller than I previously thought. A whole lot fucking smaller.

"I just realized we don't have each other on Instagram," I said quickly. "It's the only app I use mostly."

"I hate social media anyway. I never use it," he admitted.

"What's your Instagram handle?" I asked.

"Uh, jaspersworldtravels. Why the sudden need to find me? I thought we were talking about you being my date at a wedding."

Not answering him, I typed in his account name. A profile picture of him in Santorini popped up in the little circle. As did the one name I was looking for.

Followed by tommygreen95

"You've gotta be fucking *kidding* me!" I piped up.

Jasper cocked his head. "What?"

I spun the phone screen around.

"Is this the Tom who's getting married to Bruce?"

He squinted at the screen. "Um, yeah. Why? You know him?"

"Yeah, I fucking know him!"

"What? How?"

I was unable to contain myself. "Oh my god, freaky. I met Tom—well, *Tommy from London* I used to call him—when he was over here in Australia. We met on Tinder for god sake. Hooked up a few times when I was in an open relo with my boyfriend at the time. Then he met Bruce."

"Oh wow, that *is* freaky," Jasper replied. "Small world, eh?"

"I think we're past the point of small world," I smirked,

looking back at the phone, at Tom's profile, which I hadn't seen in a while. "Wow, I can't believe Tom and Bruce are getting married. What the fuck. I took Tom to his first bush doof."

Jasper beamed. "Did you meet Bruce too?"

"Yeah, I did. He came to a doof with us later on that year," I reminisced, "As soon as the two of them got back from their road trip around the N.T. I think, at the time, they were having some problems in their relationship or something. I think Bruce was struggling with some mental stuff. Actually, I remember, Tom was on the news a little later on. He got lost and nearly died out in the desert in Central Australia for three days, the silly sally. Then I remember months later them both being back together. I was like, man, I can't keep up with those two."

"True, Thomas did tell me all about his moment of Aussie fame..." Jasper laughed. "From nearly dying that is." He shrugged. "I'm glad they got through it together in the end."

I swatted him playfully. "Obviously...they're getting married now."

Jasper scooped up my hand. "Well, now we've established you know the grooms quite personally, it's even more reason for you to be my date."

He gave me his enticing puppy dog face, which did settle my heartbeat slightly, until the corners of my mouth started lifting.

"Fine," I gave in, linking my hand to his and waggling my eyebrows. "I'll receive...your gift."

<u>October 2</u>

Dear Finn,

I think this is going to be my last letter for a while.

Life really is changing. Never did I think I'd be attending Tom's wedding, nor be attending it with Jasper.

What's even stranger is that, when I first met Tom on his working holiday in Australia, Brain Cinema never showed me any indication of a wedding. It showed us fooling around on the beach, then the bush doof, and nothing after that. I sometimes think Brain Cinema has a mind of its own and shows me what it wants to. I don't know.

What I do know is that this trip is coming to a close and I kind of don't want it to. It's gone so quickly, just like most things do.

I'll come to visit soon. I promise.

Forever and always,

Mack

The Journal

THEN

A diffuser pumped lavender-scented vapor into the air, which was undoubtedly better than the citrus one from the last meeting with my psychologist. I sat across from Jill, her legs crossed, eyes looking large through her horn-rimmed glasses. My hangover from the night before scratched at my brain, sending a big "fuck you" down my stomach.

"How was your week?" Jill asked ritually.

I shrugged, "It was okay."

She folded her hands together. "Anything interesting happen?"

"Uh, I mean, I was at uni most of the week. Got a few assignments coming up so I've been pretty busy."

Busy partying, I wanted to say.

"Busy's good," Jill said, unlinking her fingers and tapping them on the desk. "Keeps the purposes flowing. What are you learning at the moment?"

How not to get an STI, I nearly said. But instead, "Um, cell biology and geography have been the main topics. But it's very introductory stuff so far."

Jill lifted her brows. "I'm sure you'll learn a lot more soon."

"I've met a new friend, too," I added.

"Oh yeah? That's good. Tell me about them."

"Her name's Rachel, and she's in all my classes. She's actually so funny, and such a…free spirit. I don't know. I find it hard to connect with people sometimes, especially after everything that happened last year, with Finn and…the cutting, and drugs."

My wrists and legs still held scars.

Little faint twigs scattered across my skin.

"And what about the nightmares?"

A slight chill traversed me as I said, "Um…I haven't had any this week."

"Really good to hear, Mack. You even sound better. I've noticed a big improvement with you since you moved to Brisbane."

I nodded before my chin dropped toward my chest. "So have I. But I dunno, I still have so many thoughts about him. But I'm not obsessed with them anymore, if that makes sense."

"Makes perfect sense."

"I'm glad," I said, lifting my hands palm-up. "At least I don't think I'm a murderer anymore."

"Mack, I've said this before. If you were a murderer, you'd be in jail and not in a therapy room with me."

"True."

A pause followed.

"Have you been journaling much this week?"

"Not much," I admitted, pulling a black-covered book from my backpack. "I'm actually running out of room in this."

"And what are you going to do with the journal after you've run out of pages?" Jill asked. "Do you have a drawer you can put it in?"

"I think I'm gonna burn it," I said without hesitation.

"Mack."

"What?"

She let out a long sigh. Then, "Nothing. Burning it could be therapeutic, but don't tell anyone that I said to start a fire."

My lips quirked suddenly. "Your secret's safe with me."

I pointed to the journal on the way out of my session with Jill. "Thanks again for the gift. Honestly, probably one of the best Christmas presents."

In response, she only smiled, yet it was enough.

On the bus back home, I wrote on the top of the last page of the journal:

<u>March 22</u>

I don't want to go back. Only forward. For now.

First Clip

LATER

Even though we left early, it took us most of the day to drive from Agnes Water down to Brisbane. There was a terrible accident on the highway, which led to a beeline of cars that were banked up for several kilometers. At one point, our GPS changed the original route to a turn-off, where we tracked backward along a coastal road, and merged back onto the highway two exits to the south.

Finally, we made it to Brisbane at sunset, and while I preferred the peace of small-town life, it was refreshing to see the golden hour glow against the city. Rachel lived in

New Farm, the same suburb I did when I lived here. Ever since we met, Rachel never moved to another part of the city, and I didn't blame her. New Farm is close to the river, and walking distance to both the city center and Fortitude Valley.

Rachel was considered a long-term tenant at this point, having made her apartment home for five years. When I lived with Stu down south, we'd always come up to Brisbane and stay at Rachel's since she had a spare room that she used as a study. We would go to the clubs, dance until all hours, and Rachel usually went home early with her girlfriend at the time.

After breaking up with Stu, I realized I hadn't hung out with Rachel in quite some time. She distracted me from the pain of the breakup; took me out dancing, went hiking and looking at plants with me, and also banned me from bringing any guys back to her place. Rightfully so, I was a mess. One of me was enough to deal with in her space.

There were so many memories in this city, and, in true best-of-both-worlds fashion, I still called it home.

Things were much different now with Jasper and Lily, though, and while the road trip should've been an indication of this, it was typed into wet cement and dried when the four of us arrived in Brisbane.

"Your car is really comfortable," Jasper said early the next morning when I drove him to the airport. I could've stayed tangled in that spare bed at Rachel's all morning with him. But he had a flight to catch, already dressed in the same uniform he wore when we first met, which strangely felt like a lifetime ago.

I yawned through the awkwardness that had leaked between us. "It does the job. How are you feeling about the flight?"

"Eh, I'm pretty used to it now," he said, chuckling, "Jet lag who?"

"The last week has been a lot-who," I quipped.

"It has," he agreed. "It's been amazing."

"It has." I tapped my hand on the steering wheel. "Why does it have to end?"

"Only momentarily, right?" he reminds me. "I'll be back in Brisbane for a night on the sixteenth, which, thank god, you have off. Then, you'll be in London in a month after that."

A light quiver rippled in my stomach. "And then what? How do we make this work? You live halfway across the world."

He put forth a deep, weighted sigh. "I know," he breathed, turning to me as the airport drew near. "I guess we just need to trust that it'll all work out."

"I'll be counting down the days until I see you again," he said, looking into my eyes as we stood by the terminal, five minutes until his boarding time.

I simply nodded, which was enough of a response to tie him over until we formed a kiss.

The visions never lie. Remember that. Please, remember that.

Jasper walked away in his black uniform that so beautifully contrasted his ginger hair, and I reminded myself that this wasn't the end, over and over. That this wouldn't be the last time I'd see him. That he wouldn't get on that flight, ghost me, and then leave me with memories, including the ones that hadn't happened yet.

Even from afar, his eyes were glassy as he gave me one last wave, before disappearing from the terminal. Tears welled in my eyes on my walk out of the airport.

We're working out at Bower Creek tomorrow, my manager Craig texted that afternoon. **I'll meet you at the start of the Hume Forest Trail at 8am.**

See you then, I texted him back.

Even though the apartment I lived in was small, it had a bath which made all the difference to me. To calm the mind and the body.

After massaging soap into my legs, my phone flashed.

"Hey, handsome," Jasper greeted me in a voice message. The corners of my mouth curled upward. "So, I'm finally boarding my actual flight now. Apparently, there were engine problems with the first flight so we had to exit the plane before going anywhere, which sucked, but I flicked through our photos from the trip, which passed the time in the lounge waiting for the next plane to be ready. Lots of memories there in those photos. I miss it already. I'll uh…speak to you when I land in London. I…hope going back to work tomorrow goes smoothly for you."

I replied to Jasper via voice message, "Ugh, flight delays suck. I hope it goes well. Message me when you land. And about the wedding, I'll suss it out with my boss."

I'd just had a week off work and now I was about to ask for another week off the following month to fly to the other side of the world. Was I hoping to have a job when I got back?

"Oh hey, Craig, I forgot to mention I've got a wedding to go to next month," I told him telepathically.

Perhaps I wouldn't tell him it was a wedding.

"So how was your holiday, mate?" Craig asked me the following morning.

We trudged along the Hume Forest Trail in our yellow high-vis uniforms. Although I'd woken up early almost every day on my holiday, I was still tired.

We had a twenty-two-kilometer trail full of weeds to identify over the next few days. And to top it off, we started our walk along the trail with a god-awful smell of something dead in the forest, one of which sent bile shooting up my throat.

"It was good," I said, wincing slightly at the stench.

"Oh good." Craig bent down to study some groundsel bush, frowning. "Bet you saw some nice planties on the trip."

I wrote down a couple of weed species on my clipboard. "Yeah, we ended up spontaneously road-tripping from the N.T. through the Central Queensland Highlands."

"Ooooooh. See heaps of brigalow trees?"

"*Heaps.*"

We kept moving. Thanks to the next kilometer of the trail having mostly the same weed species to its sides, we finally got away from the rotting carcass scent.

"I really want to go on a trip soon," Craig admitted, wiping sweat from his brow.

A dose of humidity swept through the forest, more than usual for mid-October.

Making our way along the trail at a rather prompt pace, I had several chances to bring up the wedding—to tell the truth—but my worries took over, in the form of a voice in my head. Craig had never done anything to taint his title as a good boss, yet it didn't stop me from worrying he would fire me. I needed a plan, and unfortunately, it wasn't going to be fully mapped out on my first day back.

The day slipped by swiftly, and when we'd finished identifying weeds from the first half of the trail, late afternoon crept in and I opened my phone to an unexpected message. I should've half-expected it since I was now invited to his wedding and all.

Mack! Long time no speak. I just had a chat with Jasper. Such a coincidence that you two met. But like, it makes me SUPER happy! The message from Thomas read.

Then, he said you're going to be his date for the wedding. Soooo wicked! This is your (in)formal invitation btw

Jasper hadn't messaged me to let me know he got home safe. But I guessed he had arrived, according to Thomas.

I replied to his message as I hopped into my car, **yeah crazy shit hey?! Congrats on the wedding btw. I'm keen to see you tie the knot ;)**

Family Dinner

After hopping out of the shower, it was close to six and I'd received a text from Jasper. I beamed upon reading, **goodmorning handsome. I mean, goodmorning for me. Good afternoon for you haha**

It was seven in the morning in London and I'd received a message from Tom two hours ago. Never took him for an early bird. On the other hand, I didn't think he'd be getting married next month.

Good mafternoon! I replied, chuckling to myself as I pressed send.

Jasper called me as soon as he'd read my message, laughing over the phone, "Umm, did you just make up a new word."

I lay across the couch. "Yeah. Pretty sure I did."

"A plant-identifying genius and a vocabulary creator. I'm a big fan," Jasper flirted.

I chuckled. "Stop it, you. How're you settling back in?"

"No jet lag yet which is great," he said, "or maybe I'm so used to it I don't even know what it feels like anymore."

"Makes sense."

"How was your first day back at work?" he asked.

I let out a laugh. "I mean, as riveting as a trail full of weeds can be. Nah, it went okay. Was kind of nice, actually, to be out in the field again. Even if it was identifying weeds."

"Riiiiight. Well, that's good."

I wished he was there and not on the other side of the world. It wasn't the same talking to him over the phone.

After a short silence, Jasper asked me, "Did you end up speaking with your boss about the wedding?"

I knew he was going to ask. "Uh, nah, I'm still working out how to approach it without sounding as if I don't give a fuck about working there anymore."

"This is true." He paused. "Well, let's come up with an excuse—"

"An excuse that isn't a wedding I should've prepared for?" I suggest gingerly.

"Right. Hmmm. How about..." he brainstormed, "...your aunt who lives in London has a terminal illness and she's going to pass away soon?"

"Uh-ah, I'll get bad karma."

"Okay, umm," he trailed off. Then, "Your dog, which

your boss doesn't know about, died, and you need a mental health week off."

"Also, bad karma. No deaths."

"Okay." Silence. "All right, I've got it!"

"Humor me, Jasper from London."

"Your aunt is having a spontaneous wedding in London, where she lives. And she's having a spontaneous wedding because—"

I chimed in, "Because…she recently got a new job in remote Alaska where flights are too expensive and she'll be there for a long time and the original date of the wedding won't work anymore because of the new job."

Jasper clapped and cheered. "See. At least it's only half a lie now."

It could work. It could really work. More than I cared to admit.

"Look at us becoming a brainstorming duo," I said with a smirk.

"Yeah, we're pretty good."

He then said he missed me. It'd only been a day and I, too, felt like I missed him more than I should've.

"Aw, I miss you too," I said, honestly.

"What have you got planned for the night?" he asked me.

I pouted my lips. "Well, after I rid myself of the dirt, I'm going to dinner with my dad and little brother."

"Oh true. I forgot you had a little brother. You didn't tell me much about him. How long's it been since you've seen them?"

His question had the cogs in my brain melting into

gooey liquid metal. T-1000 from *Terminator 2* vibes. I didn't want to think. I'd spent the whole day thinking.

"Mmm, I dunno," I admitted, opting for the easy answer. "I saw Dad a while ago. And Lucas, I think…last Christmas."

Turned out I hadn't seen Dad in a couple of months. With work being busier than ever, sometimes working ten-hour days, and me spending most of my weekends in Brisbane with Rachel, or camping down here, I had very much neglected my father without realizing it.

"Oh, you've got your own life to live, mate," Dad brushed it off when I apologized a few minutes after arriving at his place. "Your twenties are work work work and spending time with your friends."

Lucas hadn't arrived from Brisbane yet so it gave Dad and me a chance for some quality time.

His number two unit was tucked away down a small driveway, orange and maroon brick build, cluttered but in a homely kind of way, with a few too many baby photos of Lucas and I. It, too, smelled a little like ginger every time I came to visit. He was always cooking with it for meal prep or drinking it. The man and his health kicks.

This time, though, the ginger scent was overpowered by tomato and garlic from the Spaghetti Bolognese cooking on the stove.

"At this rate, you'll be reincarnating as freshly planted ginger," I joshed when he showed me his newest garden bed full of it. It was his first attempt at growing.

Dad laughed. "I mean, at least I'd be going to good use." He paused. "Hey, I was thinking the other day, remember all the camping trips we used to go on up the coast?"

"Yeah, I mean if you call that camping," I chuckled, stifling a smirk. "We brought the microwave, kettle, a laptop, portable DVD player—"

"Yeah, yeah, buuuuuut," Dad interjected, "Do you remember when you accidentally dropped all of your camp breakfast on the ground, cried, then I made it for you again, and you did the same thing—"

"Yeah, okay okay," I piped up. "You always love to bring that one up, don't you?"

Dad shook his head with a big grin on his face. "Look, it's one of my fondest memories. I won't ever let you live it down."

My phone buzzed. A message from Jasper: **hope family catchup is going well sweet prince xx**

My mouth curved into a smile. I heart-reacted his message, not wanting to be rude on my phone while I visited Dad.

"What's gotten you blushing?" Dad pried.

I glanced up at Dad. He'd always been an intuitive man, especially when it came to how I was feeling. Even if I couldn't comprehend my own emotions at first.

"Seeing someone new?" Dad asked.

I went red in the face. "Maybe."

I filled him in, very briefly, about Jasper.

"No way. Well, I'm keen to meet him," Dad said supportively.

Rufus started barking again. The front door swung open before the now-old guard dog could even reach it. Lucas walked through, looking taller and buffer than I'd last seen him.

"Hey, mate," Dad walked forward and hugged him. He hugged back, but not with a firm grip in the slightest.

Lucas had always been quiet, but even more so now. "Hey, dad."

I smiled at Lucas after Dad had finished greeting him. "Hey, bro," I said, also hugging him.

"Hey," he mumbled, giving me a half-smile.

Dad went back to the kitchen to stir the bolognese simmering on the stove.

"Are we having spag bol?" Lucas asked.

"Yeah, we are," Dad said excitedly. "I did watch your mum very closely when she made it for you guys back in the day."

"Yeah look, you're actually getting pretty good at making it," I agreed.

Lucas rolled his eyes and groaned. "Yeah, 'cause we have it almost every time we come over for dinner."

"Hey, it's been a long time since we've had dinner here." Dad's tone plummeted. "And last time, even though it was before Christmas, we had tacos."

"I think Lucas means probably every time we came over last year," I said, patting Dad on the back. "Maybe it's time to learn some new dishes."

Lucas nodded in agreement whilst checking his phone. "Can we please make it vegan?"

"Vegan?" Dad frowned.

"Yeah. I'm pretty much vegan now," Lucas said proudly.

I glanced over at him. Lucas, vegan? The carnivorous creature, who wouldn't even eat his vegetables when we were younger?

"It's one of the best things we can do as humans to reduce our impact on the environment," Lucas explained, a little louder than he would normally say things.

"But if you want me to make a vegan dish, where are we going to get our protein?" Dad asked ignorantly.

Lucas and I rolled our eyes in unison.

"Dad, you know plant-based protein is a huge thing now," I told him. "And they're getting really good at making it taste like meat."

"Yeah, I always walk past it in Woolies." Dad took the pasta off the stove. "To be honest, I never stop to look. But maybe I will next time."

I opened the fridge. "Beers?" I suggested.

"Yes please," said Dad.

"Nah I'm good thanks."

I narrowed my eyes at Lucas. "Who are you and what have you done with my little brother?"

Lucas chuckled. "I have gym during the week so I don't drink."

"Yeah, I can see that. You're looking pretty ripped, little bro," I complimented him.

He grinned a "thank you" at me. No need for words.

"Agreed. You're looking good, mate." Dad cast him a glance while serving up bowls of spag bol.

"Thanks."

"So, how's Rufus been?" I asked Dad after telling him the spaghetti bolognese was getting better and better every time.

Dad looked down at Rufus, who was sitting there all polite, hoping we'd feed him some spaghetti. "Oh, he's great company, as you know," Dad admitted. "A big ball of excitement."

Rufus must've known we were talking about him. He wagged his tail and hopped up, his two front paws on Dad's leg. Dad pushed him off. "Get down, Rufus. On your bed!"

Rufus dropped his ears and crawled onto his bed in the living room, letting out a big dog sigh.

"Your third kid is quite the obedient one, isn't he?" I quipped.

"At least he doesn't talk back like you two did as teenagers," Dad put forth, shoving a big ball of spaghetti and sauce into my mouth. "Actually, that's a lie. Rufus does tell me in the morning when he's ready for a walk. And he isn't exactly quiet."

Lucas frowned. "He *tells* you, does he?"

"Bloody oath he does," Dad shrugged. "Through loud barks and puppy whines."

Lucas arched his eyebrows. "Okayyyyy."

Dad soon took our empty bowls over to the sink. Lucas and I stayed sitting, exhaling heavily in the hope it would help with digestion. The beer definitely wouldn't.

"Spag bol went straight through me," Dad sighed. "I'll be back in a bit."

"Didn't need to know that, but okay," I said with the simplest sprinkle of sass I could muster.

Dad left us at the dinner table to descend into our carb-heavy food comas, both of which welcomed a rather awkward silence.

"How's uni going?" I asked him. "Learnt how to make robots yet?"

Lucas chuckled. "It's going good."

"Love it up there in the city?"

"Yeah. It's great." His replies were short and lacked enthusiasm, but this was Lucas' personality, and I loved him for it.

"I always say I'll move back up to the city one day," I said, sipping down some half-warm beer, "but something always keeps me down here."

"You should," Lucas told me. "Fuck being down here. Nothing happens, ever. It's boring."

I shrugged. "That's the thing, I kinda like it. Then sometimes I don't. But mostly, I do."

Lucas shrugged. "Each to their own I guess."

"Yeah."

We sat silently, for a big long moment, staring at the walls of family photos and old music memorabilia Dad collected, The Beatles and Elvis his favorites.

Unexpectedly, while Dad was still in the bathroom, I said to Lucas, "Hey, look, I know it might be a little too late, but sorry for not being around in your life as much over the recent years."

He gave me a surprised look, completely caught off guard. Of course, he didn't know what to say, so I kept at what I needed to.

"I know it's years ago now, and so much has happened in between, but I wanna say the way I treated you when I was going through all my shit, was not okay. And I never apologized to you for it, mainly because I was trying so hard to forget about all of it."

"Dude, it's honestly okay," Lucas blurted out. "You've been living your life, and the past is the past. But thanks for the apology. Consider it accepted."

A sudden gratitude washed over me. "Okay good, because I'm not sure where that came from."

"You're always saying weird shit," Lucas reminded me.

I shrugged. "Apparently so. But I needed to get it off my chest."

"And off the chest it is," Lucas grimaced.

My phone buzzed again. Another message from Jasper: I miss Australia already.

I missed *him*. And just when I thought weed identifying day two would be the perfect opportunity to inform Craig about the wedding—my so-called aunt's wedding in the UK—our day on the Bower Creek trail was cut short due to the rain. It crept in quickly and poured rather hard, my high-vis soaked by the time we sped-walked back to the trailhead.

Craig said we'd pick up the rest of the work tomorrow, which meant I had the afternoon to myself. Jasper wouldn't be awake for a few hours, so I couldn't tell him that the time off talk had to wait another day.

Even though I was aware of the time difference between us, I sometimes completely forgot that he was on the other side of the world.

I spent the rest of the afternoon cleaning the apartment. I dusted all the surfaces, vacuumed and mopped the floors, watered the house plants, and cleaned out the fridge (which I'd been putting off for god knows how long).

Given that the rain was set in for the rest of the day, and the fact I didn't own a dryer, washing my dirty clothes from the road trip would have to wait.

By the next day, the sun hadn't returned but it stopped raining at least. I was kind of hoping the rain would stay and completely wash out the track full of weeds so we couldn't even work there at all.

I was back in Bower Creek to finish off the weed job, which was meant to be done the day before. Wet mud, caked boots, and all.

"So, Craig," I began as we finished identifying a long stretch of the same bloody weed. I decided to start the conversation while we were working instead of on a break when it could be far more awkward. "I wanted to chat with you about something."

"What's up, mate? Please don't tell me you're leaving when we've got this many jobs and not enough ecologists." Craig turned to me all worried-looking with his head cocked.

I let out a slight chuckle. Perhaps I wasn't so replaceable after all. "Um, well, no. You know I love this job."

"So, you're not thinking of leaving anytime soon?"

"I-I mean, no, not at all," I sputtered, "that's not what I wanted to talk about". We stopped looking at the plants and instead looked at each other, which intimidated the fuck out of me. I wasn't sure why. Craig wasn't scary or intimidating.

He wiped sprinkles of dirt from his hands.

"Go on, spit it out," he said sternly, stepping away from the trail. "Let's take a break." He put his backpack up against a tree, skulled some water, and whipped out a red apple.

Usually lying would be easy for me. But not now.

So, I told him the truth. Well, mostly the truth.

Hastily, I told him about Jasper, about how I knew Tom and Bruce and about their wedding over in the UK, and how Jasper wanted me to be his wedding date.

"Bit quick to be the guy's wedding date when you only met him a few weeks ago, don't you think?" Craig asked me through a mouthful of apple chunks.

At first, I didn't quite grasp how all of this would've sounded to Craig without telling him about Brain Cinema.

And with a shrug, I said, "Gay relationships tend to move pretty quickly."

Craig rolled his eyes and whipped out his phone. "Hmmm."

"Hmmm?" I replied, hoisting my eyebrows.

"Twenty-second till the thirtieth of November, right?" Craig asked me.

I nodded. "Yeah."

"You're lucky…" Craig said. "There's nothing pressing on the days you want off. But, if you don't have the previous week's bushfire management plan written up by then, would you be able to complete it while you're over there? Cause that was going to be your priority for the week in question. And honestly, I want you on the document."

"*Done!*" I blurted out.

Craig chuckled. "Woah, you must really like this guy. You look like a kid on freaking Christmas morning right now."

I beamed. "Thank you. I appreciate it."

"No more time off for a while after this, though," Craig warned me.

"Definitely not," I agreed.

I pulled my phone out of my pocket and texted Jasper, **GOT WORK OFF YAYYYYY!**

Second Clip

My excitement for the trip to London kept me on a high until the sixteenth, when I woke up early to pick Jasper up from the airport. He would only be in Brisbane for one day and night, so we figured we'd spend the whole time together.

Given it had been a busy week at work down south, I slept through my morning alarm. I awoke to a message from Rachel that read, **omg mack, I need your advice on something asap! Please call me when you can**

Once I got onto the highway, I dialed her, to which she picked up within three rings, "Ugh, Mack, thank god." She sounded distressed, desperate.

I cleared my throat and asked, "What's up?"

She let out a deep, powerful groan. "Shit's weird, Mack."

"What's going on?" I asked her.

She took a deep breath. "It's Lily."

"Oh shit," I piped up. "What's happening there?"

Rachel let out another loud groan. "Okay, so," she continued after gathering herself. "Lily's in a polyamorous relationship with another girl. She's been with this girl for over a year."

I parted my lips and cocked my head. "Oh. I wasn't expecting that."

"Um, neither was I. She dropped the bombshell on me last night when we went on a date."

"Right," I said. "And you…"

"Ruined everything? Yes," Rachel interjected. "Did I get all weird and tell her she should leave because I wanted to be alone? Also, yes."

I gritted my teeth. "Oh shit. Well, at least you know now."

"Yeah, but it's not as simple as that, mate. I wish it was."

"Why?" I asked.

"Because she asked me if I would be her girlfriend too."

"Oh," was all I could muster up. Then, "What did you say?"

"I said no. I freaked out!" Rachel exclaimed. "All I could think was that Lily was going to leave eventually anyway. And I know it's only been a month and a bit since we met—whatever—it just…it just hurt."

I nodded. "Totally understandable. You were led to believe she was single—"

"Uh, that's the thing," Rachel cut in. "Lily never said she was *exclusively* single. I just assumed, you know."

"And totally fair you assumed," I said.

Rachel sighed. "Everything was going so well. Now I don't know what to think."

"You like her though, right?" I asked.

"*Obviously!*" she shrieked.

"Well, she didn't say she doesn't want to be with you," I said, wanting the best for her but also not wanting her to do anything she wasn't comfortable with. "You never know, you might warm up to the freedom of a poly relationship. You know, building trust. 'Cause shit, there must be a lot of trust involved in one of those."

Rachel contemplated for a few moments before saying, "I do really like her. I just…I dunno. I'll think about it."

"Only do what feels right," I said.

"Duh. I ain't going into anything if it doesn't feel right," Rachel said sassily. "I'm getting too old for that shit."

"You're twenty-eight, hon," I reminded her.

Rachel scoffed. "Yeah. Please excuse me while I blink again and I'm thirty-five. Anyway, talking about almost thirty-year-olds, how's your boy Jasper? You're coming up to Brisbane today, hey?"

"Yeah, he said he's booked us accommodation somewhere for the night *near Brisbane*," I tell her, spotting a little bit of blue through the clearing clouds. "I tried to ask where we're staying, but he said it's a surprise."

"Okay mate, that's extremely cute," Rachel swooned. "And *near Brisbane,* how vague."

"Yeah, honestly," I agreed, "it could be anywhere."

"I'm sure knowing Jasper, it'll be nice," she assured me, before going on to tell me that she was going to take the day to think about what she was going to say to Lily.

The traffic wasn't too bad for a Saturday morning. Going northbound, that was. I felt bad for those in the opposite lane going from Brisbane to Gold Coast.

Despite Jasper warning me that flights run by the company he worked for were being delayed a lot recently— something to do with a company-wide staff shortage—he arrived in Brisbane on time.

After crawling forward in the pick-up queue, I noticed him immediately amongst the crowd. Might've been the ginger hair, which worked to his and my advantage in times like these.

I can see you! I messaged him.

A few seconds later, he fished his phone from his pocket, smiled at the screen, and looked up, to his right, spotting my car. His smile grew wider as he promptly wheeled his small suitcase my way. My heart was banging like a drum as I parked right next to him.

After resting his suitcase in the boot, Jasper opened the passenger door and hopped in with a loud, relieved sigh, followed by, "Morning."

Blush burned to my ears as I echoed back, "Morning."

His mouth extended into a toothy grin, and he came in for a kiss. A quick peck before we drove off.

"How was the flight?" I asked on our way out of the congested airport area.

"Well, no delays, which was brill," he said, placing his hand on my leg, which sent blood to my groin.

"That's always a plus," I said. "So, uh, where are we going?"

Jasper let a cheeky laugh escape. "Oh yeah, I forgot that I'm the creator of this weekend's mystery Brisbane escape."

"I thought you said it was *near* Brisbane," I jested.

"Well, technically, I think it's in the Greater Brisbane region," he told me. "Definitely not the city though. I already need another break from the city life, and it's only been a week from the road trip."

"That's great," I replied with a touch of sarcasm, "but I'm also not from Brisbane, so I need you to put a destination into Maps before I get us lost."

"Good point," he said as he grabbed my phone from the console.

I informed him of the passcode, and when he put an address into the Maps, it was clear that we were going to Samford Valley, about half an hour north-west of Brisbane.

"Interesting," was all I said, attempting to hide my smirk and failing miserably. "I've never been."

"Naturally, neither," Jasper said. "I got us early check-in too. So, is there any significance with your phone passcode?"

I squeezed his thigh playfully. "June 5th. My birthday. When's yours?"

"August 12th," he chuckled. "Funny we've seen far into

the future yet we're only finding out each other's birth dates just now."

It really was crazy, but it was our crazy.

As we drove further from Brisbane, the suburbs were soon replaced with forest and farmland.

When I was living in the city those years ago, I never thought to come out this way, nor did I know a quaint country village like Samford existed so close to Brisbane. I didn't know a lot of things back then.

I sure didn't know my life would end up like it was now. Anything but.

After driving past Samford Village and further into the valley, I discovered we were close to our destination, which seemed to be a property hidden down a dirt road, within a thick nook of forest. On the acre block was a beautifully white Queenslander home with a wrap-around balcony.

"Oh my gosh, what is this place?" I marveled as we crunched closer to the fenced property.

"Farm stay, baby," Jasper said with impish glee, hopping out of my car to open the gate.

Once he did, I smiled at him through the windscreen as he poked his tongue out at me, and accelerated through the gate, parking in the designated spot at the back of the house.

At the back of the house was a paddock occupied by two alpacas and a miniature pony.

"Hello, honeys, we're home!" Jasper called out to the animals as I exited the car.

"You honestly know me too well," I said, looking around to the outdoor fireplace area which was canopied in festoon lights.

"You'd want to hope so," he hummed, positioning his hands around my waist, bringing his lips to mine for a long kiss.

We could kiss for as long as we wanted now. Or rather, for as long as we wanted for the next twenty-four hours. Then four weeks after that, I'd be off to London.

"This is literal home goals," I said, my mouth hanging agape as we took a tour through the house.

Although only one would be getting used while we were here, the house boasted three spacious bedrooms, two with ensuites. The master bedroom, where we were staying, had a massive bathroom with an airforce blue bathtub below a window that occupied most of the wall. From it, you could see out to the lush garden and trees that grew to the side of the house.

The bathtub and view—from first glance—looked strikingly familiar. And it only took me all but two seconds to realize that I'd seen it before, albeit briefly, in a snapshot that didn't even last a second. It looked better in real life, though. And I couldn't wait to spend sunset submerged with Jasper, just like the vision had shown.

We spent the morning with a long brunch with the fresh croissants and coffee provided for us. The house's owners even had a coffee machine, so once we moved to the balcony, sitting at the oak table with a view of the valley, it felt as if we were dining at a café, Jasper and I being the only patrons.

As we sipped our lattes and bit into the flaky buttery pastries, I told Jasper about Rachel finding out that Lily was in a polyamorous relationship.

Jasper rolled his eyes. "Yeah, unfortunately, Lily is still with Margot."

I pressed my lips together with force before saying, "Wish you would've told me before Rachel went and fell for her."

Jasper furrowed his forehead slightly. "I just didn't think it was my place to talk about her personal life with someone I hardly knew…you know what I mean. Besides, Lily has been having issues with Margot for a while now. Then Rachel came along, and yeah. I know she likes Rachel a lot though. She told me. Said she hasn't felt this way in a long time."

I sank further back into my chair and looked out to the rolling hills in the distance. "That road trip really was a big deal for all of us, wasn't it?" I said after a pause.

"Um, yeah, it was!" Jasper declared. "It's not every day you meet two strangers at a music festival, fall for these new people, and then go on a road trip across state with them after, what, three days of knowing each other."

A smile formed across my cheeks. "Yeah, that's true."

What was also true: the sunset from the bathtub that evening, its pink and orange glow exactly how I'd seen it in the vision.

We soaked together, our heads at the ends of the tub. It was big enough for us both. Just.

Although options for dining out were limited in Samford, we weren't bothered to cook, so we hit the local pub for dinner, grabbing a pizza to share in the beer garden, accompanied by a bottle of rosé.

We got carried away talking about Tom and Bruce's wedding, and how Jasper wanted to take me to his favorite restaurant in London.

"It's a shame you aren't coming over for longer," Jasper said, stroking my palm with his pointer finger. "We could've taken a quick trip to Paris…or Italy."

I raised a cheeky eyebrow at him, the wine clearly gone to my head. "I'll just ask my boss for *more* time off."

Jasper squeezed my hand. "No, you won't. Because I've already booked your flights."

"Oh, really?"

"Yeah," he said, sipping back the last of his wine. "I just need to send you the booking confirmation."

My mind prickled with discomfort at the mere mention of Jasper paying for the flights.

But it didn't stop me from saying, "Thank you again for bringing me over to London. I still can't believe it."

"You'll believe it when you're packing your bags," he quipped. Then, "Should we get another drink?"

We drank a couple more wines and watched locals partake in some truly terrible rounds of karaoke, from Taylor Swift's *Love Story* to Dolly Parton's *Jolene*, before deciding we'd had enough.

After a quick trip to the bathroom, I went outside the pub to see Jasper unlocking the car.

A sudden coldness expanded in my core. "What are you doing?" I asked bluntly.

"Gonna drive us home," he said confidently, a slight slur in his voice. "Then, I'd like to make love to you."

"You're kidding, right?" I snapped. "You've had nearly a whole bottle of wine and you should know how I feel about drunk-driving."

His face faltered as he blurted out, "Oh, shit. Mack. I'm sorry. Fuck. I'm an idiot. I wasn't thinking."

I shook my head; eyes narrow at him. "Yeah. You really weren't."

He walked forward, putting his arm on my shoulder. "I'm really sorry, okay?"

I brushed him off. "Whatever. Let's just get an Uber."

But the moment I whipped out my phone, he pulled his out and announced, "I'll get it."

We didn't speak much on the drive back to the house, or when we got ready for bed. I considered writing a letter to Finn, but I'd run out of room in my journal.

I was reminded internally—once again—that when it came to the accident eight summers ago, there was no fixing to be done, only steps backward and forward, living with it.

"I'm sorry, mister," Jasper said when we lay in bed with the light on. "I know how much it still hurts you."

After a lengthy exhale, I said, "It's not your fault. It wasn't something that happened to you, so how are you to know, right?"

He twisted on his side to face me, running his finger

over my forearm. "It didn't, no. But I can relate…to grief anyway. I know what it's like to lose someone, and to have to live without them. So, while I didn't have the exact experience you did, or experience the guilt you do, I can still understand it. And you know you can talk to me about it whenever you want. I'm here for you, always. We're stuck together, whether you like it or not. Whatever this universe is, has decided that it's you and me."

I also turned to face him, only a few inches apart. "I know, and it scares me to know that sometimes."

"I know, me too," he breathed. "And it's not like there's a guide to any of this. Most of the world doesn't even know about what we can see."

My eyes drifted sideways, then to him again. "I wonder if they will one day."

"Maybe. But it's also kind of nice them not knowing. It's like we get to live in our own little world. Our own little secret. Secrets aren't all bad, you know. They can be beautiful, too."

"Like you," I said.

The ends of Jasper's lips crept outward. "I'm so glad I met you, Mack."

A warmness bloomed inside me. "Me too. Once I finally got over the initial shock."

He shook with laughter for a few seconds before saying, "Yeah. Same. At first, it scared the fuck out of me. Now, it's starting to feel light…and right. Who knows, maybe we'll live in a house like this one day."

Jasper turned onto his back, and I followed suit.

"You didn't get any hints in your vision?" I asked him.

"Nope. Not one."

"We know you like your surprises, Jasper, so maybe this one's for the best."

I once thought that about Finn's family farm. That it was in my best interest to never return. But the following week, once Jasper returned to the UK and I was back at work, I found myself driving there.

The Farm

I'm not sure what urged me to drive to the Bower Creek farm after all these years. But on my way home from work, I cruised over and parked on the grass outside.

The first thing I spotted was the "for sale" sign planted to the right of the driveway.

I didn't even know if Finn's parents still lived there. This could've been the third owner in eight years. I didn't know. However, what was certain: the farm was up for sale.

I tried to spot the house between the trees. By the looks of it, it appeared almost the same as when I'd last seen it. You'd think if someone new moved in, they would've rebuilt or at least renovated to fit their style.

I hopped out of the car, locked it, and walked toward the rusty metal gate.

Hesitating for a moment, I sighed.

I opened the gate, shutting it behind me.

The massive fig tree still towered over the driveway, yet it seemed somewhat different when I strolled past it. Might've grown in the past eight years. Might've been greener after the rain. Might've been because as an ecologist, I now saw flora differently.

The closer I got to the end of the driveway, the stronger the wind grew, gusts blowing against me with such force.

The wind wasn't as brutal when I reached the end of the driveway. In fact, the field before the farmhouse was quite calm, and green. The sun beamed down on the courtyard where Finn and I would play chess from time to time. He almost always beat me, but it didn't stop me from playing.

I sauntered to the farmhouse as slowly as I could, taking it all in.

Casting my gaze to the fields in the distance, I could remember the walks down to the creek.

The creek.

Our special place.

The dirty white Ute wasn't there, nor was the dark blue sedan. Instead, there was a navy SUV parked in front of the house.

I peeped around the side of the house where the clothesline was.

She was hanging out a load of washing, pegging up the

last shirt in the basket. The crunching of my feet on the gravel caused her to turn around.

"Mack?" she called out, her mouth falling open. Kerry looked almost the same. Aside from her curled hair, which had a few strands of purple in it. She wore blue denim shorts with a T-shirt tucked into them, and brown boots as high as her knees.

Upon first glance, it seemed as if she'd recently been to a rodeo or country music festival or something.

Stunned, I stood there with a blank face for a moment.

"Hey, Kerry," I said awkwardly, a patch of sweat pooling on my forehead. It wasn't even remotely hot anymore.

I thought she was going to ask me to leave. Tell me I was the reason her only son was gone and that she could never forgive me.

But instead, her face softened and she stepped on the pebbled stones toward me.

"What a surprise," Kerry said with a half-smile. "I was actually thinking about you the other day."

"Funny that," I said back.

Her facial features flattened. Flustered and a little lost for words, she asked, "What brings you here? It's been so long. You're looking good."

"Thanks. I was just, ah, working in the area and decided to drive past and pop in."

Half-true.

Her smile grew a little wider. "It's good to see you, Mack." She held her gaze with me for a few seconds, as if this was just as hard for her as it was for me. She gestured her hand toward the house. "Come inside. Would you like some tea or coffee?"

The inside of the farmhouse was less cluttered than I remembered. The wooden interior of the kitchen was cleaner too. The musky incense smell, however, still remained.

For a place that once had me feeling more at home than my own, I'd never felt more disconnected.

"I've only had one coffee today," I said, glancing around, "But I know if I have one this late, it'll keep me up. Tea would be great, thanks."

"Good choice," Kerry said, filling up the kettle and lighting the gas stove.

She opened one of the cupboards above her head. "What tea do you want? We've got lots. English Breakfast, Earl Grey, Strawberry and Raspberry, Chamomile…"

"Hmmm…Strawberry and Raspberry sounds nice," I decided.

"Again, good choice, it's my favorite at the moment." She reached into the red-colored box and fished out two tea bags. "It doesn't really need any sweetener either, which I *love.*"

I managed a smile.

"So…what have you been doing with yourself?" Kerry asked. "I know it's a broad question to ask someone you haven't seen in almost a decade, but yeah. You been keeping well?"

"Uh, yeah, I have. I'm an ecologist now, which I love," I said, trying not to lose my breath.

"Oh, great. And how did you get into that?"

"Uni for four years. I studied in Brisbane and lived there before moving back to work here."

Kerry arched her eyebrows. "The big city hey?" She paused. "Must've been different."

"Oh yeah. Very," I agreed.

She chuckled softly, looking outside. "I remember telling Finn it would be *very* different than what he was used to on the farm."

My smile grew and I said, "Yeah, he really thought he was ready for the city lifestyle, didn't he?"

The kettle started squealing right as Kerry was about to say something. She turned around to take it off the stove.

Half of the reason I went to live in Brisbane immediately after high school was because Finn wanted to. And if he were still alive, we probably would've gone together.

After pouring our teas, she handed me a white mug with a bright red wattle tree on it, which perfectly matched the now-crimson color of the hot water.

"What about you?" I asked. "What's new with you? I saw you're selling the farm?"

Kerry rolled her eyes, taking a small sip from her mug. "Yeah. It's been a big job getting it all cleaned up, and an even bigger decision to make. But now that Delayne has two kids and lives with her husband, Charles and I have decided to downsize finally. Don't get me wrong, the farm's great and there are lots of memories here. But it's just too hard to manage and we're not getting any younger."

We stepped outside to drink our cuppas in the courtyard.

"Totally understandable, though," I said, taking a sip and letting the hot tea slide down my throat. "Where will you move to?"

Kerry chuckled. "We've actually been looking at this unit which is just down the road from here, so not far."

I chuckled too.

"It's small, but it has a big backyard with a nice garden I can make all nice," she explained, gazing off into the distance.

"Sounds great."

"Yeah, it's been a slow process of selling, since it's a bit out of the way of the booming coastal properties. But hopefully, the right person buys it one day soon."

"Oh, it'll happen for sure," I assured her. I cleared my throat after another gulp, looking to the fireplace, the same one which kept me warm on more nights than I could count.

I could feel it.

A flood, about to burst from a full river.

I broke down in tears, accompanied by loud sobs.

Kerry exhaled heavily, shimmying over so she now sat next to me rather than across.

She softly rubbed my back, which made me cry even harder.

"Hey. It's okay," she breathed, a slight shake in her voice.

"I'm so sorry," I wept. "I still b-blame myself and I always think about what I would do to change things."

"Oh, honey, it was life, and it happened," Kerry comforted.

I soon sat up straight again, mumbling, "I know you probably hate me deep down."

"No, Mack, I don't hate you," Kerry said, "And I'm sorry for the way I treated you after the accident. I was consumed. And I did blame you for a long time after Finn died. But I realized you aren't to blame for his decision to drive the car, even if it was your car. He made that decision all on his own."

"But I could've been more forceful and said no," I sniffed.

Kerry sighed and closed her eyes for a moment before opening them again. "At the end of the day, we can't change things, hon," she said softly. "Life is going to happen, and we just have to let it happen. And try to be at peace with it."

I wiped my eyes and nodded.

"Hey, c'mon," Kerry told me, standing up. "I wanna show you something."

She ushered me back inside immediately as the mosquitos began buzzing for blood. I followed her into the living room. She switched on a light and stopped in front of a cupboard topped with a bunch of belongings.

A shrine. In the middle of it was a large wooden-framed photo of Finn in his high school uniform. I remembered the exact one. It was in year ten before he got a buzz cut in year eleven and kept it that way.

Surrounding the photo were only a few things I recognized—his Playstation controller for one—powdered in dust and covered in stickers of things he fancied. *Call Of Duty*, *Far Cry*, *Grand Theft Auto*, and the TV show *Spartacus*. The skipping rope he would use in his home workouts was also there, a little dusty, too, like the rest of it. There was also a crinkled piece of paper with a sketch of a vaguely-drawn city on it. Skyscrapers penciled in blue, and the windows in orange.

Kerry watched me study the drawing. "I guess he was already thinking about leaving the farm, even in kindergarten," she said.

My mouth quirked at the thought of Finn so young. So innocent. So unaware that thirteen years later, he would make an actual plan to escape to the big city. A plan he would never keep. A plan I would eventually live out for him, in the hope he was watching down, or up, from wherever the fuck we go when we die, experiencing everything he thought his future would hold.

Kerry picked up the Playstation controller, dusting it off with her fingers. She looked at me, her hands stretched out with the controller in them.

"He would've wanted you to have it," she said, placing it in my hand. "I know you two always used to play together."

The number of times we'd verse each other in *COD* and because we were both sore losers, we'd wrestle each other right after the game until one of us tapped out, which was almost always me.

"Dunno if it'll get much use now, but thanks," I said, wiping more dust off so the stickers appeared a little brighter. "I appreciate it."

Kerry looked back to the photo of Finn. "You know, there isn't a day that goes by where I don't think about him."

I nodded in agreement.

"I'm sure he misses you. You two had an amazing connection," Kerry told me, which crossed me quite unexpectedly. She let out a soft laugh, locking her eyes with mine. "He didn't have to say anything, but I knew something was going on between you two."

Turned out I didn't have to come out to her if the conversation led to it.

I cocked my head. "How'd you know?"

"I just knew. Mothers are intuitive. We know. We get a feeling."

I sighed because I wished he was there, so I could have one more moment with him.

Kerry fixed her bold eyes back on me and said, "He'll always be with you. As he is with me."

"Finally," Finn breathed a sigh of relief. "You're here."

I'd gone down to meet him at a lookout in Brisbane. We'd been here before, to this exact spot. I used to always come down here for sunsets when I was at university. The river, The Brown Snake, sparkling in the sunshine. Story Bridge and the towering skyscrapers. The purple jacarandas in spring.

"How are you?" I asked him.

"As good as I'll ever be," he was quick to say.

"Oh yeah?"

"Yeah."

Twenty-six-year-old Finn still rocked the buzz cut. Twenty-six-year-old Finn was as lean as I'd remembered him.

"Why am I meeting you here?" I asked him.

I was utterly confused yet he seemed calmer than ever.

"We've lived here since we left school, mate," he told me. "Are you feeling okay? Did the session from Saturday night go to your head or something?"

I nodded and said, "Maybe. I dunno."

He put his arm around me.

Warm, like bodies under a blanket.

He planted a kiss on my cheek, his mustache brushing against my stubbled skin.

I twisted my head toward the view before us.

"Life can get so hectic sometimes, can't it?"

Before I could answer him, he said, "But beautiful places make it worth it. I wanna live here forever with you."

The sun disappeared suddenly, applying a dark filter to the cityscape. The once-glistening river turned a murky grey. Dark, dismal clouds grew in the distance at such a speed I'd never seen. With it came a wind I couldn't even feel.

"There's a storm coming in," I said, to state the obvious.

He chuckled and shoved me playfully. "Oh whatever, Sarah Connor."

Thunder growled loudly.

For a moment, even when I first woke from the dream, I thought it was real, that Finn was still alive again and I was actually seeing him for the first time in eight years. But the dream world disappeared about as quickly as I'd awoken.

Four Weeks Later

For the first time in a long while, I sat on a flight and didn't think about the plane's engines malfunctioning, or what would happen if the aircraft burst into flames. Sitting in peace, I refrained from eye contact with the passengers and crew, minus Jasper, of course.

I left the perspiring humidity of Australia behind and reveled in my excitement for the other side of the world.

Jasper walked by my seat in his slick black and orange blazer, stifling a smirk every time he strolled down the cabin.

At one point on the long-haul journey, I imagined myself strutting into the cozy plane bathroom and Jasper following me in. We'd have our ways with each other, then walk out as though nothing happened. Perhaps while the passengers and crew were in an uncomfortable but still-distracted slumber.

As tired as I was, sleeping on the plane proved mighty difficult. It might've been the elderly woman snoring loudly next to me, or being cooped up in a seat with nowhere near enough legroom.

But eventually, with my earphones in, listening to binaural beats, I dozed into my neck pillow.

Once I woke, five hours later, surprisingly, most passengers on the plane were asleep, while the other night owls, who I presumed physically couldn't sleep in a seat, either watched a movie or show or listened to music whilst staring into the abyss of darkness A.K.A. the night sky.

Jasper must've been sleeping in his seat at the back of the plane; not spotted until the end of the flight.

"Good morning, passengers. We're descending on London Heathrow Airport a little earlier than scheduled," a voice announced over the speaker. I could've sworn it was Jasper but it happened rather quickly, so I wasn't quite sure.

Passengers began to wake, followed by a sea of yawns. "Our estimated arrival time is twenty-two past seven in the morning, local time."

We began to edge beneath the clouds with some turbulence. Nothing to become alarmed about.

Jasper and I found each other's weary eyes, reeling a smile out of each other.

From the half-fogged-up window in my row, skyscrapers protruded below, lights still flickering from some. By the looks of things, it was going to be a cloudy day.

After a relatively smooth landing, Jasper told me to connect to the airport wi-fi as soon as I got inside the terminal, that he would message me when he was done with all the post-flight particulars.

After collecting my suitcase, I pulled up at a coffee bar and cast docile glances at the passersby, trying to comprehend how busy the airport was. Everyone on airport time, and not seven-in-the-morning time.

Screeching from the nearby coffee machine was almost music to my ears compared to the laughing in earshot.

And once a latte hit my lips, everything was immediately fine again. The laughing trailed off into faint background noise.

If my blood cells had legs, they certainly had regained the much-needed spring in their step.

After messaging Jasper and telling him my whereabouts, he soon popped up behind me, the smell of his freshly sprayed cologne the embodiment of cozy date night dinners, those of which I eagerly awaited to experience with him. We'd been to a festival together, sat in a car for several hours without killing each other, fed farmstay animals as if they were our own, and now we'd traveled to the other side of the world.

"This…" I said after a succulent piece of duck curry melted

in my mouth, "…has gotta be some of the best food I've ever had. It kind of makes up for it being *so* fucking cold."

"It definitely does," Jasper agreed. "It is really cold for a November night, I must say."

He and I locked eyes and shook our heads in disbelief. So completely and utterly satisfied it should've been illegal.

Jasper massaged my palm with his thumb. He looked immaculate in his dark blue button-up shirt. Mine were all crinkled from being in my suitcase, so I'd borrowed one of Jasper's maroon ones, which I jokingly said I was going to steal. It was a joke at first. But perhaps I'd turn that joke into a reality.

"I couldn't not bring you to my favorite restaurant in London," Jasper beamed. "They're always changing their menu too."

I waggled my eyebrows, looking around at the dark cozy restaurant full of minimal brown interiors and yellow strip lights. "Gotta try it all."

He tossed me a guilty grin. "I'm bad, babe. I'm here usually once every two weeks."

I shrugged. "You've got the money, so why not spend it, right?"

Jasper pursed his lips. "This is true," he said, taking a sip of Prosecco from his flute. "Actually, I'm thinking about investing in a farm in Australia."

I cocked my head. "I'm listening."

"Well, I've been thinking about it," Jasper replied, properly chewing his food before continuing, "I think I wanna build an adoption retreat on a farm. For orphaned or homeless kids who don't have a forever home as of yet, and to nurture them and provide education services and therapy and whatever else they need until they move on. And you know, parents who do want to adopt could come to the retreat and get to know the kids, and they'd be in safe hands with the carers until then."

I stared at him for a hot minute, shaking my head in awe. "Wow, that's beautiful, mister."

The more Jasper conveyed his vision, the more it reminded me how much of a gift he really was. Someone who wanted to care for others. Who wanted nothing but the best for those around him.

I thought about Kerry's farm for sale in Bower Creek.

"I'm imagining a big rural playground for the kids," he went on, waving his hand in level with his head. "Activities. Fun stuff." He turned his excitement down a notch when he said, "It's what I wish I had when I was in the foster care system. I wanna give them hope, make them feel cared for. Because my experience, up until I was adopted, was quite royally fucked. My carers didn't really give a shit about me. They treated me like I was just a number, a temporary job task." Jasper took a moment. "When my foster mums took me in, I was numb, you know. I didn't know what being loved was, and it was hard to grasp. I needed therapy, especially in my teens. And it did help. But not as much as the two women who saved my life. I really owe it to them. Honestly."

"I know one of your foster mums passed away, but what about the other one?" I asked, "Do you see her much?"

"Yeah, we chat all the time, when we can," Jasper said.

"We're both pretty busy, but we make the time. I'll take you to meet her while you're here."

"I'd love that," I said, squeezing his hand.

The indistinct chatter of the restaurant diminished abruptly, leaving the dining room conspicuously quiet.

Most diners were focused on whatever was outside. Some even left their tables to get a better look at the other side of the glass.

"No way," Jasper gaped, looking over at the wall-sized glass window a few tables away. "In *November*?"

"What is it?" I asked curiously.

Jasper grinned. He stood, grabbed my hand, and led me over to the window where a few others looked outside.

A blanket of little white flakes fell from the sky.

"I've never seen snow before," I piped up, the sight of it eudaemonic in its own way.

Jasper's eyes extended. "It doesn't snow in London very often," he said, turning in my direction and wrapping his arm around me as we watched the snow shower. "It's our lucky day."

"Wanna put up the Christmas tree?" Jasper called out, a big fat grin plastered over his face. He held a large tattered white box.

I scoffed. "It's November, babe."

"And?" he replied sassily. "Who's to say when you put your Christmas tree up?"

I shrugged. "This is true. I'm down. Let's deck the fuckin' halls—"

"With like, boughs of all the merry shit?"

"Yeah, you could say that," I said.

After shifting some of his plants to different window view spots, we carved out an ideal space for the tree in the living room, in a corner between it and the kitchen.

An unusual cold snap had hit the city, so the snow kept on falling.

"The years keep going quicker and quicker, don't they?" I said as we stuck baubles on the tree.

"They do," Jasper agreed. "Guess it just means we need to do the things we want to do, even if we feel as if time's running out."

"Exhibit A: putting up a Christmas tree in November," I said.

Jasper swung me a smirk. "Exactly. Because, why the fuck not?"

We set up the last few baubles. Instead of a star on top of the tree, Jasper came out with a rainbow tree topper which I couldn't be any happier to see.

"It's perfect," I said, kissing him on the cheek.

We gazed at the sparkling lights on the tree, which flashed through the living room.

"It was nice meeting your mum today," I said, massaging his neck.

Jasper chuckled. "Yeah, you two got along brilliantly. While you were in the bathroom, she said she likes you loads."

"Well, I'm honored for the approval," I said, going a tad red in the face. "She's so cool."

"Yeah, she's great. She seemed to love the idea of me moving over to Australia."

I held onto him, resting my head on his shoulder. "She'll miss you, but yeah."

"I know. I'll miss her too. But I guess this is my next journey. We can always come visit."

"Oh yeah," I agreed. "When you told her, her face really lit up hey." I kissed him again, but on the neck this time. "And I loved that you introduced me to her as your boyfriend."

"I just thought, why fuck around with waiting when we already know," Jasper said, pressing his lips onto mine.

As we pulled away, my smile faded and my gaze fell.

"Everything okay?" he asked.

Tell him.

And so, I said, "I have something I need to tell you. I don't want to keep it from you anymore, and I think you deserve to know. I'd want to know."

"Mack, what is it?"

I exhaled heavily, regathering my breath, thinking of the words to use next. "When I first saw you on the plane, I uh…saw us have some amazing memories together. Most of which haven't even happened yet—"

"Me too," he cut in, a twinkle in his eye.

"But." *Say it.* "I also saw you die."

His half-moon smile deflated, and for a moment, I thought he was going to yell at me for lying to him, perhaps kick me out of his apartment like we'd reached the third act break up in a romantic comedy.

"You saw me die?"

I shrugged. "Yeah," not sure what else to say yet.

"I need more information here. How does it happen? Is it soon? Should I start writing a will?"

"Sorry, I've never had to have this kind of convo," I said, my mouth extending into a grimace. "I'm trying to be considerate. But sounds like you want to know details, so let's go."

"I'm patiently waiting over here," Jasper said, folding his arms.

"Okay, sorry, yeah. So, it's not for a while. You've got at least ten years, I think. I don't know for sure; you definitely had some grey hair. I don't know how it happens, or any dates, or specifics. But I do know that I'm there, because…" I paused. "You die in my arms."

His eyes were a little glassy, so I wasn't sure if he was about to cry or not. Instead, his lips curved into a smile and he said, "Phew. I've got time."

I was genuinely shocked at how well it looked like he'd taken the news. "You're not mad I kept it from you?"

He flicked his hand forward. "Oh no. Babe. We're all going to die. Death is natural. Unless you're a vampire. I just wish I could return the favor so you could find out when you were going to die. Sadly, I didn't see it in my visions when we first met."

"No shit, because you die before me," I said. "That's why you didn't see me die. But you never know, you might come back as a ghost and haunt me or some shit."

He narrowed his eyes, smirking. "Oh, I will. Don't you worry…"

After a moment, he said, "We're going to have to *really* make the most of it now, aren't we?"

I didn't even need to say yes. Instead, I kissed him, my lips more clear than any words spoken.

London Snow

"What do you want to do today?" Jasper asked, following his question with a kiss on my neck.

"Well, it's still snowing." I gestured my hand toward the living room window, to the flurries falling from the sky outside, onto the surrounding apartments.

Everything was blanketed in white, with more on the way by what the weather forecast had predicted.

"You want to go walking in it, don't you?" Jasper breathed into my ear from behind, kissing his way across my shoulder.

"Yeah, I do," I said, but my cock argued the moment Jasper massaged the outer sides of my thighs.

My shaft extended and pushed against the front of my jeans.

Jasper started sucking on my earlobe, his breath loud when so close.

The front of his shorts popped out, a hard bone rubbing against the outside of my jeans, right between my arse cheeks.

He reached around and grabbed my pulsing cock. Meanwhile, I pushed my arse against his dick. And although it was pure dry-humping, it made my cock throb even more.

The snow fell harder.

We got harder.

"You want to go to the bedroom?" Jasper huffed, his hand now down my pants, kneading the head of my dick.

"No," I panted, throwing my right hand around the back of his neck, pulling him in closer so I could feel his hard-on tighter against me.

"Fuck me right here," I said. "Look at that view."

"As you wish, handsome," he said. "But I can assure you, the snow won't be my focus."

Without hesitation, he unbuttoned my jeans, releasing my cock and grasping it firmly in his hand. I gasped at his carnal touch.

He pulled down his shorts and threw his cock between my bare cheeks, moving his shaft up and down, teasing me, having me squirming while he cradled my balls.

"Should we get lube?" I giggled, pressing back into him.

Amorously, my eyes wandered out the window again, to the apartment balconies in view. As long as we didn't take our shirts off, it would look like, from the outside, two gay guys having a moment of innocent adoration, cuddling, watching the snow fall.

"I've got a better idea," Jasper offered, bending me over the window sill slightly, spreading my arse apart.

He buried his face in my hole, and as soon as his tongue hit my sphincter, my mouth formed an O and I couldn't help but moan.

"Fuck that feels so good."

"Mmmhmm," was all he managed in response, his tongue deep.

"I want you inside of me," I groaned, right as he hit another sensitive spot. "Oh, fuck. Yes!"

He stayed eating my arse for what felt like a blissful eternity.

As my eyes were shut, thinking how good it felt, he spat on his cock and bent me over further.

As he entered me, the wind outside howled, blowing in a thick shower of snowflakes. And it only got stronger at each thrust.

I reached around and grabbed the back of his neck again, pulling him in closer as he fucked me with force, writhing as his dick prodded my prostate.

He licked the back of my neck.

The Christmas lights on the tree beside us had changed rhythm and now flashed at a fast pace.

"Oh, fuck yes, you feel so good!" Jasper cried out, thrusting into me as deep as he could.

I gaped and moaned, close to bursting.

After a few deep, slow thrusts, Jasper started pounding

me faster, and I didn't need eyes on the back of my head to know that my arse cheeks were red.

My dick began to leak the harder he fucked me.

It was almost blizzard-like outside.

"I'm getting so close, baby," I whispered.

"Fuck yeah, me too," he gasped for breath.

He collided with a spot I didn't think anyone had ever hit.

"Oh my god, I'm coming."

Without hands, silver wet jets started to shoot from my cock, onto the ground, causing me to shudder.

"Fuck yes," Jasper groaned, scooping up some free semen from my dick and slurping it up.

He fucked me hard until he pulled out, ropes of thick warm come hitting my back and running down like droplets on glass.

The snow cleared, now only falling in tiny flakes.

The Christmas lights stopped flashing.

I stayed bent over in a daze until Jasper cleaned his jizz off me.

We kissed, before I asked, "Ready for a walk?"

As an Australian who had never walked in snow during the day, my initial burst of excitement lasted a whole ten minutes. Until my fingertips started to numb at the end of my gloves.

"All this snow really is quite rare," Jasper said as we sauntered through a local park, shaking a tree branch, which resulted in a showering of white flakes. "I've lived here nearly my whole life, and this may just be the thickest it's ever been."

"You're welcome," I said, pointing at my chest.

He waggled his eyebrows and pushed me playfully. "Yeah, either that or climate change. But let's go with your unrivaled presence."

I blushed as he kissed me against the snow-dusted tree.

Jasper switched his gaze from me to the tree's branches. "Want to know some English history and folklore about these trees?"

I studied the thick trunk and white-powdered leaves. "An English oak tree."

"Correct. Have you heard the history and folklore behind this tree?"

"Mister, I'm an ecologist, not a historian."

"Well, do you want to know?"

Giddy with excitement, I said, "If it involves plants, you should know by now that of course I want to know."

"This is true. Noted. Okay so, based on what I learned in history class, ancient druids worshipped in oak groves," he explained, moving his hand along the rough trunk. Not so much in a sexual manner, but my indecent mind thought otherwise. "Couples would marry under the oak trees."

"I wonder how many of them were gay."

Jasper shrugged. "Who knows, maybe a few did marry in secret."

I sighed. "We're lucky. Many weren't."

Jasper placed his mitten on my cheek. "We are lucky. *I'm* lucky to have met you."

I chuckled. "Right back at you."

He then suggested, "Maybe one day we can get married under an English oak tree, like this one."

Marriage. Me? Never in my wildest dreams. Except if the dream was a vision. Which, turned out, very much had been. If I closed my eyes, I could see the jade ring. But I didn't want to think about the ring too much. Because if I thought about the ring, I thought about Jasper's face. But with his eyes unblinking. And it brought me great sadness because even though he was right next to me, promising me, without words, that he'd chosen me, a part of me wondered how long we really had together. A thought that wouldn't occur only once, twice, or even a handful of times. I'd often be reminded. But it didn't mean I couldn't make the most of the moments, even knowing what lay ahead, the exact timeline utterly unclear.

Instead of replying to the idea of an oak tree wedding, I said, "So, you know how when we first spoke in the Blue Bar?"

"Mmmyes."

"And we were talking about secrets and yours was that you first drove a car when you were eight. Do I get to hear this story now?"

He laughed. "Ahhh, I mean. It's not exactly a good one. I could've died."

After his smile deflated, I was quick to say, "Oh, you don't have to tell it if you don't want to. I was just thinking back to the night we met and it came to mind."

He grabbed me reassuringly by the waist and pulled me in. "It's okay. If I didn't want to talk about it, I would say I didn't want to talk about it."

"So, you're okay to talk about it?" I asked, my lips not-so-subtly leaning toward a smirk.

He waggled his eyebrows. "Yes, if you really want to know."

"I mean, it is an intriguing statement to come out and say you first drove a car when you were eight. So, it's only natural that I'm curious to hear all about it."

He rolled his eyes. "This is true. Goddamn secrets." He sighed. "Okay, so basically, when I was eight, my biological mother and I were shacked up with one of her questionable boyfriends and apparently at the time, I was a serial sleepwalker. I'd get up and walk around the house, sometimes get the juice out of the fridge, pour cereal thinking it was breakfast. All sorts of shite." He laughed. "And one night, I'd grabbed my mother's car keys to the literal bomb of a vehicle she owned at the time. And I went outside, turned the car on, and reversed out of the driveway and hit the mailbox, which was this, like, big solid brick mailbox."

My mouth was agape with my hand covering it. I quickly removed it and blurted out, "Oh my god. How did you know how to turn on a fucking car?"

Jasper chuckled, beaming at the trip down memory lane. "Well, I can remember there were a few times when I would ask my mum to show me how to turn on the car and she even let me do it myself one time. So, I think that's how I subconsciously knew how to turn on the car and achieved it while I was still asleep. But yeah. It wasn't long afterward that she really went downhill. I think I was in foster care six months later."

His eyes were glazed over, the mere mention of his upbringing still forcing a flicker of sorrow, even if it resulted in laughter.

"I'm sorry, babe. I should've known this memory of yours might bring your mother up."

He shrugged. "It's okay. The past can't be erased. You know that as well as I do."

I nodded my head, and after a pause, proceeded to ask him something but stopped.

"What?" he asked.

"I was just going to ask if you ever think about her," I said, hoping it was okay to bring up.

He didn't hesitate in saying, "Yeah, I do sometimes. And to tell you the truth, I've thought about trying to find her loads of times, to see how she's doing, to see if she's still alive. But I kind of prefer to think of her as a reminder now. That sometimes, you find your own family."

The snow soon turned to rain, the white powder melting to slush. We spent the afternoon making terrariums with equipment bought from the hardware store and nursery. Jasper said he was bored, which is when I'd suggested the idea of making something, to which he sprung up and fumbled for his phone and wallet.

Beside each other in comfortable silence, we planted moss into glass boxes, studying the process intricately.

Deep in thought and needing to share what was on my mind, I said, "There was something I was thinking about on the plane ride here."

Jasper smiled at his mossy terrarium. "What's that?"

"So, when you're on a plane, you look around and see everyone in their own little bubbles. But it also made me think about the fact being in a plane is one of the only times we're truly disconnected, you know. From what's below."

To this, Jasper let out a short laugh. "Yeah, until they start to introduce free Wi-fi on every plane, which could be likely. Most international flights have wi-fi you can pay for. Others are trialing free wi-fi."

I looked over to Jasper. "I personally find the time in a plane, without any contact to the outside world, to be calming."

"Relatable," he said, staring off into the distance. "Being a flight attendant all these years, moving through time. Backward, forward, disconnected. Making people feel welcome."

"You do have a welcoming charm," I added, immediately being transported back to when we first met.

Welcoming people into an establishment of some sort.

Was it manifestation or destiny?

Jasper soon said, "I know we've only known each other a while, but I think I want to say that…I love you."

Time was irrelevant here.

"I love you too," I said back, following his gaze to the half-built terrarium. "But you already know that."

We both did.

We Already Are

Tom and Bruce stood facing each other, both wearing dark blue suits that boldened their facial features. An intimate crowd of fifty or so gathered before them, among them Jasper and I.

"Do you, Thomas Green, take Bruce O'Brien to be your lawfully wedded husband?" the marriage officiant asked. "To live together in matrimony, to love him, comfort him, honor and keep him, in sickness and in health, in sorrow and in joy, to have and to hold, from this day forward, as long as you both shall live?"

Tom's best friend and groomswoman, Courtney, was dressed in a silky blue dress to match the getups of the grooms, her long blonde hair curled and coruscating.

I'd met Courtney when the two of them came to Australia two years prior. I also kind of used her and Tom for a lift when we first met. Now, look where we were.

Behind the groomsmen and groomswomen, rolling hills glistened against the sunlight. The farmland venue had families of alpacas scattered through the paddock. And with the snow fully cleared, it sure made way for all the greenery.

"I do," said Tom, his yearning eyes fixated upon Bruce: taking a leap, an oath.

Tom and Bruce looked much paler than when I'd seen them in Australia, not that I was surprised.

The officiant nodded. "And do you, Bruce O'Brien, take Thomas Green to be your lawfully wedded husband? To live together in matrimony, to love him…"

I turned to Jasper, grasping his hand.

The officiant's voice began to blur the longer Jasper and I held each other's gaze.

"I do," Bruce said.

The officiant's voice grew louder. "I now pronounce you husband and husband."

Thomas and Bruce kissed, to which the crowd clapped and cheered. To see Thomas and Bruce so happy, walking down the aisle together, arms linked, with exuberant grins on their faces brought me, and every single person in the crowd, immense joy.

As he and Bruce sauntered past our row, Tom and I locked eyes for a short full-circle moment.

The wedding reception was held in a revamped barn on the farm. Even though Tom had grown up in London his whole life, and Bruce in Ireland, the two settled on a spot that gave them a little taste of both.

I lined up for my third helping of brie cheese and crackers. After the ceremony, my hunger skyrocketed to borderline ravenous.

"How *good* is the cheese, though," a familiar voice chirped from behind me.

"Courtney…hey!" I crowed, putting my plate down to hug her. "You look great!"

"Bit different than our bohemian bush festival attire, right?" Courtney winked, pointing at herself. "So, how's the UK winter treating you?"

Her raised sarcastic eyebrow had me shaking with laughter. "Fucking cold. But wow, beautiful with all the snow. And the wedding."

"Oh my god, I know right," she said, turning her head over to the main table near the stage, where Tom and Bruce were eating and laughing. "Those two are…so imperfectly perfect for each other."

I raised my cup. "They really are."

After a last plate of cheese and crackers, I discovered that I'd overdone it in the food department. So, I asked Jasper if he wanted to step outside into the night for some fresh air. The air was that, and much more, even with a puffer jacket on, my breath akin to an exhale of vapor.

We weren't the only ones outside. A few people were huddled around a fire, Tom and Bruce being two of them. They sat on a bench next to the fire, eyes fixed on the flame.

"Look who it is!" Tom piped up as we emerged from the shed.

They both stood from the bench. Tom embraced me in a hug.

"Huge congrats, Tommy from London!" I cried out. "The wedding was beautiful. Ugh, you both look so good!"

"Aw, thanks for coming," Tom said gleefully, "All the way from Australia too!"

Bruce moved forward and hugged me next while Tom hugged Jasper.

"It's honestly been an amazing break, especially from the humidity," I admitted.

Bruce arched a brow. "Oh, I bet."

Tom stepped in front of us. "Loving this by the way," he said, pointing from Jasper to me. "When Jasper told me, I couldn't believe it. I was like *no way*."

Jasper looked at me pensively. "Life is fucking strange, isn't it?"

"The strangest," I said, already getting lost in his eyes.

The few people around the fire stepped back inside now that Kylie Minogue started playing over the sound system.

"So, what have you hoes been up to?" Jasper asked Tom and Bruce. "Other than getting married of course."

They both flashed their rings.

"Go on, give us a look," Jasper said to them.

Their matching handmade wooden rings had a blue strip of aquamarine in the middle.

"Oh wow," I gasped, taking a closer look.

"Yeah, it's koa wood," Tom mentioned. "We both love

the outdoors, so we thought why not bring a bit of nature to live on us forever?”

Bruce must've thought this was one of the cutest things Tom had ever said, because he swooped in and kissed his husband several times.

“But yeah, other than the wedding,” Tom answered, “we've honestly been staying at home loads. We moved into a new apartment not too long ago. It's a charming mix of me screaming into the void when I fuck something up on one of my paintings, and Bruce sitting there wondering what he's going to write next. But yeah, it's going well. We've got a good steady income, a nice place together. Can't complain.”

Bruce gave me a look as if to indicate he wanted to tell us something. A deep burning secret perhaps.

“I swear, Mack,” Tom went on, “When I found out you were coming to the wedding with Jasper, it really took me on a trip down memory lane. I kept thinking back to that frosty morning at the first bush rave you took me to, and I'm pretty sure if it wasn't for the chat we had in the field, I would've kept sleepin' around on Tinder. I don't think I would've started chatting to Bruce. Well, actually having a conversation and not just a one-night stand.”

I waggled my eyebrows. “I'm glad I could be of service in being some sort of catalyst to this.” I swished my hand around swiftly from Tom to Bruce.

“I would've found you one way or another,” Bruce said to Tom, casting him a smirk. “There wasn't gonna be anything keeping me from you.”

"You two are too cute," Jasper commented, holding onto me from behind.

"Says you two, still in the honeymoon phase…" Tom blurted out. "Oh, to be back there again."

"We're going on our honeymoon in a month," Bruce said sassily.

"Which I'm super excited for…*obviously!*" Tom piped up.

"Where are you guys going?" I asked.

This had a grin growing on Thomas' face. "We've got an overwater bungalow in the Maldives."

"Fucking jealous, lad," Jasper piped up, then turned to me. "Once I move over to Australia, we should plan another holiday."

I eyeballed him, responding sarcastically, "Oh yeah, I'll just ask for another week off. No biggie! Maybe ask me in six months."

"Wait, you're moving to Australia?" Bruce interjected.

Jasper smiled. "Yeah." He went on to tell them all about his plans of buying a farm and now Tom and Bruce were the jealous ones.

"If the grooms could please return to the shed," Courtney called out over the microphone.

"We're being summoned," Tom cooed, leading Bruce inside.

Jasper and I followed, too cold out there for our liking. Besides, the fireplace inside warmed us handsomely as we stood beside it, thawing our hands out.

"This is a song Thomas and Bruce were fond of when they first met," Courtney explained to the crowd while the grooms stood next to her at the front of the stage. "It encapsulates their love for one another, and the wicked journey they've been on the past couple of years." Her voice started to tremble. "I love you both like my own brothers." She hugged them both.

The lights in the shed dimmed to a blue glow. A cover of *Truly Madly Deeply* started playing. Thomas and Bruce took to the stage, swaying slowly in each other's arms.

When the chorus came, Courtney joined them with her boyfriend, then Thomas' father Harry, and his girlfriend Abigail, followed by the rest of the groomsmen and groomswomen.

Jasper nudged me. "Wanna dance?"

"I thought you'd never ask," I said flirtatiously.

He took my hand, our skin warmed by flame.

He led me over to the dancefloor, which gradually filled with people dancing together.

In the middle of the crowd, Jasper positioned his arms around my waist. Not too tight, not too loose. Mine sat on his shoulders comfortably. His gaze didn't feel all-consuming like it did when I saw him at the petrol station in Central Australia, right after running away from him.

With his eyes glued to mine, Jasper said, "I love you, Mackenzie."

I cocked my head to the side, taken by surprise. "That's the first time you've called me Mackenzie."

"There's a first time for everything."

I paused before saying, "I love you too, Jasp."

He cocked his head slightly. "No one's ever called me that."

"There's a first time for everything," I reminded him.

He waggled his eyebrows. "Like…buying a farm."

I linked my fingers with his. "I might actually know a place."

"Oh yeah?"

I nodded. "Yeah. I'll tell you all about it tomorrow."

He beamed. "Well, I look forward to it."

We turned our heads to the newly wedded husbands.

"If we can be anything like them, I'll be happy."

"Oh, darlin' boy," Jasper breathed, softening to a whisper. "We already are."

I didn't question it.

I already knew it was such a small world after all.

So large—full of life—yet small enough to form even the most synchronized connections. Ones which sometimes made you think perhaps there was something bigger at play.

An explanation behind all of it.

Or maybe there wasn't, and it, by nature, was the way it was.

I don't know.

I couldn't tell you.

Featherstone Retreat

NOW

Wistfully, I stare out the window, at the gloomy, fog-filled farm. The one Jasper and I have lived on for two years now. The Bower Creek farm, passed down from Kerry to us. Home.

A knock at the front door snaps me out of a daze. Quickly, I leave the room, passing the study on my way down the hall. Jasper's frantically typing at the antique wooden desk which was passed down to us by my granddad a year ago. It'd been a quest to maneuver it up the stairs, but we figured it deserved a spot in the big new house.

"Babe, they're here," I say, pointing downstairs.

He shuts his laptop in a hurry and stands. "Okay, coming. Oh my god."

"This is it," I tell him for the third time this morning.

He pecks me on the lips, and it still makes my heart swell as much as our first kiss had, four years ago.

"This is it," he echoes, leading me down the hall and stairs.

We share a smile and I look at the jade ring on my finger before opening the oak door.

On the other side stands a woman, dressed neatly in black with her hair slicked back. When I look into her eyes, I receive a vision, though it's extremely brief, as if this might be the only time I meet her.

Beside her is a boy, who I assume must be Taj. He's eight years old, yet his age speaks no numbers compared to the fear in his eyes, in his bitten fingernails.

MACKENZIE'S BRAIN CINEMA ACTIVATED

First clip: me showing Taj plants around the farm.

Second clip: Taj and several other kids enjoying a movie night at the manor with Jasper, Lily, Rachel and I.

Third clip: Taj dressed in a suit (it looks like his year ten or twelve formal).

Fourth clip: Taj and I standing beside a grave, crying, an arm around each other's shoulders.

With a handshake, Jasper greets the woman. "Claire, is it?"

He quickly turns to the boy. "And you must be Taj."

Taj nods, standing closer to Claire. From the corner of my eye, I see Jasper's pupils go glassy.

"When I heard about your place, I thought it might be the perfect place for Taj," Claire says, looking around at the enormity of room between the front door and the grand staircase. "We've tried to get him in with a foster family, but it's hard in the area at the moment."

Taj's eyes dart around each corner of the manor, which is the main dwelling of Featherstone Retreat, thanks to the inheritance money from Jasper's mum, as well as a government grant to build the manor house.

Jasper and Claire start chatting about the foster care system in the lounge room. I overhear the mention of Bower Creek and how we want to create a nurturing environment here at Featherstone.

Meanwhile, I tap Taj on the shoulder. "Hey, let's go get you settled, bud."

He mumbles a soft, "Okay," and follows me upstairs.

No one needs to tell me, but I can tell Taj is triggered by talk of the foster care system. We walk up to the same room I'd made the bed in. Science Hour on the radio has been taken over by a local indie rock band's new song. I turn off the speaker.

"So, this is going to be your room," I tell him.

With natural relief, he looks around for a moment, then approaches the window, the misty valleys now thick with clouds.

"It's the best view in the house," I say, hoping it helps, but briskly realizing he's eight and probably doesn't care about a postcard vista. He'd likely rather play a video game.

I point out the window. "You can walk right up to the top of the valley there. Most of the time, there are lots of wallabies hopping about, too."

Taj turns around and looks me in the eye for the first time, before saying, "I've never seen a wallaby before."

I smile. "Well, kid, we're going to change that real quick. Perhaps when the weather's a little better." A beat. "I'm also planning to run gardening and plant workshops, to teach you and the other kids how to harvest on the farm."

"Will I learn how to grow carrots?" he pipes up.

"Of course," I say, already feeling a sense of accomplishment, even though I haven't taught Taj anything. "Any reason carrots in particular?"

"They're my favorite vegetable," he says.

I make a tick in the air with my finger. "One carrot growing workshop coming right up."

Our property already generates ample amounts of fresh fruit and vegetables for the local community here in Bower Creek, and the kids who stay at Featherstone will learn all about this and help continue the cycle. The whole place runs on renewable energy, too.

"Where do you and Jasper stay?" Taj asks.

Ushering him closer to the window, I point to a little cabin in the distance. "There."

Taj deflated.

"But Lily, our house mother, will be here to look after you. She's lovely. And you'll get to meet Rachel, and other kids are expected this week. Oh, and also Marco, the cook. He makes super yummy food."

Rachel and Lily are still together, and they live in a small shipping container home on the property. Lily is no longer in a relationship with Margot. She ultimately decided she only wanted to be with Rachel around a year after they started dating.

"Will you and Jasper be here for dinner?"

"Yes. We'll be here for dinner," I say, my smile stretching further. "And if you ever need anything from us, do ask. Don't hesitate, okay? We're a family here."

Taj flinches at the word *family*, but only a fraction before Lily enters the room.

"Hey there, Taj. How are you, little dude?" she says, enthusiasm radiating from her.

So much so that it draws a smile out of Taj. "Good," he says shyly.

"Want to play some video games?" Lily asks.

"Yes please!" he replies without hesitation and rushes to the door.

Lily hands me a paperback book and says, "I loved it. Thanks for letting me borrow."

"I'll be sure to let Mum know," I tell her.

Taj gives me a trusting look before leaving with Lily.

I look down at my copy of *Alyssa's Brain Cinema*, Mum's latest young adult novel. The story of a teenager who discovers she can see the future relationship timeline of every new person she meets. Mum's publisher thought it to be a fantastic idea for a book. And they've never found out that it's based on Mum's life, that after its release, several readers, including myself, would reach out to Mum and thank her, tell her that the story was extremely relatable and that they'd had similar experiences. What experiences exactly, they didn't say, but Mum and I did wonder how many of those people were like us, baffled that an author had crafted an idea that made them feel like they weren't so alien in this world. Though, if they do have a Brain Cinema of their own, they still live in secret like us, hiding behind a novel branded as fiction.

Jasper keeps talking to Claire about particulars so I step out to the still-dewy lawn and walk to our tiny home right above the creek. We didn't want it too close to the water because of flooding dangers. Yet our home is relocatable, so we'll move it higher in the future if we must.

Everything has its dedicated space in our two-bedroom cabin. There's storage under the bed, more storage under the couch, and collapsible drawers.

With not much on for the rest of the day (which hardly ever happens), I give our space a spruce-up.

Since the opening of Featherstone Retreat, things have been extremely busy, which means on odd occasions, cleaning gets neglected.

As I'm sorting through a box in our bedroom, I find two old journals, one twelve years old, the other four. They're dusty, of course, but not tattered in the slightest.

The first journal recounts the summer leading up to Finn's death and the days, months, that followed. Although I told Jill I would, I never burned the journal—I couldn't, as much as I wanted to forget everything written in it.

And I'm glad I didn't, as it only took a few years later to find it and for it to inspire me to write a second journal: when I first met Jasper in Alice Springs, the festival, road trip, and lead-up to London.

Four years ago.

Jasper thinks there's a book in those pages, that I could rewrite them to form some sort of coherent literary piece, but I'm not sure if I'm ready to consider that. Who knows, though, maybe I will end up following in Mum's footsteps.

But first, Jasper and I need to get Featherstone Retreat running smoothly. And once that's done, we've got a wedding to plan. Our wedding.

When the sun is centered, Jasper and I lay on the biggest, flattest rock by the creek, our bodies adjacent on towels, the tops of our heads touching, pressed against one another as water cascades below.

"Hey, Jasper."

"Yeah?"

A soft wind rustles the leaves of the river oaks.

"Nothing."

He fixes his gaze on me. "What were you gonna say?"

I shake my head, chuckling, "It's stupid."

"Go on," he insists.

I sigh, twisting to face him. "Do you think we would've done less if we didn't know what was coming?"

His eyes wander heavenward, before saying, "No. This was the plan all along."

Before I can reply, he swoops in, kisses me, and I immediately surrender.

Jasper always reassures me when I have a flicker of doubt. He reassures me that without rocks, a waterfall won't make the sound it does. Much the same, without moments passed, we aren't who we are today.

He says, "I could get used to this."
     And I say, "So could I."
     I know it won't be forever, though.
     One day, I'll have to let go.
     One day, I'll have to learn how to live without him, too.
     But today isn't that day.
     Because today is for now.
     Tomorrow is not certain.
     But for us, it's okay.
     Better than okay, in fact.

Acknowledgments

Firstly, I pay my respects to the Traditional Owners of the places in which this story was written and mentioned in its pages.

Australia is full of incredible destinations to visit, and I'm grateful that I was able to explore a lot of the spots that Mack and Jasper did in this book. It definitely helped bring the setting for *Such a Small World* to life.

As did some incredibly talented and supportive people. Writing a book is mostly solitary, but what happens after is very much a collaboration.

Thank you to the team at Deep Desires Press for publishing my work, and for all the editing and support. Publishing a book gets overwhelming behind the scenes, but having these people in my corner has made me feel far less alone during the process. Big shout out to Craig, Margaret, Ethan, Francisco, and others that I've worked with there.

To the incredibly talented Tal Lewin at Caravaggia13 for the stunning cover illustration. Thank you for bringing my boys to life. I was floored by the colours and detail when I first saw it, and still am.

A huge thank you to the booksellers for continuing to support my work (special shout-out to the teams at The Bookshop Darlinghurst and Shelf Lovers in Brisbane). To all the Bookstagrammers, reviewers, and media who helped get my debut romance novel *When Things Happen Together* off the ground with their lovely posts, articles, and reviews.

And to the readers who messaged kind words. To know that a story I wrote has helped someone feel seen and represented inspires me to keep doing what I'm doing. I never thought my words could have an impact in this way, and I'm stoked knowing that people have found a sense of belonging in my stories.

Such a Small World is my most personal work yet, and while it's mostly fiction, a lot of the content, like Mack struggling with grief and identity in his teenage years, are feelings that I felt when I was his age.

To those who've ever felt different but refused to stop existing, this one's for you.

And finally, to my friends and family for being part of my life.

Much love to you all!

About the Author

Jordan Clayden-Lewis was born and raised in Australia, and loves queer stories of all sorts. These stories have ultimately inspired him to write his own.

When Jordan's not reading or writing, he's parenting his overactive dog Misty, hiking a trail in the forest somewhere, or thinking about Mexican food.

Such a Small World is a standalone sequel to Jordan's debut romance novel *When Things Happen Together*.

Read the beginning of
Thomas and Bruce's
love story in

When Things Happen Together

Two travelers on the ultimate Australian road trip. Two numbers that will change their lives forever.

Thomas is in need of a change. Being an aspiring artist from London, he hopes a working holiday in sunny Australia will be the muse he's been waiting for. But it isn't Australia's vast landscapes that are his source of inspiration…

After a string of unromantic dates, Thomas meets Bruce, a handsome Irish traveler with alluring almond-colored eyes. The more time the pair spend together, however, the more they start seeing the numbers 1122 everywhere. Are the numbers just a coincidence, or is something greater at play? Is Bruce really who he says he is, or is there more to him than he's letting on?

A story about seizing the moment, finding a sense of home, and embracing love when it comes knocking.

OUT NOW

Also from Deep Desires Press

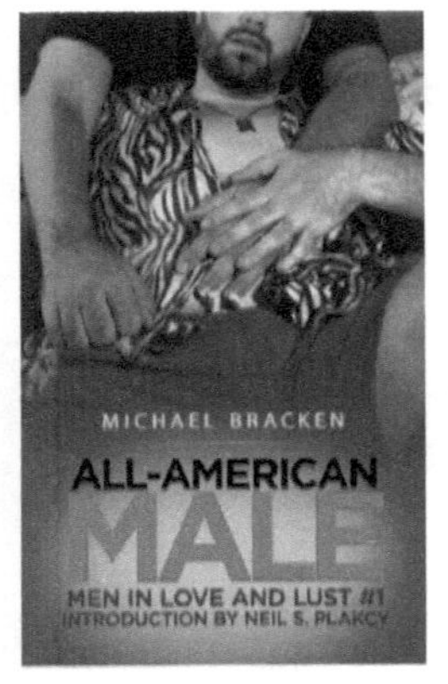

All-American Male
Men in Love and Lust, Book One
Michael Bracken

When college student Bernie is dragged to a Christmas party where he knows nobody, the last thing he expects is to be naked and between the thighs of the sexiest man he's ever met.

While older men aren't usually his thing, there's something about Professor Maeyer that gets Bernie going in ways he hasn't felt for a long time. So, when the party ends and everyone's gone home and it's just Bernie and Professor Maeyer, he gets a deeper education, the kind that can't be taught in class, the kind that can only be taught in the bedroom.

Bernie's about to learn just how much Professor Maeyer can blow his mind (and his load).

"Learning Curve" is just one of nineteen scorching hot and smutty-as-hell stories in this sweaty, throbbing, pounding collection of gay erotica from Michael Bracken, acclaimed author of erotic short fiction.

Available now in ebook and paperback!

**Also available in Michael Bracken's
Men in Love and Lust series**
Queer Bait
Sporting Wood

Also from Deep Desires Press

The Line of Succession
Harry F. Rey

Families are built on secrets, but when it's the royal family, the stakes—and the secrets—can be deadly.

Fifteen years ago, Prince James's father, Prince Richard, was killed in a mysterious helicopter crash, along with his secret Irish lover. The young James became heir to the British throne over his twin sister, Princess Alexandra.

With Queen Victoria II turning ninety, James's personal life, now that he's thirty, has come more into the public spotlight as he's expected to marry and produce an heir. Known for his playboy lifestyle, he'd gladly accept that reputation to hide the truth that he's gay and in a secret long-term relationship with his best friend and press secretary, Andrew.

His twin sister knows his secret, and plans to use it to create a scandal that will help her take the crown for herself, but her plans rely on trust, and she will soon learn her allies are not as trustworthy as she thought. Will James win his throne, while keeping the love of his life? Or will the monarchy topple in the face of naked ambition and public scandal?

Available now in ebook and paperback!